THE DEMON ERUPTION

DEMON HUNTER BOOK THREE

KERRY ADCOCK

The Demon Eruption
Paperback Edition
Copyright © 2022 Kerry Adcock

CKN Christian Publishing
An Imprint of Wolfpack Publishing
5130 S. Fort Apache Road 215-380
Las Vegas, NV 89148

cknchristianpublishing.com

Paperback ISBN 978-1-63977-254-4
eBook ISBN 978-1-63977-914-7
LCCN 2022944691

THE DEMON ERUPTION

PROLOGUE

THE MS SCHWENLAND, a German ship of 8,500 gross tons, steamed away from the coast of Antarctica, propelled by twin diesel screws at a speed of 12 knots. Carrying a complement of over 80 men and two Dornier Wal seaplanes, they had successfully accomplished their mission. The seaplanes were used to photographically survey 600,000 square kilometers of the frozen land as well as drop dozens of aluminum flags to mark areas. The initial plan was to claim parts of Antarctica for Germany to protect the whaling industry, but also for a more nefarious reason.

Standing on the bridge, *Kapitan* Krueger watched as they left the cold arctic waters and headed back toward Germany. A bearded veteran of World War I and a loyal member of the *Kreigsmarine*, he'd been assigned this mission. His second in command, *Fregattenkapitan* Mergkoff, a younger officer, stood nearby looking out at the sea through binoculars.

"It looks like clear sailing." he remarked.

Kapitan Krueger nodded.

"Do you think they can create a working base?" asked Mergkoff.

"I hope so," replied Krueger. "This will give us a strategic base in which to take back what we lost in the war. The submarines are already approaching the location to begin their work on our hidden base."

The ship sailed safely back to Germany but never returned to Antarctica as it was sunk during World War II.

CHAPTER ONE

Tex-Am Drilling Platform
Highway 177
Andrews County, Tx
Present day

SAM DONALDSON SAT in the well-used single-wide mobile trailer used as an office at one of Tex-Am's oil drilling sites. The fifty-eight-year-old owner of one of the largest drilling companies in the nation had successfully completed another directional drilling. The site was located just north of Odessa, Texas, and he looked forward to returning home to celebrate. His current crew consisted of three 4-man crews working 8-hour shifts operating the rig, a tool pusher and sometimes a drilling engineer. Soon he'll need his three-man logging crew for wireline work or a one/two-man staff for logging or measurement while drilling. He rolled up his charts and maps to leave when he heard frantic yelling near the drilling platform.

What's going on?

Sam jerked the trailer door open to see what the trouble was and stood, shocked at what he saw. Dozens of hideous creatures had swarmed the platform. Two of his men had already been killed, and the other two were running towards a truck to escape. Sam grabbed a long pry bar and ran towards the oil rig.

"Run, Mr. Donaldson!" yelled one of the crew just before a large reddish-colored creature with huge black wings impaled him with a long claw.

Sam swung the pry bar and struck the creature, it merely turned and hissed at him. The creature jerked the bar from his hand and shoved Sam to the ground. The abomination raised the bar over his head when another equally hideous creature resembling a huge vulture yelled, "Stop, Tarnac wants him alive." The ugly creature dropped the bar and placed his foot on Sam's chest to prevent him from moving.

"You're lucky, this time." said the creature, spewing decaying flesh and saliva onto Sam.

Sam was unable to do anything to help his crew and was forced to lay and watch as the last one was slaughtered.

———

Yellowstone National Park
Old Faithful Geyser
Present Day

AFTER PARKING and walking the one hundred yards to the semi-circle wooden platform next to the famous geyser, Jake Taft and his new bride, Ellie, sat on the wooden benches waiting for the next eruption. Old Faithful erupted about every 45 minutes, and when it did, it sprayed water high into the sky.

"This is amazing," said Ellie with a smile. "The whole park has been amazing."

Jake Taft, an Army Special Forces veteran, turned Texas cattle rancher—wearing jeans, western boots, a light jacket, and his Stetson cowboy hat—grinned and hugged his wife. "It's a beautiful park, and you make it even better."

Ellie, a pastor of the Shady Oak Community Church in Shady Oak, Texas—wearing jeans, hiking boots, and a Yellowstone

National Park sweatshirt—sat back and laughed. "You sure know how to impress a lady."

"Are you disappointed that we didn't go to some tropical island for our honeymoon?" asked Jake.

"Absolutely not," replied the dark-haired Ellie. "As a child, growing up in the east, I've always wanted to come to Yellowstone and see the geysers and the wildlife. We can go to the tropics or somewhere abroad later. After our adventure in Germany, I'll stay around here for now."

Jake laughed out loud. "You mean you didn't enjoy being smuggled into Germany and fighting Nazis and demons?"

"No. I hope that's the last of them for a while. I'm worried that they never found that half-demon clone of Hitler though."

"I agree," said Jake with a nod. "So far, he's eluded authorities, but they'll find him." Jake thought back to the events over the last few years. He remembered being recruited by the heavenly angel, Malachy, to help stop a demon uprising. He had memories of saving the President's daughter and fighting a demon lord named Ghazi. Along with the FBI, he stopped Ghazi from unleashing biological poisons over major cities. Then the Nazis began experimenting with demon, animal, and human DNA, which resulted in a demon clone of Adolph Hitler. They'd planned to detonate a small nuclear bomb at a global summit in Berlin but had been thwarted in the end.

"We're so fortunate that Malachy helped us stop them. He saved us and the world leaders." added Ellie.

Jake faked a look of pain. "I helped a little."

Ellie elbowed him in the ribs. "Of course, you did. You being able to see demons and kill them helped save us all. After all, they call you the demon hunter now."

Jake moaned. "Ugh, don't remind me."

———

THEY WALKED BACK to their rented car and drove southeast, back towards the center of the park. As they drove along Lake Yellowstone, Jake glanced out the window and suddenly pulled over and stopped.

"What's wrong?" asked Ellie.

"Demons." replied Jake. He pointed out the window towards the distance across the lake. "I see demons flying across the sky."

"Where are they going?" asked Ellie. Only Jake could see them unless they wanted to be seen. "Are they coming this way?"

"No, they're flying away from us."

"Well good," said Ellie with a sigh. "We've had enough of them for a while."

"Yeah, I hope so." replied Jake.

"But why hang around Yellowstone Park? There's nothing but nature and animals."

Jake shook his head. "I don't know. I hope it's just random." But somehow, he knew better.

CHAPTER TWO

Northwestern Volcano Observatory
1001 N. Walton Ave
Five Corners, Washington

DR. WENDI HAMILTON, a thirty-six-year-old, raven-haired woman, sat on a stool in the laboratory of the newly opened Northwestern Volcano Observatory. A part of the United States Geological Survey, the building was only six months old and had the newest equipment used to study volcanic activity. She was studying some of the latest charts when Tina Williams, a twenty-three-year-old black college student, walked by.

"Are you going to be there all day?" she joked. "It's nearly time to go home."

Wendi laughed. "I'm almost done."

Tina shrugged her shoulders. "Well, ok, you know what they say, all work and no play."

"I just need to check this last chart, and then I'll be done." She glanced at Tina walking away, put the chart down, got up and walked to the door. "I'll walk out with you."

The two women left the building and walked to the parking lot.

Tina caught sight of a shadow flying overhead, and when she looked up, she stopped and stared. Wendi stopped and looked at her. "What's wrong?"

Tina pointed to the sky and Wendi looked up to see two huge shapes descending towards them.

"What are they?" asked Tina.

As the objects got closer, Wendi saw that they were ugly creatures with wings. She turned to Tina, "I don't know, but run."

Tina ran to her car, fumbled with her keys, but was able to get the door open and threw herself into the car. She slammed the door and peeked out from the side window.

Wendi had made it to her car, got in, and slammed the door. Tina could see her trying to get the keys into the ignition when one of the things that looked like a giant warthog landed next to the driver-side door. With no effort, it ripped the door off and pulled Wendi from the car. An equally ugly creature grabbed Wendi from the other and flew off into the evening light with her. Tina sat and stared for a few moments, not sure if she saw what she did, and then dialed 911.

Tex-Am Drilling Platform
Highway 177
Andrews County, Tx

BOB CONNER WAS EARLY for his evening shift at the oil rig. He drove his pickup down the dirt road towards the oil rig platform to take over his shift. He drove into the drilling compound near the trailer they used as an office and parked. It was getting dark, he didn't see any activity around the rig, and no one had turned on the large lighting system.

Those slackers, now where could they have gone?

He got out of his Chevrolet pickup and started walking toward the rig. He then noticed Donaldson's suburban still parked, and no lights were on in the trailer.

"Mr. Donaldson," he yelled. "Hello, Sam? Anyone here?"

When no one answered, he walked over to the trailer and saw that the door was open. "Hello, anyone in there?" He turned on the lights, but the trailer was empty. He turned and looked back towards the rig and, in the dim light, saw what looked like someone on the ground.

"Sam, Rob, is that you? C'mon, this isn't time for jokes. Billy? Alex? Tom?" He walked over and looked down.

Rob was lying face up, with a huge hole in the chest. Bob stumbled back and looked around in a panic. He saw another crumpled body on the ground, so he ran over to it. This one had a body, but the head was missing. By the clothes and the build, he thought it might be the new guy, Alex, but wasn't sure. Bob stepped back, tripped, and fell into the dirt. He turned and saw Billy staring wide-eyed at him, except his eyes were glazed over, and the bottom half of his body was missing. He got up, ran to his truck, and pulled his shotgun from behind the seat. He looked around, but all was quiet. He pulled out his phone but there was no signal, so he climbed into his truck and sped back towards the highway.

CHAPTER THREE

Northwestern Volcano Observatory
1001 N. Walton Ave
Five Corners, Washington

CLARK COUNTY SHERIFF'S Deputy Stan Banes drove his patrol car into the parking lot of the observatory. In the fading sunlight, he saw an ambulance and another county patrol car were already on the scene. The fifteen-year police veteran climbed out of his car, hitched up his gun belt, and approached the back of the ambulance. He saw a young black woman sitting in the back with a blanket wrapped around her. She was wearing an oxygen mask and the paramedics were checking her vital signs. He turned to one of the paramedics who was writing down her information on their clipboard. "So, what's her story, Phil?"

Phil shrugged and motioned for him to step out of the woman's hearing. "Man, I don't know. She says that one of her friends, a doctor who works at the lab, was kidnapped by monsters."

"Monsters?"

Phil nodded. "Yep, that's what she said. They flew down and took her friend away."

"Aren't these the scientists that study volcanos and earthquakes and stuff?" asked Banes.

"I think so." replied Phil.

Deputy Banes glanced over the woman. "Do you think she could be on drugs or may have had a nervous breakdown?"

"Beats me. She seems normal, just terrified."

"Thanks." said Deputy Banes. He walked over to the woman. The young woman was visibly shaking. "Ma'am, I'm Deputy Banes with the sheriff's department, can you tell me what happened?"

Tina pulled the oxygen mask down. "I know you're going to think I'm crazy, but Doctor Hamilton was kidnapped by monsters. I saw it all."

Deputy Banes took his notebook out of his pocket and began writing on it. "Ok, let's start with your name."

"Tina Williams."

"Ok, Tina, and do you work here at the observatory?" asked Banes.

Tina nodded. "Yes, I'm a research assistant. I go to the university too. I was about to leave and saw Wendi, I mean Dr. Hamilton, working. It was getting close to quitting time. I told her that she needed to go home too. She walked out with me. We were walking to our car when these things flew down at us. Dr. Hamilton said for us to run, so I did. I got to my car and was able to get in. I locked the doors. I looked out. One of those creatures pulled her door completely off, like it was made of paper, it grabbed her, and flew off with her."

Deputy Banes wrote down the information. "Now, what did they look like?"

Tina sat and thought for a moment, then shivered. "I only got a look at one of them. It looked like a flying warthog."

"A warthog with wings?"

"Yes, yes, a giant warthog." she answered. "You don't believe me. There's a security camera for the building that will prove me right."

Deputy Banes looked at the building and saw a security camera on each corner of the building. "Do you think you can show me the video footage?"

Tina looked around, not sure what to do.

"It's ok, you're safe now. It would help us get your friend back."

She nodded. Deputy Banes pointed to the other deputy on the scene. "Tina, this is Deputy Luna, she will take you inside to see if you can get us a video of it."

Tina got up and walked with Deputy Luna towards the building, keeping the blanket wrapped around her. Deputy Luna had her arm around her and was talking softly to her as they disappeared into the building. Banes walked over to the missing woman's car. The driver's door was on the ground about ten feet from the car. It had been ripped from the hinges.

Something sure happened, but what?

Sgt Murphy of the sheriff's department arrived at that moment, parked, and walked over to Deputy Banes. He looked at the car and whistled softly to himself. "So, what happened, Banes?"

Deputy Banes looked at his fortyish, thick-built, bald sergeant. "The woman said some monsters flew down, ripped this door off, and kidnapped a scientist who works at the observatory."

Sgt Murphy looked at Banes with a frown. "Cut the crap, what really happened?"

"Honest, sarge, that's what the woman said. She went inside with Shelly to look at the outside video cameras."

Sgt Murphy scratched his bald head. "Alright, you wait for crime scene to get here while I go inside and see." He walked into the building, which was empty since everyone else had gone home already. He called Deputy Shelly Luna on his radio and asked for their location. She directed him down the hall and to the left. When he arrived at a door, Deputy Luna waved him inside. Tina was sitting at a desk typing on a computer with a large video monitor in front. Tina looked up.

"I'm Sgt Murphy, did you find anything?"

"I'm finding the correct time to get the recording." She answered. After a few moments, she located the time on the camera of them walking out. She got up and backed away. "All you have to do is hit the play button. I'm not going to watch." She backed out into the hallway.

Deputy Luna sat down and pushed the play button. They both watched the two women walk down the sidewalk and into the parking lot. Tina stops and points to the sky and Dr. Hamilton looks up too. She looks frightened and says something to Tina. They both run across the parking lot to their cars. Tina gets into her car as she said she did. The two law enforcement officers watch in horror as a creature, described exactly as Tina explained, lands next to the scientist's car. It rips the door off and pulls her from the car. Another creature, a tall black one with no nose but long sharp teeth and a long-spiked tail, lands and takes the woman. They both fly off out of sight of the camera.

Deputy Luna looks up at her sergeant. "What she said is true."

Sgt Murphy nodded. "I'll call the undersheriff. This is way above my pay grade."

———

Tex-Am Drilling Platform
Highway 177
Andrews County, Tx

ANDREWS COUNTY DEPUTY Tim Sutton drove up and stopped on the highway behind a couple of pickups. His car's headlights illuminated several men congregating around one pickup. From their appearance, they were roughneck oil rig workers. He carefully got out and approached them. He shined his flashlight at the group who were obviously upset. One of them—a thin, bearded man in his twenties—rushed towards him, which alarmed Deputy Sutton, so he backed away.

"You've got to help me," he said, "They're all dead."

"Dead. Who's dead?"

"The crew at the rig, someone killed them, and our boss is missing." replied the man.

"Ok, calm down. What is your name?"

"Bob Conner."

"Ok, Mr. Conner. Now what is going on?" asked the deputy warily.

"I work for Tex-Am drilling. I went to the site for our evening shift, and all the men are dead. Murdered."

"By whom?"

Bob shook his head. "I don't know. But one of them is missing his head, and another is missing half his body."

"Where is this site?"

Bob pointed off into the dark. "It's a few miles down that dirt road back there."

"Who are these other men?" asked the deputy.

"They're the rest of the crew. I was the first one to get there. I told them to stay away, so we waited here for you."

"Good idea. Alright, tell the others to wait in their trucks. I need you to show me where it is. I'll get backup to go with us." explained Deputy Sutton. He walked back to his car and radioed for another deputy to come assist.

About 20 minutes later, another Andrew County car pulled up. Deputy Sutton walked up to the car. Deputy Juan Montoya rolled his window down. "What's up?"

Deputy Sutton leaned down. "This guy says his coworkers have been murdered at an oil rig site."

Deputy Montoya stared at him. "For real?"

"He's adamant about it, so I figured I needed someone else to back me up just in case."

"Who are the other guys?"

"Other co-workers. I told them to stay here."

"Well, let's do it, but you go first. I'm following you." Deputy Montoya said with a smirk.

Deputy Sutton rolled his eyes. "You're my hero. Just keep an eye out in case this goes bad. Weird people out here these days." He walked back to Bob's truck. "Mr. Conner, we'll follow you. When you get to the rig, park away from it so we can check it out."

Bob Conner nodded, got in his truck, and turned it around. The two deputies followed him down the dirt road in the dark. When they arrived, Bob pulled over to the side and allowed them to drive closer. They parked and shined their car spotlights around.

Deputy Sutton spotted one body closer to the rig. "I see a body over by the rig, Juan, do you see another one?"

Deputy Montoya shined his light around and spotted another body near a pickup. "There's another one over here. I see two more maybe by the other trucks."

"Ok, you keep an eye on Conner, in case he really did the killing and he's tricking us. I don't want to get shot in the back." The six-foot tall veteran deputy walked over to the body nearest to the rig and shined his light down. It appeared to be a male, but his head was missing. He shined his light around but couldn't find it. He radioed back to Deputy Montoya. "Hey, Juan, the guy was right, this man's head is missing."

"Wow!" replied Deputy Montoya. "Dispatch, it appears we have at least one dead body out here. Can you notify the Sergeant and call crime scene.?"

"10-4," replied the dispatcher over the radio.

Deputy Sutton walked over to another body and saw that he had a huge hole in his chest. "Here's another one." He shined his light around and found the man missing his lower half.

What on earth could have done this?

He only found a large pool of blood as proof of the last man. There were drag marks that went into the darkness. Deputy Sutton decided not to follow them.

Deputy Montoya had gotten out of his car and walked over. "So, where's their boss?"

Deputy Sutton shook his head. "I don't know. Conner said his boss was gone. He's either kidnapped, or he's the mass killer."

CHAPTER FOUR

Northwestern Volcano Observatory
1001 N. Walton Ave
Five Corners, Washington

FBI AGENT STEVE COLLINSWORTH parked his car in the lot and climbed out. Dressed in a tan shirt, brown slacks, and a black FBI jacket, he looked around and saw a couple of Clark County patrol cars, and a crime scene van was parked near a small white Hyundai. They'd made a perimeter around the car with yellow crime scene tape. A local news station van was also parked nearby.

Agent Collinsworth lifted the yellow tape, ducked under it, and then walked up to a young, short, female deputy with her hair in a tight bun. He showed the deputy his FBI credentials. He looked at her name tag, which said Luna.

"Your department called our office?" he asked.

Deputy Luna nodded. "Yeah, a woman was kidnapped. This one is really weird."

"How so?" he asked.

Deputy Luna thumbed over towards the car. "Door has been ripped off, and the woman was taken."

Agent Collinsworth shined his flashlight on the vehicle, walked over to the car door, and bent down. The hinges had been pulled directly out of the frame. He noticed the top of the door frame was crumpled and looked like a huge hand had simply pulled the door off. It reminded him of when the fire department uses the jaws of life to extricate people in car wrecks. He shook his head. "Any note of any kind left?" he asked.

"Nope." answered Deputy Luna.

"I was told that you have a witness?"

Deputy Luna nodded. "Yes, she went to the hospital to get checked out. She was very upset. We got her statement before she left. She said monsters did it."

Agent Collinsworth raised an eyebrow. "Monsters?"

"Yep, winged monsters."

"Any way to prove that?"

Deputy Luna pointed towards the building. "Sgt Murphy's inside with our crime scene guy. They have it all on security video."

"Thanks." replied Agent Collinsworth as he walked towards the building.

"Once you go in, turn left, it's the fourth room on the left." yelled Deputy Luna.

Agent Collinsworth waved without turning around and entered the building. He found the security office where she said it was. Inside was a sheriff's department sergeant, a male in civilian clothes, and a man in plain clothes with a jacket that said "Crime Scene" on the back who was working on the video system. Agent Collinsworth showed them his badge.

"Thanks for coming," said Sgt Murphy. "The undersheriff said to call you. Besides being required to notify the FBI on all kidnappings, we thought this is unusual."

"No problem," said Agent Collinsworth. He turned to the other man. "And who are you?"

The middle-aged black male shook his hand. "I'm Cedric Reynolds. I'm the supervisor of this facility. We're part of the National Geological Agency. We're all shocked about what happened."

Agent Collinsworth nodded. "We'll get to the bottom of it. Any phone calls demanding money or anything?"

Cedric shook his head. "No, nothing. We don't know why anyone would kidnap Wendi."

Agent Collinsworth took out his pocket notebook and looked at it. "Wendi Hamilton is what I was given."

"That's correct. Dr. Wendi Hamilton. She's our head volcanologist."

"A what? A Vulcan what?" asked Agent Collinsworth.

Cedric smiled. "Not Vulcan. She's a volcanologist, someone who studies volcanos."

Agent Collinsworth smiled back. "Oh, right. Any idea why someone or something would kidnap her?"

Cedric shook his head.

"Do you want to see the footage?" asked Sgt Murphy.

"Yes." replied Agent Collinsworth. He looked over at the screen as the crime scene officer played the tape. He watched the scene unfold and the creatures taking Wendi. In his 12-year career in the FBI, he had never seen anything like this, but knew who had. He rubbed his head and turned to them. "We have a special unit in the FBI that needs to look into this." He handed them his business card. "Send me everything you got."

CHAPTER FIVE

J Double T Ranch
Sutton County, Texas

IT WAS EARLY in the morning in West Texas, and Ellie had left to go to the church in their new Ford F350 pickup. They'd traded in her car for it as broad-shouldered Jake couldn't fit in her small car very well, and they didn't think it was good for her to drive his dented, scratched-up old red pickup.

Jake walked towards the barn, followed by his loyal friend, Roscoe, a huge half-wolf dog. Roscoe had wandered up on the ranch one day and decided he liked it. Since then, Roscoe had been an integral part of their lives, often saving Jake from demons, he had the scars to show for it. Jake and Ellie had arrived home late last night from their honeymoon.

When Jake and Roscoe entered the barn, he saw his only employee named Roy, a fiftyish, short, thin man with a handlebar mustache and a quick smile. Roy was feeding the horses and talking to Ned Parker, an older man with a bushy mustache and lambchop sideburns. He wore the same broadcloth shirt and brown pants stuffed down inside old worn-out boots. The odd thing about Ned is that he's what most people call a ghost, but he prefers to be called a disembodied spirit. He's the original owner of the land, and even though he died many years ago, he loved the place so much he stayed. Jake is the only person that can see ghosts and demons unless they wish to be seen. Ned had grown fond of Ellie and Roy, so he allowed himself to be seen by them.

"Good morning." said Jake.

Roy looked up and smiled. "Good morning, how was the trip? I saw y'all got back late so I didn't want to bother you."

"You love birds have a nice time," said Ned with a wink.

"Yes, it was nice to go somewhere that I'm not being bothered with demons and creatures of the night." replied Jake.

Roy nodded. "That's good, and it's been quiet here at the ranch, just us hard workers."

Jake laughed. "I'll bet."

"Where's Miss Ellie?" asked Roy.

"She already left, she's headed to town, to the church."

———

Shady Oak Community Church
2203 E. Hollis Street
Shady Oak, Texas

ELLIE TAFT DROVE into the parking lot of their newly built church. The church had been finished, thanks to a national Christian magazine that donated money in exchange for an interview with Jake, and a portion of the proceeds from a book written by her best friend, Pamela Martin. Previously they had a couple of modular buildings and a large storage building, which had been removed as the new building will house all their needs.

She entered and was met by Janet Pearston, a cheerful and bubbly part-time administrative assistant and receptionist. "Welcome back Ellie," she said. "I hope the honeymoon was awesome."

Ellie hugged her and smiled. "Yes, it was fabulous, but now it's time to get back to work. I guess George is at his store?"

Janet nodded. "Yes, he said he'll stop by later."

George Tillon was the church's part-time associate pastor who owned the local feed store. Ellie walked to her new office and sat behind her desk for a moment. She laughed to herself because her previous office in the portable buildings was small. Jake said it was the size of a broom closet.

She began checking her emails when her best friend, Pam, a thirties, feisty blonde, who owned the local newspaper and coffee shop and was also a book author, came in.

"Hey, stranger," said Pam. "How does it feel to be Mrs. Taft now?"

Ellie laughed. "It will take some getting used to."

"So, have you been able to change Jake yet?"

Ellie rolled her eyes. "Jake is just fine the way he is. It's just you that he likes to annoy."

Pam pulled up a chair and plopped down. "So, what's on your agenda?"

"Oh, just the normal church things."

"Did you hear what happened over in Andrew County last night?"

Ellie shook her head.

"Four men were murdered at an oil rig, and the owner of the company is missing. They don't know if he was kidnapped or if he is the killer."

Ellie raised her eyebrows and sat back in her chair. "Did they say if they knew why?"

Pam shook her head. "Nope, but I talked to Deputy Cole in town earlier, he talked to one of the deputies in Andrew County. They told him that it was a massacre. One of the men was missing a head, another had a huge hole in his chest, and another was missing half his body. They found parts of the fourth guy. That's about all he could find out."

"That sounds ultra-violent. I wonder if demons were involved?"

"Who knows."

"I'll let Jake know later."

Lubbock County Medical Examiner
4434 S Loop 289,
Lubbock, Texas

DR. CHARLES DURBIN and his assistant, Ann Graft, had begun working on the autopsies of the men brought in from Andrew County. They had taken fingerprints of the headless one, just to ensure they had the correct identity. Dr. Tamatha Welch was working on the man with a hole in his chest in another exam room. The man with only half a body was in the morgue, along with a few body parts they found of the fourth man. After going through the normal procedures, Dr. Durbin examined the neck area of the headless man. He looked for any serrated areas indicating it had been cut, but instead, it appeared to have been by blunt force.

"Hmmmm, this looks odd." he said to his assistant.

Ann looked closer at the wound. "Yes, it does. No cut marks."

"Did they say how he was decapitated?"

"No, the report said he was found lying in the middle of the oil rig area."

Dr Durbin walked around to the other exam room where Dr. Welch was working.

"Tammy, have you noticed anything odd about your autopsy?" he asked.

Dr. Welch looked up. "I was just going to ask you the same thing. Come look at this."

Dr. Durbin stepped up and looked at the huge hole in the victim's chest.

"Look at the edges of the wound." she said.

Dr. Durbin looked closer and noticed that there were tear marks.

"This must have been done by some sort of animal. It must be." said Dr. Welch.

"Did you take samples?"

Dr. Welch nodded. She then pointed to the cadaver's left shoulder. "Take a look at that."

Dr. Durbin looked and saw claw marks like he had never seen. "These are not normal animal marks."

"It looks like something held him with one clawed hand and ripped a hole in his chest with the other."

"Could it be someone who was wearing some kind of clawed attachment?" asked Dr. Durbin.

Dr. Welch shrugged. "Who knows. That's why I took a sample for DNA."

"I came to see you because the other victim had his head ripped off, not cut." explained Dr. Durbin.

Dr. Welch lifted her plastic face shield. "Something had to use a huge amount of force to do all this."

"That was my thinking." replied Dr. Durbin.

"Let's go look at the other ones."

The two medical examiners walked to the morgue freezer and pulled the door open. They rolled out one of the corpses and unzipped the body bag. They looked at the man they identified as Robert Adams, who only had half his body.

"This is brute force too." said Dr. Durbin.

Dr. Welch pulled out the other man, or what was left of him. She unzipped the bag that held a leg, part of the torso, and his head with his face frozen forever in terror. She looked closely at the wounds. "Charlie, look at this. There looks to be teeth marks."

Dr. Durbin leaned in and examined the ribs and leg. "You're right. This man was ripped apart and eaten."

Dr. Welch zipped up the body bags and they rolled them back into the freezer. They walked out into the hallway.

"I think I need to call the feds. These claw marks and teeth marks aren't normal." said Dr. Durbin. "I suspect this isn't involving a human. Weren't there demon attacks a couple of years ago over in Sutton County involving that rancher they call the demon hunter."

"Jacob Taft?" said Dr. Welch.

"That's the guy." replied Dr. Durbin.

CHAPTER SIX

Hell's Corner
New Orleans, Louisiana

THROUGHOUT HISTORY, the New Orleans area has been hit by hurricanes and major storms, more than twenty in just the last thirty years. They recover and rebuild most areas, but there is an area that has never recovered. This section is outside the city and has never been rebuilt, leaving the remnants of houses. Recently, the parish bulldozed the crumbling shacks and houses, but no one ever built on that section because of what lay farther out.

An area of rundown buildings and bars used by drug dealers, prostitutes, gangs, and other dredges of society. This became known as "Hell's Corner".

The local parish law enforcement made many attempts to clean up the area, but being understaffed and having too large of an area to patrol kept them from properly controlling the crime. By the time any law enforcement vehicles crossed into "Hell's Corner", the criminal element would be evacuated and the area seemed to be empty and quiet. Their attempts to tear down and bulldoze that section always ended in the equipment being mysteriously damaged or disabled and workers going missing. Eventually, it became off limits to most law-abiding citizens.

In the middle of this decrepit section sits an old southern mansion, or at least it used to be a mansion. The three-storied home looked as if it was specially made for every horror movie.

In one of the rooms on the top floor sat Wendi Hamilton. The room was dark and musty and the windows were boarded up, but there was enough light coming in through the cracks for her to see the walls. They were covered in obscene graffiti, claw marks, and demonic symbols.

After being snatched from her car by that horrible creature, she was brought to a van where three men waited. They tied her up and put a hood over her head. She lost track of time as they drove almost nonstop, except for bathroom breaks. She was always accompanied by one of the thugs who never spoke to her. She was fed inside the van.

Upon arrival at their destination, she was jerked out of the van and marched into the mansion with the hood still over her head. The hood was removed when she was shoved into the room and the door closed. Wendi had no idea where she was or how long she had been in the room when the door opened and a huge ugly demon glanced down at her. His head was large but flat on top. His small yellow eyes stared out from under a thick forehead. He had no neck as his head came straight out from his massive shoulders. A large black sword hung from a belt around his huge waist.

"Come." he said with a voice straight out of hades.

Wendi slid back into a corner. "Where am I going?" she asked in a trembling voice. "Why am I here?"

"Stupid human. Come or I will drag you."

Wendi struggled to her feet and followed the creature down the stairs to the second floor. She was shocked to see all types of hideous creatures and humans, who looked more like zombies, moving around. They stopped at a door where an equally hideous demon stood. They spoke to each other using grunts, clicks, and squeaks. Wendi looked around for a way to escape, but there was none. The demon opened the door and shoved Wendi inside when she didn't move.

She stared in horror at a large ballroom with boarded-up windows. The walls were painted black and had various satanic symbols scribbled on them. Attached to the walls were shackles, chains, and all types of torture devices. A human corpse, with maggots crawling in and out of it, hung from one of the shackles attached to the wall. The stench almost made her faint, and she covered her mouth with her hand. Several large candelabras stood around the room, casting weird lighting throughout the ballroom. Incense burned in the room, but it did nothing to cover up the smell of death and decay.

Wendi was prodded to the far end of the ballroom to an upraised platform. A figure sat in an overstuffed chair with animal horns, skulls and bones of all types attached to the chair, making it some sort of horrific throne. Through the candlelight, Wendi could make out the creature which made her step back in shock. He had a large, oval-shaped head with glowing yellow eyes, and one eye had a vertical scar through it. His snout was like that of a crocodile or alligator, with large teeth and fangs that protruded below the jaw and curved around in a semi-circle. The creature's body was large and muscular with a large tail. To one side of the throne sat a large bong, which Wendi assumed was used to smoke narcotics. He had a large black sword resting across his lap. He leaned forward and stared at Wendi.

"Step closer." he said in a deep gravelly voice. When she didn't move, the demon escort shoved her forward, causing her to fall forward onto her knees amongst skulls, bones, and decaying flesh on the floor. Wendi vomited. He stared at her for a few moments and then motioned for the escort demon to leave.

"You're Wendi Hamilton? You're the volcano expert?" he asked.

Wendi wiped her mouth and stared at him wild-eyed but nodded.

"Good, I have use of you."

"W…w…who are you?" she asked after finally finding her voice.

The creature sat back. "I have gone by many names over time.

The ancient Egyptians worshipped me as Sobeck, and in South America, they called me Supay, but you can call me Tarnac."

"What do you want with me?" she asked.

Tarnac grinned, showing his sharp teeth. "Why, you're going to help me destroy this world so it can be rebuilt the way lord Satan and I want it."

Federal Bureau of Investigation
Office of Deputy Director of Paranormal Activities
935 Pennsylvania Avenue Northwest
Washington, D.C.

DEPUTY DIRECTOR OSCAR RUIZ was finally settling into his position after being promoted to deputy director after a previous corrupt deputy director was killed by demons two years ago. He'd helped Jake Taft stop demons from trying to take over the world several times, so when the opening became available, he was appointed. After the world finally accepted the idea that demons did exist and were a threat, the FBI created a special unit to deal with them. Sadly, he only had a handful of agents to utilize, but he did have the assistance of some half-demons who wanted to help. They were the result of experiments the Nazis completed when trying to combine human, animal, and demon DNA. After they were abandoned in Arizona and Nevada, three of them decided to help the FBI fight the powers that had created them. While browsing through reports and news items that might involve the paranormal, his phone rang.

"Deputy Director Ruiz," he said.

"Deputy director, this is Agent Collinsworth in the Vancouver office. I think I have something that might interest you."

Oscar picked up a notepad and pen. "What've you got?"

"We have what we think is demon activity up here. Two women were walking to their cars when two creatures we believe to be demons attacked. One woman was taken."

"Where did this happen?" asked Oscar while he wrote down the details.

"It occurred in a small city called Five Corners in the parking lot of the Northwestern Volcano Observatory." replied Agent Collinsworth. "We got the details from the woman who was not taken."

Oscar sat back in his chair. "Did she have any idea why the woman was kidnapped?"

"No, sir."

"What is the missing woman's name?"

"Wendi Louise Hamilton."

"What does she do there?" asked Oscar.

"She has some sort of PhD in volcanos." replied Agent Collinsworth. "We've put a bulletin out through NCIC, and the local sheriff's department gladly turned everything over to us. I'll send you all the photos of the crime scene and the witness statement if you want this."

Oscar rubbed his temple. "How do we know this is demonic?"

"Sorry, sir," answered Agent Collinsworth, "I forgot to mention we have building security footage of the abduction. They flew in, ripped her door off her car, and flew off with her."

"Ripped her door off and took her in broad daylight?"

"Yes, sir, about 5 pm yesterday when they were leaving for the day."

"That's blatant of them." said Deputy Director Ruiz. "Ok, send me the report along with the witness statement, photos and video."

"Yes, sir, and good luck."

"Thanks." Oscar said, and he hung up. *Now why would demons snatch a woman out of a parking lot in broad daylight?*

J Double T Ranch
Sutton County, Texas

IT WAS EVENING, and Ellie was almost finished with getting dinner ready. Jake and Roy had just parked the pickup after their daily chores out on the land. Ellie stepped out on the porch and saw Ned sitting in a rocking chair, smoking his pipe.

"It's dinner time, you two. Hurry up, or it will get cold." she yelled.

"That's one thing I miss, a good meal." commented Ned.

Ellie smiled and watched the two men walk toward them. Roy was short, thin, and bowlegged, wearing a red shirt and jeans with a dusty black cowboy hat. The wide-shouldered, six-foot-three Jake was dressed in his usual work shirt, jeans, a worn Stetson hat, and boots; they looked like they'd just stepped off the pages of a western novel. Roscoe followed beside him. The huge wolf laid down next to Ned on the porch. Jake bent down and kissed his five-foot-four wife. "We could've helped fix dinner. You're busy at the church too."

Ellie shrugged. "I got here early, so I thought I'd go ahead and fix us dinner. Wash up and let's eat."

They all sat and ate dinner while discussing the day's activities. "Pam came to see me today."

"Was she as annoying as ever?" asked Jake.

Ellie laughed. "She's just Pam. Anyway, she said that there was a mass murder over in Andrews County. The whole crew of an oil rig was murdered, slaughtered would be precise. A deputy over in Andrews County told Deputy Cole that one was beheaded, and another ripped in half."

"Andrew County?" said Roy with a shake of his head. "I used to work at a ranch up there, and I used to do a little oil rig work too."

Jake sat for a minute. "Sounds horrific. Did they say if anyone saw any demons?"

"She didn't say," answered Ellie. "The owner of the company's missing. They don't know if he's dead or kidnapped. She said there are rumors that he may have killed them."

"What company?"

"Tex-Am oil."

Roy raised both eyebrows. "Wow, that's Sam Donaldson's outfit. He worked his way up from working on rigs to being a company owner. I'd be surprised if he slaughtered his own workers. He's a decent man."

"I'll give Oscar a call and see if he's heard anything." said Jake.

———

LATER THAT EVENING, Roy had already gone to bed, and Jake and Ellie were sitting in the living room of his single-story ranch. It was split into two buildings connected by the porch. One side was the kitchen and formal area, and the other side held the two bedrooms.

They were relaxing and discussing minor things that needed to be done at the ranch and her work at the church when a huge figure suddenly appeared in the living room. He was seven feet tall with skin the color of golden brass. He was dressed in white clothing with a golden belt, and on the belt was a scabbard covered in jewels and etched with strange symbols that contained a huge golden sword.

"Malachy." said Ellie with a huge smile.

"Greetings, Jake and Ellie, from the Most High God." said Malachy in his usual deep voice and a wide smile.

Ellie and Jake got up. Ellie hugged him while Jake shook the giant's hand.

"It's good to see you, my friend." said Jake.

"Yes, it's always great to see you."

Malachy's face then became serious. "Sadly, this isn't a cordial visit. The fallen are up to something, and I'm afraid you'll be needed."

Jake nodded. He learned never to question the big angel who had been watching over Jake for years before he even knew he was there. "Does it have to do with the men that were killed at the oil rig?"

"Yes," replied Malachy. "Demons attacked them and took the owner, Sam Donaldson. Also, there was an attack in a small city in Washington that we believe to be related. They're up to something, and it's never good."

"I was telling Jake earlier about the massacre at the oil rig." explained Ellie.

"I'll call Oscar and make sure he knows about both." said Jake.

"Good, and be careful." said Malachy before he disappeared.

Jake went to the kitchen and returned with two cups of coffee. They sat in silence for a few minutes, absorbing the information.

"I wonder how Malachy knows so much, but doesn't know when and where the devils are all the time? He comes from heaven after all." said Jake.

Ellie set her coffee cup down on the coffee table and sat back. She curled her legs up on the couch. "I've wondered that myself many times. Our human brains can only understand so much about the heavenly world. Angels are created beings just like we are, so they aren't omniscient. All I can figure is that God gives them information when he deems necessary, just like he does us. That's the best I can figure."

Jake slowly nodded. "Things are run differently in heaven that's for sure."

Ellie laughed. "That's a unique way to put it, but yes, I think they are."

"But I think things are about to get busy again."

CHAPTER SEVEN

Private Airfield
Northern Mexico

SAM DONALDSON FELT like his life had gone from bad to worse. After being carried away from the oil rig by those murdering monsters, he was deposited nearby, where several men in a large SUV tied him up with zip ties and blindfolded him. His shoulders ached and had small punctures from the claws when they carried him through the air. He was forced into the SUV and driven for several hours, only stopping to get gas, he assumed. They would let him urinate on the ground outside the SUV but kept him blindfolded. He asked several times what they wanted and said that his family would pay for his release, but the men never answered.

Sam lost all track of time and even slept for small amounts of time. The SUV stopped, and this time he was jerked out and walked to a building. Once inside, he was left alone in a room which gave him the opportunity to take his blindfold off. He blinked, waited for his eyes to adjust to the light, then looked around. He was in a small room with a window. He looked out, and the only thing he could see was cactus, scrub trees, and Mexican palms.

I'm down near the border.

There was a table with some water bottles, which he drank. He hoped they would let him go once the ransom was paid.

———

Hell's Corner
New Orleans, Louisiana

WENDI HAD BEEN LED out of her nightmare room and down the stairs, where she was tied again, and a hood was placed over her head. She was walked to a van, and after a brief ride, it stopped. She was removed from the van and could hear an engine revving up. She was guided across a flat surface, helped into some type of vehicle and strapped in. She was told not to take the hood off or else. She sat in fear as she heard the engine wind up and the vehicle moved. It accelerated, then she felt herself lift and she realized she was in an aircraft. The sounds around her were loud, and after several minutes, she took the chance and removed her hood. She blinked at how bright it was around her. When her eyes adjusted, she confirmed that she was in an eight-passenger prop plane. There was a pilot and another man in the copilot seat. He glanced back at her but didn't say anything about her hood being taken off. She looked out the window and could only see water. They were flying low over the water, obviously trying to avoid detection. She peeked over the shoulder of the pilot and saw the GPS screen on the aircraft. The screen showed that they were leaving land and were headed out over a large body of water. She looked around inside the cabin and saw behind her stacks and stacks of compacted rectangular packages. They were about twelve by fifteen inches and several inches thick.

Drug smugglers?

She sat back and after several hours she spotted land. Soon she could make out beaches, hotels, resorts along the coast and palm trees. She glanced again at the GPS screen, saw that they had turned and were flying directly inland, and then about an hour later, they landed at a private airstrip. The man in the copilot seat motioned for her to put the hood on. She was removed, walked to a building, and left inside a room. Believing she was alone, she removed her hood but was surprised to see a man sitting in a chair with a bottle of water.

He smiled and handed her the water. "Howdy, I'm Sam Donaldson. Welcome to my private hell."

———

Federal Bureau of Investigation
Office of Deputy Director of Paranormal Activities
935 Pennsylvania Avenue Northwest
Washington, D.C.

FBI AGENT STEPHANIE WILLIAMS parked her government vehicle in the parking garage. She was wearing a light blue blouse, jeans, and an FBI windbreaker. She walked to a secure door, entered it using her keycard, then took the elevator to their designated floor.

Agent Williams was a blonde, mid-thirties, no-nonsense veteran FBI agent with three vertical scars on her cheek from a demon attack a few years ago. She and then Agent Ruiz were trying to locate the President's daughter when they were attacked by two demons. Only Jake's intervention saved them from being killed. Now, as a hard-core member of the paranormal unit, often called the "Ghoul Squad" or "MIB for Demons", she was running late for a meeting with Deputy Director Ruiz about possible new demon activity.

After exiting the elevator, she walked down to a conference room and entered. Deputy Director Ruiz, her partner Agent Terrell Pyle, and several unusual others were already there.

Also attending were three half demons. Depending on how the Nazi experiments went, they could be a mixture of demon, animal, and human DNA. The Nazis had only assigned them by numbers, but since then, the half-demons gave themselves names. One was half demon and half woman named Eudora. She had been one of the Nazis' most successful experiments. She had no hair, one blue eye and one yellow eye, which is typical of half-demons, extraordinary demonic strength for her five-foot-eight frame, but otherwise looked human. Another was named Kong, part ape, part human, and part demon, who stood eight feet tall and had the strength of several white-backed gorillas. He also had the typical normal eye and one yellow eye. He had human intelligence, and either couldn't speak or declined to. He'd become Eudora's close friend and self-appointed bodyguard who rarely left her side. The last unusual member was part man, part demon, and part eagle. He resembled a comic book character, except he was real. His face and upper body were human, but his lower half was eaglelike, and he had huge wings. The Navajo's called him Soaring Eagle, so he kept the name. These half demons had saved Ellie and Pam from death at the hands of the Nazis and helped stop the killing of half of the world leaders at the conference in Berlin. Most of the "half-demons", as they have come to be known, lived peacefully in Arizona on the Navajo Reservation, but these three had volunteered to join the FBI to help stop demons they call "full-bloods", or anything else with evil intent. Eudora had emerged over time as their leader. They consider themselves a new species but haven't come up with a proper title.

Agent Williams took a seat next to her partner, Agent Pyle, a black ex-NFL player turned FBI agent who also had been instrumental in stopping the Nazis.

Deputy Director Ruiz began his briefing. "Now that Stephanie has had her extra beauty sleep, we can begin." he said with a grin. Agent Williams frowned, Agent Pyle elbowed her in the ribs, and Eudora snickered.

"We have been made aware of two possible demonic activities recently." said Ruiz. "In front of each of you is a case folder with the reports and photos. The first is an attack in a small city near Vancouver, Washington. A woman who works at the Northwestern Volcano Observatory was taken by two demons. A co-worker was not taken and gave us the information, there is also a security cam video of it. I sent the video to your email. Since her abduction, we haven't heard from or about her. Comments? Thoughts?"

The group sat and looked through the photos and reports.

"Ransom possibly?" suggested Agent Pyle.

Deputy Director Ruiz shook his head. "I doubt it. She doesn't have money, nor does her family. She's a woman with a PHD who works hard studying volcanos."

"Volcanos?" said Agent Williams.

"Yep, that's her specialty."

"Anything on her bank account or credit cards?" asked Agent Pyle.

Deputy Director Ruiz shook his head.

"Could it have just been random?" asked Agent Pyle.

Eudora shook her head. "Demons may kill randomly, but they don't snatch women out of their cars in daylight for no reason."

"I agree." said Agent Williams. "If it had been random and just for kicks or just to kill her, we would have found her body. They're up to something."

"Ok, the next one is a mass killing in Texas. We believe demons attacked an oil rig, killed four men, and took another one. The man they took was the owner of one of the nation's biggest oil drilling companies." explained Deputy Director Ruiz.

"Now this one could be for ransom." suggested Agent Pyle.

"Possibly." said Deputy Director Ruiz.

"How do we know that demons are involved?" asked Eudora.

"We received a call from the medical examiner's office in Lubbock. While doing the autopsies, they noticed that all the injuries were by brute force. Also, the bodies had large claw marks and one had been eaten partially."

"Sounds like demons." said Agent Pyle.

Agent Williams rubbed her forehead, "So two kidnappings within a few days, but in different parts of the country, and no contact or ransom demands that we know of."

"So, we aren't certain they are connected." added Agent Pyle.

"They didn't kill the witness in Washington, but slaughtered four men in Texas." added Eudora.

"And that's not far from Jake's ranch." said Agent Pyle.

"They kill four men but take one." said Soaring Eagle. "The full-bloods will kill for sport but won't take one alive without a good reason."

"Or they were ordered to by their leader." added Eudora.

"Any idea who is the leader of this area." asked Deputy Director Ruiz.

Eudora thought for a minute. "I can't recall."

"I've heard rumors that the current leader is a demon called Tarnac." said Soaring Eagle.

"Tarnac?"

Soaring Eagle nodded.

"Didn't Jake have dealings with a demon named Tarnac?" asked Agent Williams.

"I'll have to check, but I remember reading in a report that he did. I'll contact Jake and ask. I think we need to talk to the kidnapped man's family and then go from there. He has money, so there may be a random demand and the family has kept it quiet. Stephanie and Terrell will go out there and talk to them. Since Jake's close, I'll see if he can go too. Eudora and her people can see what they can find out from their sources."

"Any word on the half-demon Hitler they created?" asked Agent Williams.

Deputy Director Ruiz shook his head.

"We haven't heard anything either." added Eudora. "It's like he disappeared."

"That's what worries me." replied Deputy Director Ruiz.

The meeting was adjourned. *Volcanos and oil rigs?* Thought Deputy Director Ruiz.

CHAPTER EIGHT

J Double T Ranch
Sutton County, Texas

ELLIE HAD ALREADY LEFT to go to the church in town while Jake cleaned up the breakfast dishes. He stepped out on the front porch to head to the barn when he remembered to call Deputy Director Ruiz, so he pulled out his cell phone and dialed.

"Deputy Director Ruiz." answered Oscar on the third ring.

"Oscar, it's Jake. How have you been?" asked Jake.

"Busy as usual. These things never seem to stop. I was just about to call you about something."

Jake laughed. "I was calling you about something too."

"You go first."

Jake sat down in one of the rocking chairs on the porch. "I had a visit from Malachy last night. He said demons attacked an oil rig near here and took the owner. Also, there was an attack in a small city in Washington."

"Yep, he's right." said Oscar and then he chuckled. "It's nice to have friends in high places. It's a shame he can't tell us more."

"I guess he tells us what he knows or what he's allowed to."

"I guess so." replied Oscar. "So, a woman in a small city near Vancouver was kidnapped by demons. We have it on video surveillance, but we have no idea why. Her family isn't rich. The one in Texas is much worse. Four men were slaughtered, and we believe that the owner was taken."

"Sam Donaldson?" asked Jake.

"Yes, he owns a large oil drilling company. Do you know him?"

"No, but Roy used to work the oil fields and knows about him. He said the guy is upstanding, hard worker, and wouldn't have killed four of his people." explained Jake.

"We agree but can't rule it out yet. I'm sending Stephanie and Terrell out there to talk to the family in case there's been a ransom demand that we don't know about. Can you meet with them and go see the Donaldson family?" asked Oscar.

"Of course, I can. Can you send me what you have on these two incidents so I can get up to speed when I go visit them?"

"I'll send them to Ellie's email. When are you going to get an email address? This is the 21st century." said Oscar humorously.

Jake laughed. "I leave the modern technical stuff to my lovely wife."

After he hung up with Oscar, Ned turned to him. "Looks like you're going off on another adventure."

Jake chuckled. "I wouldn't call it an adventure but it looks like I have to go to Odessa about a kidnapping and murder."

Ned got up and walked towards the barn grumbling, "Odessa? The world's gone crazy, worse than when I was alive."

Jake grinned and shook his head.

When he was alive?

He called Ellie. "Hey, I just got off the phone with Oscar."

"The way you said it, it sounds like he wants you to do something." said Ellie.

"Yep, you're right. He wants me to meet Terrell and Stephanie tomorrow so we can interview the Donaldson family in Odessa, in case they know more." explained Jake.

"That's great. It will be good to see them again."

"Ellie, honey, this isn't a friendly visit." replied Jake.

"I know, but maybe I can be of some emotional help to the family."

Jake rolled his eyes. He knew better than to argue with her. "Ok."

"I love you." said Ellie, and then she hung up.

Jake sighed and shook his head. "Women." he said out loud.

Roscoe, who had been sitting nearby, barked.

"A lot of support you are," said Jake. "You're on her side."

Roscoe barked again.

"Come on, we have work to do."

———

Private Airfield
Northern Mexico

IT HAD BEEN a rough night for Wendi Hamilton and Sam Donaldson, sleeping on the floor. The captors had removed their bindings and given them food, water, and blankets but nothing else. They'd been escorted down the hall to a bathroom when they needed it, but that's all they were allowed to see or do.

Last night they had talked about who they were and what they did for a living, but not much more as they were exhausted from their ordeal.

Their guards had brought them some tortillas for breakfast.

"Tortillas and water, they spared no expense." said Sam sarcastically.

Wendi smiled slightly. "Have they said what they want you for?" she asked.

Sam shrugged, "Ransom, I guess. I don't know what those creatures have to do with it though." He thought back to his crew and how they were slaughtered, causing him to shudder.

"I don't know exactly why I'm here, but the monster that I talked to said they wanted to destroy the world and rebuild it."

Sam stopped chewing and stared at her. "Are you serious?"

Wendi nodded.

"But I just drill for oil and gas." he explained. "I wouldn't have anything to do with destroying the world."

Wendi just shrugged, and they ate in silence. A few minutes later, their guards entered and escorted them down the hall to the hanger portion of the building. They weren't blindfolded this time. Inside the hanger was a single-engine Daher Kodiak turboprop aircraft. It's capable of holding ten passengers but also able to carry cargo, and can land on gravel, dirt, or grass runways.

A man they assumed was the pilot was checking over the plane. Their escorts ordered them aboard the aircraft.

"Where are we going?" demanded Sam.

One of the men shoved the butt of the rifle into Sam's stomach, causing him to fall to one knee. "Shut up and get on the plane." snapped the man in a Mexican accent.

Sam and Wendi climbed into the plane and settled into their seats. Two of their captors also boarded, sat behind them, and buckled in. The pilot started the engine and taxied out onto the dirt runway, where they accelerated into the sky to their next unknown destination.

———

Midland-Odessa International Air and Space Port
Midland, Texas

IT WAS MIDMORNING when Agents Williams and Pyle landed at the Midland-Odessa Air and Space Port, located midway between the cities of Midland and Odessa, Texas.

They gathered their luggage and obtained their rental car. Agent Williams called Jake and advised him that they were on their way and said they would meet them at the Donaldson's. They drove west on the freeway towards Odessa.

Agent Pyle looked out the window and frowned. "What's that horrible smell?"

Agent Williams laughed. "Well, city dweller, that's natural gas. This area is oil and gas heaven."

"I don't know how they stand it." he replied with a frown.

Agent Williams smiled and shrugged. "Big baby, I guess you get used to it just like the pollution from cities."

Agent Pyle shook his head. "Why would demons snatch someone from around here?"

"That's what we're supposed to try and find out."

14351 Glendale Park Drive
Odessa, Texas

JAKE AND ELLIE left early that morning and drove northwest the two and a half hours to Odessa, where they stopped and ate breakfast. They followed the directions to the Donaldson's gated community and parked outside the gate.

Twenty minutes later, the two FBI agents drove up in their rented Toyota Corolla. They pulled up alongside Jake and Ellie.

Agent Pyle rolled the window down and looked over the new Ford F350 King Ranch pickup. "So, you finally broke down and got a decent truck?" he asked with a smile.

Ellie smiled. "Yes, I made Jake get us something a little more comfortable."

Jake leaned over and said, "There's nothing wrong with my old truck."

The two agents laughed. "Except for the dents, demon claw marks, scratches, and faded paint job?" said Agent Pyle.

"I hate to interrupt your truck admiration, but we need to go talk to the Donaldsons," said Agent Williams. "I called a few minutes ago and they gave me the gate code, so follow us."

Jake nodded. Agent Pyle drove up to the gate, entered the code, and the gate swung open. They drove through the expensive subdivision until they came to the Donaldson's residence. Their home appeared to be a two-story, 5,000-square-foot residence, brick mixed with rock, and a circular driveway. They parked, and the two agents exited their car wearing casual business clothes with jackets that had FBI embroidered on the left pocket.

Jake climbed out wearing his usual western attire, complete with his Stetson. Ellie was dressed in a dark blue jacket with a matching skirt. They approached the two agents and Jake shook their hands while Ellie hugged both.

The group walked to the door and Agent Williams rang the doorbell. A man answered the door and Agent Williams showed him their FBI credentials. The man was dressed in a suit, appeared to be in his thirties, muscular, and had a no-nonsense face. He led them into the large main living area where two women sat, most likely Mrs. Donaldson and a woman who looked to be a younger version of her. Another tough-looking man in a suit stood nearby.

The older, slim, blonde-haired woman rose from a couch and gave a weak smile. "I'm Sharon Donaldson." She pointed to the younger blonde woman who sat on a different couch. "This is our daughter Allison."

She pointed to the two men in suits. "We have three men for our security. This is Thomas and Edward. Kenneth is out walking the property, keeping a watch out."

Agent Williams stepped forward and shook her hand. "I'm Special Agent Williams and this is my partner, Special Agent Pyle." She motioned toward Jake and Ellie. "This is Lt. Colonel Taft and his wife Mrs. Taft. Lt. Colonel is a consultant with the FBI, and Mrs. Taft is a pastor of their local church."

Jake removed his hat, smiled, and nodded. Ellie stepped forward and shook her hand. "If there's anything I can do, just let me know."

Mrs. Donaldson thought for a moment and then pointed towards Jake. "Don't you live on a ranch south of here? Aren't you the one they call the demon hunter? I saw you on the news when you saved the President and other world leaders in Germany."

Jake frowned. "Yes ma'am, that's me. The news has nicknamed me that, but I'm just doing what God called me to do. And these three other people here also helped save everyone in Berlin, not just me."

"Do you believe these demon creatures did this? Is that why you're here?"

"Yes, ma'am."

Allison turned to Ellie. "As far as helping us, we need for you to find my father." she said with tears welling up in her eyes.

Agent Pyle spoke up. "That's why we're here."

Agent Williams looked at the two security men suspiciously. "How long have you had bodyguards?"

"Our board of directors suggested we get security after what happened." answered Mrs. Donaldson. "That is until we find Sam and get him home." She pointed to the couches and other chairs in the large living room. "I'm sorry, please sit down. How rude of me to keep you standing around."

Agent Williams shook her head. "No problem, you've been under a lot of stress."

Jake remained standing behind the couch where Ellie and Mrs. Donaldson sat. The two FBI agents sat in two overstuffed chairs.

Agent Williams reached in her pocket and pulled out a small recorder. "I'm going to record this because it's easier than scribbling down a lot of notes. This way, we can just talk."

The two Donaldson women nodded.

"Has there been any recent threats from anyone?" asked Agent Pyle.

Mrs. Donaldson shook her head repeatedly. "No, no, no one has done anything like that."

"My father is loved by everyone." added Allison. "He's a great man."

Agent Williams smiled. "Everything I've read says that too. Has there been any ransom demands of any kind?"

Both women shook their heads. "No one has contacted us." replied Mrs. Donaldson. She began to tear up. "Why would someone kidnap Sam if it's not for money? I've been told that the four men that were at the rig were killed violently. Is that true?"

Agents Pyle and Williams nodded solemnly. "I'm afraid so." said Agent Pyle.

"But could it have been men in costumes?" asked Allison.

Agent Williams glanced over at Agent Pyle before continuing. "I don't want to make this any harder than it is, but the four men's deaths indicate demonic activity."

Allison started crying and put her face in her hands. Ellie got up, went over to the other couch, and sat beside her. She carefully reached around and put an arm around her. Allison leaned into her. "What would demons or monsters want with daddy?" she said while she wept.

Allison looked up at Ellie. "You're a pastor? Why would God let this happen to him?" she asked.

"God loves us and gives us freedom of choice, even angels." explained Ellie. "But some choose the wrong path, even angels. These demons are fallen angels that chose to go against God. He grieves too when even one person turns the wrong way."

Jake walked over, knelt on one knee, and looked at the young woman. "That's what we're here to find out, Allison, but I promise we'll do everything we can to track them down and get your father back. There's an angel who's my friend, and even they are trying to help. We'll get through this, together."

Allison lifted her head and reached for a tissue off the coffee table. "I'm sorry, I just don't know what to think about all this."

"It's perfectly understandable." said Agent Williams. "What exactly does your husband do? I know he owns oil and gas drilling."

Mrs. Donaldson got up, sat on the other side of Allison, and held her hand. "Sam's company drills for natural gas and oil. There's nothing different or unusual."

"Has anyone asked him to do anything lately that he refused or any dealings that have gone badly?" asked Agent Pyle.

Mrs. Donaldson shook her head. "Not that I know of, but I don't get deeply involved in his business dealings. He hasn't mentioned anything unusual. Nothing I can think of that those devils would want him for."

"Anything from his credit cards or bank account?" asked Agent Pyle.

"No," replied Mrs. Donaldson. "The bank and credit card companies have alerts on everything but so far, nothing."

"You mentioned a board of directors." said Agent Williams.

"There are only four, counting Sam. I can't imagine any of them wanting to hurt Sam. We've known them for years. Steve Peterson is Allison's godfather and Sam's best friend. The other two are business partners." answered Mrs. Donaldson.

"We just want to cover all of our bases just to be sure." said Agent Pyle. "We might need to talk to the others and see if they know of anyone that might want to harm your husband."

"Harm him." said Allison suddenly. "Why would anyone want to harm him."

Agent Williams frowned at Agent Pyle. "We don't know of any reason anyone would want to harm him."

"Do you think he's dead?" asked Mrs. Donaldson wide-eyed.

"No," replied Agent Williams. "We just have to consider every angle."

Jake had stood back up and turned to Mrs. Donaldson. "I can tell you from my experience with these creatures, if they or someone had wanted him harmed, they would have done it at the oil rig. They took him for a reason, and that's what we need to find out."

Mrs. Donaldson thought for a moment and nodded.

The third security man walked into the room. They looked up, and Mrs. Donaldson said, "This is Kenneth, our other security man."

In one smooth motion, Jake reached inside his jacket, pulled out his Colt .45 semi-auto handgun he had in a holster on his belt, and shot Kenneth in the knee.

Kenneth fell to the ground in pain. The other two security men pulled handguns and pointed them at Jake, which caused Agents Williams and Pyle to pull their weapons and point them at the bodyguards.

Before anyone had a chance to say anything about Jake's sudden act of violence, they were all hit by the stench of ashes and sulfur. Mrs. Donaldson pointed at Kenneth and screamed. They all looked at the security man on the floor who had changed from a man to a hideous green demon with yellow wings. It reminded them of a deformed gecko with sharp teeth and leathery yellow wings.

All the armed people in the room turned their weapons on the creature.

Ellie had helped Mrs. Donaldson and Allison get up and back away. Agent Pyle moved and stood in front of them, shielding them.

Agent Williams spoke to the other two security men. "Lower your weapons."

The two men lowered their handguns but kept them ready.

Jake stepped forward and pointed his gun at the demon. "Why are you here?"

The demon hissed at Jake.

Jake stomped his foot on the heathen's injured knee. "Why are you here?"

The thing hissed and snarled.

Jake ground his boot into the demon's wound, causing him to hiss even more. "I will only ask one more time. Why are you here? Who took Sam Donaldson?"

"I was ordered to observe and report." said the demon in a high-pitched voice. "I can't tell you who took him."

"Yes, you can."

The glowing yellow eyes glared at Jake, who ground his boot even harder into the wound. "Where is Sam Donaldson?"

The creature screeched, grabbed a dagger hidden behind him, and plunged it into his own chest.

"No." yelled Mrs. Donaldson.

Agent Pyle knelt next to the creature. "Where is Donaldson?"

The demon laughed, gurgled, fell back, and died.

"That's a first." said Agent Williams dryly. "Never seen a demon commit suicide."

"He must've been more afraid of whoever ordered him here than us. Enough to kill himself." commented Jake.

Agent Williams turned on the two security men. "Do either of you know him?"

Thomas shook his head in shock. "No, I was hired from a security firm. I never met him until we came to work here." He looked over at Edward.

Edward stared at the rapidly decomposing demon. "I only

worked with him a couple of times. I swear, I didn't know he was a monster. How can he do that?"

"Demons have the ability to change their appearance to look human." explained Jake.

"How did you know?" asked Mrs. Donaldson.

"I can see them as demons, even when they change their appearance to look human." answered Jake.

Mrs. Donaldson and Allison put their hands to their mouths. "It smells horrible." said Mrs. Donaldson.

"After they die, they decompose at an incredible rate." said Agent Williams.

"Let's go into a different room." suggested Ellie. "No need to keep looking at this."

They all walked into the dining room, where Mrs. Donaldson and Allison sat down.

Mrs. Donaldson shuddered. "This thing has been walking around here the whole time and we didn't know."

Agent Pyle nodded. "There was no way for you to know it. This helps us believe your husband is still alive, and they wanted a spy to know what's going on here."

Agent Williams turned to the Donaldsons. "I agree. For now, just allow these two security men here. No others. I will ask for a couple of FBI agents to be stationed here as well."

"Of course." said Mrs. Donaldson.

"There's no doubt now that demons are involved." said Agent Pyle off hand.

"I'll call our supervisor and let him know what happened. We'll have a cleanup company come take care of this… mess." said Agent Williams.

The FBI agents gave her their business cards before leaving. Once outside, Agent Williams frowned. "We're no closer to finding out what's going on."

Jake nodded. "Yes and no. We know for sure that demons are involved in both situations, we just don't know if they are related."

"When demons kill themselves rather than talk, it gives me a bad feeling about this." said Ellie.

On the drive back to the airport, Agent Williams called Deputy Director Ruiz and briefed him on what happened. She hung up and looked at Agent Pyle. "Oscar's going to brief Director Chisom."

Agent Pyle nodded. "What do you think? You've been doing this longer than I have."

"Yeah, but I didn't get swallowed by a giant snake and beat up by a demon." replied Agent Williams with a smile.

"Hey, Stephanie, that's not fair." said Agent Pyle pretending to be offended. "I was tied to a chair at the time."

Agent Williams laughed. "Good point. In answer to your question, I know that anytime demons kidnap people, it's not just for fun. They're planning something, and if a demon is willing to kill himself rather than tell us anything, that means it's something big."

"Amen to that." added Agent Pyle. "You referred to the demon as he rather than it. Are these monsters, people or animals?"

"Ellie explained it this way," answered Agent Williams. "In the beginning, they looked like angels. You've seen Malachy, who doesn't exactly look like a normal human. They're a separately created species. When some of them rebelled from heaven, over thousands of years, they have become the creatures we see today. I guess you can call them he,she or it, whichever makes you feel better."

"I'd rather not call them at all." said Agent Pyle.

CHAPTER NINE

The White House
1600 Pennsylvania Avenue Northwest
Washington D.C.

THE PRESIDENT of the United States, William Campbell, sat at his desk reading recent intelligence reports. He was in his fifties with salt and pepper hair that was becoming grayer the longer he was in office, but his bright blue eyes were sharp and clear. He was in his second term after he prevented a biological attack on the nation's capital with the help of Jake Taft and the FBI agents. Then his administration subsequently exposed a conspiracy between an FBI deputy director, a demon, and a corrupt congressional senator.

Since then, besides being at the global summit in Berlin last year when the Nazis tried to detonate a small nuclear bomb, his current term had been routine, dealing with domestic issues, terrorism, and foreign policy.

There was a knock at the door. His administrative assistant opened the door and looked in. "Do you have a few minutes, Mr. President?" she asked.

"Of course, Gladys. Do you need something?"

"FBI Director Chisom wishes to speak with you." she answered.

"Send him in by all means."

Director Chisom entered the oval office and shook hands with the President. "Have a seat, Bill." said the President.

Director William "Bill" Chisom had started out as a field agent, and in forty years, he worked his way up to director. He kept fit; he was in his mid-sixties, gray hair but kept a crew cut. He was well-liked in the bureau and trusted without question by the President. "I didn't want to make this an official situation until we get more information, but I wanted to give you a heads up."

The President nodded. "Domestic or international?"

"So far, domestic and demonic." replied Director Chisom.

The President sat back with a sigh. "Can't it be normal terrorism? What are these abominations up to now?"

Deputy Chisom handed the President a file. The President put on his reading glasses and scanned the reports as the director briefed him on the events in Five Corners, the Tex-Am oil rig, and the incident at the Donaldson residence.

The President took off his glasses and tossed them onto his desk in frustration. "So, we know both were demon related?"

Director Chisom nodded. "Yes, sir, as you read, we have video of the abduction of the woman in Washington. The medical examiners in Texas have ruled it as an attack by a creature other than an animal at the oil rig. No news on the owner we believe was taken. We weren't positive that he was kidnapped and not part of it until the incident at the Donaldson's house when Jake shot the demon. Also, Jake's angel friend, Malachy, told him they were."

"And he didn't tell Jake more about it?" asked the President.

Director Chisom shook his head and shrugged. "I appreciate their help no matter what. They seem to show up at some times and not at other times."

"Absolutely, he saved us all in Berlin, but even with what Malachy said, we're still not positive that Donaldson isn't in cahoots with the demons." said the President.

"True, Mr. President," replied Director Chisom. "But from all we can tell, he was a decent man, but the two agents working it will still keep that in mind."

"Agents Williams and Pyle." commented the President. "They're good people. Tell them to be careful."

"I will, sir."

"So, for now, we don't have enough information to bring this up to another level. You'll keep me updated, of course."

Director Chisom got up to leave. "Of course, Mr. President."

After he left, the President shook his head. "Not more demons." he said.

———

Texas State Highway 137
Crockett County

JAKE AND ELLIE were about halfway home when Ellie noticed that Jake kept looking in the rear-view mirror.

"Is something wrong?" she asked.

"There's a white van that's been following us." he replied with a frown.

Ellie looked over her shoulder at the van. "Well, there aren't many major roads through here. Just coincidence?"

"Maybe so, but they've been following us since we left Odessa. Even after we stopped for gas in Barnhart."

A few miles farther, the van accelerated to pass, and as they came alongside, the van swerved and collided with their truck.

Ellie jumped and Jake swerved to the right onto the shoulder to avoid another collision.

"What on earth do they think they're doing." said Ellie.

"Hang on!" snapped Jake as he slammed his foot on the gas pedal, which resulted in the van being left behind.

Jake looked in the mirror as the van sped up. "Try your phone for a signal."

Ellie looked at her phone. "Sorry, no signal."

Jake frowned as the van closed on them. The passenger of the van leaned out and began firing at them. The rounds peppered the tailgate and shattered the rear window.

"Get down!" yelled Jake.

Ellie ducked down just as another volley of bullets hit the truck. Jake swerved back and forth, trying to throw off their aim. The van raced forward and tried to clip the rear quarter panel, but Jake slammed on the brakes bringing the van even with them. He glanced over and saw two men with masks. As they rounded a curve, the passenger aimed a rifle at him, so Jake slammed the truck into the side of the van, forcing the van across the road and into the ditch. The van continued until it hit a fence post and steam came from the front of the van.

Jake accelerated to put as much distance between them, even though the van seemed to be disabled. They drove for a few more miles when Ellie announced they had a cell signal and dialed 911.

"Crockett County 911, what is your emergency?" asked the dispatcher.

"My name is Ellie Taft, we've been shot at and almost run off the road."

"What's your location?" asked the dispatcher.

"We're between Barnhart and Highway 190." explained Ellie.

"Is anyone hurt?"

"No, we're fine. The van that attacked us went off the road and hit a fence, so we're not sure if they're injured."

"You said they shot at you?" asked the dispatcher.

"Yes," replied Ellie. "They also tried to run us off the road. It's a white panel van."

"Ok, I'll have deputies headed in that direction. What are you driving?"

"We're in a dark blue Ford crew cab pickup. Our back window is shot out, and we have bullet holes all over the truck." replied Ellie.

At that instant, something large landed on top of the cab.

"What was that?" asked Ellie.

"What's going on?" asked the dispatcher.

As if on cue, several large claws punctured the roof of the cab and began trying to pull the metal on the roof back. Jake once again swerved left and right to dislodge the creature.

"Something landed on the roof of the truck, and it's trying to rip the roof off." said the startled Ellie.

Jake pulled his Colt 45 out of the holster and fired twice through the roof resulting in a high screech.

"Are shots being fired?" asked the dispatcher.

"Yes!" yelled Ellie. "My husband is shooting at a demon!" said Ellie.

"Demon? Did you say demon?" asked the dispatcher.

The truck was suddenly rocked by a blow to the side. Jake glanced out the window and saw a huge demon, the size of a rhino on steroids, aiming right for them. It slammed into the side, causing the truck to slide sideways and roll over on its side.

When the truck slid to a stop, the windshield was ripped off, and an ugly winged gray demon tried to reach in.

Both Ellie and Jake were stunned briefly. The winged abomination tried to grab Ellie, who avoided the creature's claws as Jake fired more rounds at the demon. The rhino-like demon rammed the truck, causing the truck to spin, and Jake hit his head. Jake saw spots and everything started spinning. Through his rapidly darkening vision, Jake saw that the gray demon had grabbed Ellie's arm and was trying to pull her from the truck. He wanted to reach out and stop the thing, but his arms didn't seem to work. He caught a glimpse of a golden sword cutting the devil's arm off right before everything went black.

———

AGENTS WILLIAMS and Pyle were at the airport waiting for their return flight when her cellphone rang. She answered and listened, her face becoming angry.

"Where?" she asked. "Are you both ok?"

"What's going on?" asked Agent Pyle, but Agent Williams waved him to be quiet. "What hospital? We'll be there as soon as we can." she said and hung up.

"So, what happened?" asked Agent Pyle.

"Sorry, Terrell, that was Ellie." said Agent Williams. "The Taft's were attacked on their way home."

"Do they know who it was?"

Agent Williams shook her head as she got up. "No, she said some men in a van and then by demons."

"Are they okay?"

"Yes," replied Agent Williams as they walked back out of the secure area towards the ticket counter. "They're at a hospital in Eldorado. Let's get our luggage."

"Is their new truck okay?" asked Terrell.

Agent Williams stared at him, rolled her eyes, and punched him in the arm.

"Just kidding." said Agent Pyle while rubbing his arm. "You hit hard."

"Ex-NFL wimp." she said.

CHAPTER TEN

Elflein 4000
Buenos Aires, Argentina

WENDI HAD GIVEN up trying to keep up with how long they had been gone or where she was. The small aircraft had hopped from one small airfield to another, stopping only long enough to refuel and use the facilities. Some of the airfields were just dirt or grass landing strips with a shed as a building.

Sam had tried to talk to the pilot or some of the people on the ground, but none of them would speak to him.

She obviously knew that they were not in the United States anymore since they had been flying south, and she could see jungles and mountains not associated with the U.S. Lately, they had stopped flying low over the jungle and were flying along a coast. She soon saw a large city in the distance, the aircraft flew over a large bay and past the city. They then landed in what appeared to be a private airstrip. They taxied to a series of buildings and parked.

A brown windowless van pulled up and they exited the small aircraft. Wendi and Sam were escorted into the back of the van and sat inside with two serious-looking men with guns. They drove for some time, perhaps an hour, but it was hard to judge. When the van stopped, and the rear doors were opened. Three men in suits ordered them out. When they climbed out, Wendi and Sam were able to look around at their new surroundings and were amazed. They were in the rear driveway of a magnificent three-story modern English mansion with an immaculate landscape and garden.

They were herded in through a large kitchen, into a marbled hallway, past an elevator, and into a huge library.

A man with white hair stood at the window and turned when they entered. Another man sat in a chair facing away from them.

"Greetings from Buenos Aires." said the man with a slight accent. He was dressed in a starched white shirt, dark slacks, and expensive shoes. "I am Herman, you're now guests of my estate." he said.

"Guests?" said Sam abruptly. "We've been kidnapped, threatened, flown across the continent under guard, and now we're guests?"

The man named Herman dismissed Sam with a wave of his hand. "Yes, yes, I must apologize for the transportation, but we had to be secretive."

"Why?" asked Wendi. "What do you want with us?"

"There will be time for questions and answers later." replied Herman. "First, you must be exhausted from your ordeal. My people will escort you to your rooms where you can rest and freshen up."

Sam looked over at the man who sat in the chair.

Herman saw him look over. "Oh my, how rude of me." he said. "Forgive my lack of manners by not introducing you to my new associate."

The man got up and turned around with a smile. "Good afternoon, my name is Adolf Hitler II."

Sam and Wendi stared in disbelief at the man who looked identical to a young, clean-shaven Hitler, except that he had one yellow eye.

Schleicher County Medical Center

102 N US Highway 277
Eldorado, TX

A MEDICAL TECHNICIAN pushed Jake in a wheelchair down the hall to his ER room after getting a CT scan. He had a small bandage over his left eyebrow where a cut had been stitched up. As he grumbled that he could walk just fine, the technician rolled him into the small ER room, where Ellie and Pam waited.

"Oh, great, a headache and now Pam." growled Jake.

"I came to check on Ellie." she said with a grin. "Oh, and you too."

Ellie giggled. "I bet you two are actually brother and sister?"

Jake just frowned and Pam rolled her eyes.

A few minutes later, a Crockett County deputy came in. "Afternoon, I'm Deputy Sherrod. I came to check on y'all."

Ellie smiled. "Thank you for checking. We're fine."

"Except for Jake," said Pam. "His sense of humor has been damaged."

Deputy Sherrod didn't know whether to laugh or not, so he just kept talking. "Your truck was towed into the impound lot." He handed Ellie his card. "Here's my info and the report number to give to the insurance company."

"Anything on the van?" asked Jake, who had gotten out of the wheelchair and sat on the edge of the bed.

"The van was stolen out of Odessa," explained the deputy. "Crime scene processed the inside but was only able to get one good print, the rest have been wiped clean. Not much to go on."

"I figured it would be stolen." said Jake.

Deputy Sherrod handed Ellie a box. "Mr. Taft's handgun is in here. The ambulance people gave it to us when he was transported. He might need this if monsters and demons are after you. The roof of your truck was pretty much ripped to shreds. I've seen news clips of these things but never actually seen anything until now. The dead one we found at the scene decayed so fast, and it stunk."

"Yes, demons stink and decay fast, and I hope you never have to see a live one." said Ellie.

The deputy left and Ellie's cellphone rang. She answered it saying, "We're in trauma room 4. It should only be a few minutes; we're just waiting for the doctor to come in." And then she hung up. "That was Stephanie and Terrell. They just pulled into the parking lot."

A few minutes later, there was a knock, and the two FBI agents came in.

"Long time no see." said Pam. She went over and hugged both.

"So, how are our patients?" asked Agent Williams.

"I'm ok, just a few bumps and bruises." replied Ellie.

"Jake's grumpy." said Pam.

"I'm right here. I can hear you." growled Jake.

"So, he's normal." said Agent Williams with a grin.

Agent Pyle looked at Jake with his bandage and bruises and smiled. "You look like crap."

"Do you two want something, or did you just come to make fun of me?" grumbled Jake.

They all laughed.

"So, what happened?" asked Agent Pyle.

Jake and Ellie explained the two attacks and what the deputy told them.

"Wow, lucky Malachy showed up when he did." said Pam.

"Yes, Malachy killed one of them and the other got away." explained Ellie.

The doctor came in. "Well, Mr. Taft, I have good news, all the scans are clear. You might have a mild concussion, so I recommend a week of rest."

His comment brought a round of muted snickers and giggles.

"Thank you, doctor." Ellie said while suppressing a grin.

The doctor left and they were gathering up their belongings to leave when Agent Williams spoke up. "Did Malachy say anything else?"

Ellie hesitated for a minute but finally answered. "Yes, he did."

They all looked at her.

"And?" asked Agent Pyle.

She glanced at Jake before answering. "Jake was out of it from his bump on the head, and Malachy had pulled him from the truck, so he didn't hear what he said." She hesitated again.

"What did he say?" asked Jake.

The others looked at her in anticipation.

"He said that Tarnac is involved." she said softly.

"Not Tarnac." said Pam wide-eyed.

"Tarnac? Who's he?" asked Agent Pyle.

By then, they were walking out of the hospital while Jake explained. "Tarnac is a demon lord we encountered in New Orleans a couple of years ago. He gave us information about Ghazi. We ended up shooting our way out of his lair."

Ellie thought about her and Pam having to dress up like drugged-up prostitutes to sneak into the mansion with Jake. She remembered fleeing the mansion, driving their suburban at a breakneck speed, while Jake shot demons who were hanging on. She shivered at the thought.

"Oh, that Tarnac." said Agent Pyle. "I read the reports. Didn't Soaring Eagle say something about Tarnac in our last meeting?"

"Wait, you can read?" said Agent Williams.

"I'm not just another pretty face, you know." answered Agent Pyle.

"And yes, Tarnac was mentioned in the meeting."

Jake's jaw clenched. "Looks like we need to pay him a visit and see what he's doing."

CHAPTER ELEVEN

Elflein 4000
Buenos Aires, Argentina

THE MANSION WAS LOCATED on the prominent Elflein street in the exclusive area of 'Las Lomas'. Besides the kitchen, dining room, reception area, and library, the first floor consisted of three suites, each having a jacuzzi and bath. There was also a gym and workout room. Wendi and Sam were allowed the freedom of the interior of the house but were restricted to the first floor. They were watched constantly by either the staff or the guards.

Their captors had conveniently provided them with several changes of clothes, so they didn't have to wear the same ones every day. Sam and Wendi wandered around the large first floor.

"Well, at least our prison's nice." said Sam.

Wendi nodded. "Yes, and the clothes they gave us are our sizes. This dress cost more than I make in a month."

Sam nodded. "They planned well." He was wearing a light blue shirt and tan pants while Wendi wore an expensive sundress.

"But they still haven't told us why we've been brought here. Have they told you anything?"

Sam shook his head in frustration. "Not a word. It's like they're waiting on someone."

They sat down on one of the couches.

"Can you believe that Hitler guy?" asked Wendi.

"I was shocked, but surely he can't be Hitler. He said he was Hitler II. Maybe a look-alike to fool people. They can do all kinds of things with plastic surgery."

Wendi shrugged. "Maybe, but he was creepy with that one yellow eye, like those monsters."

"Those things have two yellow eyes." commented Sam. "Seems odd he would have only one. I wonder how he figures into all this."

Wendi looked around and saw one of their constant guards standing by the door, but just outside in the hallway. "Do you think we can escape?" she whispered.

"I've been thinking about that too." whispered Sam. "Maybe we can get to the U.S. Embassy."

Their conversation was interrupted when Herman came in wearing a silk shirt and dark slacks. He walked over to his desk and sat down. "I hope you're rested."

"What do you want from us?" demanded Sam.

Herman reached over, opened a box, and removed a cigar. He smelled it, then snipped off the end and lit it. He inhaled it and blew out the smoke. He looked over at them. "All will be explained when the other member of our group arrives."

"Who are you people?" asked Wendi. "Why do you have a Hitler imposter?"

Herman smiled. "Oh, my dear, he's not an imposter, he's the real thing."

"That's not possible." argued Wendi. "He would have to be nearly 100 years old."

"I didn't say he was the original Adolph Hitler."

"So, he is a fake." said Sam.

Herman shook his head. "No, technology has enabled us to make another Hitler."

"A clone." said Wendi.

"Of sorts," replied Herman. "Our organization has been able to obtain Hitler's DNA, and with the help of others, we've done the impossible. We created another Adolph Hitler."

"And who is your organization?" asked Sam.

Herman puffed on his cigar and smiled. "Why, the Third Reich, or in this case, the new Fourth Reich."

"You're Nazis!" blurted Sam.

Herman nodded.

Sam heard rumors that the Nazis came to South America after the war to avoid war crimes, but never believed it to be true. Then it dawned on him. "So, you are part of that group that tried to kill the world leaders in Berlin."

"No, we're separate, but still under the same flag. It's a shame that Frau Getman didn't accomplish her task, but she was able to succeed in making us a new Fuhrer."

"But why?" asked Wendi.

Herman smiled brightly. "Why, to continue our quest for domination."

"You're insane." snapped Sam.

"Sanity is relative." replied Herman. He got up from his chair and walked towards the door. "Now, who wants an exquisite lunch?"

———

J Double T Ranch
Sutton County, Texas

PAM DROVE up to the ranch house in her Ford Explorer and parked. She had driven them home since their truck was obviously not drivable, and still in the auto pound. Roy came out with Roscoe following. "Welcome back." he said. "So, y'all had an exciting time on the way home."

Ellie smiled. "It was definitely a trip to remember."

Roscoe trotted up and Ellie gave him a belly rub. Jake pulled their luggage from the back of Pam's Explorer. "The truck is totaled. I called the insurance company. They weren't too happy, but will replace it. We can go pick it up in a day or so."

"So, how's your head." asked Roy, noticing the bruises and bandage.

"The doctor said he's ok but wants him to rest for a week." answered Ellie.

Roy chuckled. "Good luck with that."

"Why does everyone laugh about that?" grumbled Jake.

"Honey, do you plan to do that?" asked Ellie.

"Of course not." replied Jake.

"Exactly." said Ellie with a grin.

Jake shook his head and carried the luggage into the house.

"He still has a headache from the crash." explained Ellie.

"Whatever." said Pam sarcastically.

Ellie giggled as Pam got into her Explorer. "Thanks for bringing us home. We can use Jake's old truck to go get the new one."

"So, what about Tarnac?" asked Pam.

Ellie shrugged. "I'm not sure. Stephanie and Terrell are going to talk to Oscar, then decide from there."

Pam nodded. "I feel sorry for Tarnac if Jake still has a headache when he gets there."

Ellie grinned. "You're bad."

Federal Bureau of Investigation
Office of Deputy Director of Paranormal Activities
935 Pennsylvania Avenue Northwest
Washington, D.C.

IT WAS LATE when the two FBI agents arrived back in Washington. Deputy Director Ruiz had insisted that he would wait at the office for them.

Agents Williams and Pyle came into his office and flopped down into two chairs.

"Rough day?" asked Deputy Director Ruiz.

"Long day." replied Agent Williams.

"You said on the phone that Jake and Ellie were ok, but are they really?"

Agent Pyle nodded. "Yes, sir, they both have a few bruises, and Jake has stitches above his eyebrow. A lot better than it could have been."

"Doc said Jake might have a mild concussion and recommended a week's rest." said Agent Williams.

Deputy Director chuckled. "That won't happen. He's too bull-headed; nothing will slow him down. So, what do we know and suggestions on what to do?"

Agent Williams began. "Like I said on the phone earlier, the Donaldson family have not received any ransom demands, but that demon was watching them."

Deputy Director Ruiz nodded. "So, obviously they're involved, but we don't know to what extent."

"Right." said Agent Pyle. "The van was stolen, but they got one print. It comes back to a local thug in Odessa. The local police will pay them a visit. Ellie said that after Malachy killed the demon, he told her that Tarnac was involved."

"And Soaring Eagle mentioned him too, so I think our next step is for me to talk to Director Chisom about going to New Orleans." said Deputy Director Ruiz.

The two agents got up to leave. "I would imagine Eudora and her people will want to go too." said Agent Williams.

"Without a doubt." answered Deputy Director Ruiz. "Now, get some rest. I have a feeling the next several days are going to be busy."

———

Elflein 4000
Buenos Aires, Argentina

IT WAS evening when Wendi was sitting out on the terrace looking at the lights of Buenos Aires glisten and flicker, wishing she wasn't a captive and could enjoy being there. Her constant guard was nearby.

Adolph Hitler strolled out and sat down in a chair. "Beautiful, isn't it?"

Wendi shrugged and frowned. "Yeah, if I wasn't a prisoner."

Hitler nodded. "I'm sorry, but Herman said that you and Mr. Donaldson are crucial for their plans." he explained.

"Which are?" asked Wendi.

"I'm not at liberty to tell you."

Wendi stared at this so-called new Hitler for a moment. It was amazing how he looked like the photos she'd seen of the Fuhrer. Except for the one yellow eye. "You said it was their plans? Are they not your plans?"

Hitler thought for a moment. "I'm told that the original Hitler, whose DNA I have, wanted to unite the world under him and make it a better world. I don't think that's a bad idea."

Wendi shook her head at hearing his reason. "Is that what Herman told you?"

Hitler looked over at her. "Of course."

She shook her head slowly in frustration. "Did it ever occur to you that he could be lying? Hitler was a monster. He was responsible for the death of millions of Jews, as well as the death of millions of soldiers and others during the second world war. And he started the war."

Hitler jerked his head around at her. "That's not true!" he snapped.

Wendi was taken back as his yellow eye glowed.

Hitler realized that he had frightened her and calmed down. "I'm sorry. I shouldn't have reacted in such a way."

"Do you have any memories of Hitler, your DNA donor?"

Hitler shook his head. "No, I have no memories of anything until I was rushed away during a gun battle in Germany. I was brought here almost immediately."

Wendi nodded and looked quizzically at him. "So, your first realization is when you became conscious in Germany?"

"Yes." answered Hitler. "I was in a huge tube, and then I was wet and cold. The men wrapped me in a blanket and rushed me out. I learned later that it was in Berlin. Herman has been so kind and helped me learn everything."

Everything? He has been brainwashed, thought Wendi. *Tread carefully, girl, this guy has demon DNA too and could turn ugly.* "Do you know that you have demon DNA also?"

Hitler's eyes widened. "Of course not, demons don't exist." he answered. "Where did you get such a ridiculous idea?"

My god, what have they not told him? She rubbed her temples with her fingertips. "Why do you think you have one yellow eye?"

"Herman said that it was from the chemicals and the DNA process." he explained.

Wendi decided to try one more time to convince him of his misinformation. "Did they tell you demons have yellow eyes? Did they tell you that the Nazis wanted a master race, which was one specific race of people, and the rest would be eliminated?"

Hitler abruptly got to his feet. "I'm tired of these lies." He stomped off.

Sam came through the door and almost collided with him. He sat down in the chair that had been vacated by Hitler. His hands touched the metal arms of the chair, which made him look down. The arms of the chair had been bent and indented, as if someone had squeezed it and left their imprint. "Did you see this?" indicated Sam.

Wendi looked over and gasped. "Wow, he did that. I was talking to him and tried to convince him that they've been lying to him. He got angry."

Sam whistled softly. "I guess his demon part gives him that type of strength. I guess we'd better be careful not to rile him up."

"I was just telling him the truth." said Wendi. "He doesn't believe he's part demon. Mr. Herman Nazi has been filling him with lies about the original Hitler. He's made him look like a hero."

Just out of sight of the two, Hitler listened in on their conversation. A few minutes later, Wendi and Sam went back inside and Hitler walked back outside. He looked down at the chair with a puzzled look, felt the arms of the damaged chair, and then stared at his hands.

CHAPTER TWELVE

The White House
1600 Pennsylvania Avenue Northwest
Washington D.C.

DIRECTOR CHISOM ENTERED the oval office and noted that a group was already assembled, waiting for him. He'd called and asked for a meeting with the President, but obviously, he had invited others. Waiting in the oval office with the President was Secretary of State Phil Jennings, Chief of Staff John Wohlman, and Homeland Security Chief Sarah Ornelus.

"Have a seat, Bill, as you can see, I called a few others just in case." explained the President.

Director Chisom sat down in one of the overstuffed chairs. He nodded to the others. The President sat in the other overstuffed chair while the rest sat on the couches that surrounded a large coffee table.

"So, what's the latest? Your call sounded more urgent." said the President.

Director Chisom brought the rest of them up to speed on the past events.

"So, these monsters are at it again." said Chief of staff John Wohlman.

"I'm afraid so, John." said Director Chisom. "We have four dead people, two possibly kidnapped, and the Taft's attacked to show for it."

"Has there been any activity on their credit cards or bank accounts?" asked Homeland Security Chief Sarah Ornelus.

Director Chisom shook his head. "No, nothing. It's like they disappeared off the face of the earth."

"Well, we know they're somewhere." said President Campbell. "Either they're victims or in cahoots with these demons."

"We're looking at both aspects." explained Director Chisom. "The fact that demons were spying on the Donaldson family makes us lean more towards him being kidnapped and not a party to it."

"And Colonel Taft killed the demon?" asked Secretary of State Phil Jennings. "I wish he'd been able to get more information."

"Colonel Taft didn't kill the demon." corrected Director Chisom. "The demon killed himself."

"That's a first, isn't it?" asked Homeland Security Chief Sarah Ornelus.

"Yes, which tells me that if a demon would kill himself, then it's serious."

"I agree." said the President. "So, what's the good news, if there is any."

"Colonel Taft's angel friend said that a demon lord named Tarnac is involved." continued Director Chisom.

"Well, his angel friend would be a pretty reliable source." joked the President.

"Is this Tarnac character some sort of arch demon?" asked Chief of Staff John Wohlman.

"I believe so," answered Director Chisom. "Or whatever they call their demon hierarchy. Perhaps he's on the same level or higher than Ghazi or Degen was. Also, one of our half-demon agents named Soaring Eagle said Tarnac is big in this area of the world." added Director Chisom.

"He's the eagle-man?" asked Homeland Security Chief Sarah Ornelus.

Director Chisom nodded.

"Can we trust them?"

"Their information coincides with the angel, so we have no reason to think otherwise. These half-demons hate regular demons as much, if not more than we do. They were made to be slaves for them." explained Director Chisom.

"And they helped save us in Berlin." added the President. "I have no reason not to believe them."

"Where's this Tarnac?" asked Chief of Staff John Wohlman.

Director Chisom shuffled some papers until he found the right one. "He's supposed to be in a location near New Orleans. They call it Hell's Corner. The local law enforcement has tried unsuccessfully to get rid of it."

"Why haven't they?" asked Homeland Security Chief Ornelus.

Director Chisom looked up. "Demons can make themselves invisible or transparent or whatever you want to call it. They must materialize or become solid when they want to do anything physical. So, when law enforcement shows up, they just disappear. When the authorities try to tear the place down, the demons wreak havoc. It's hard to fight something you can't see."

"Ok, so, what do you suggest, Bill?" asked the President.

"I suggest that we eradicate that evil nest once and for all with Colonel Taft's help because he can see them even when they don't want us to. Also, the half-demon agents can see them as well. This way, they can't elude us." explained Director Chisom.

"What resources are you going to use?" asked Homeland Security Chief Ornelus.

"My plan is to use two FBI strike teams, and with permission, I would like to use the National Guard as a backup."

Homeland Security Chief Ornelus nodded and thought for a moment. "Colonel Taft and your half-demon agents are the only ones that can kill demons, what about the rest?"

"Demons can't touch or contact holy ground such as cemeteries, inside churches, holy sites, etc. So, we've developed bullets that have cemetery dirt embedded in it. It won't kill them outright, but if they're hit enough times, it can disable them or perhaps even kill them too."

"I'll call Governor Cravens and let him know what we're going to do." said the President.

Homeland Security Chief Ornelus spoke up. "I think we can have some bulldozers and wrecking balls waiting to demolish that place once and for all."

Heads nodded around the room.

"Then Operation Hell's Corner is a go." announced the President.

———

Serenity Mobile Home Park
1200 Lake Drive, Lot #32
Odessa, Tx

WEARING GREEN TACTICAL GEAR, the Odessa Special Weapons and Tactics (SWAT) team arrived at the mobile home park. After contacting the office, they parked one street over from the suspect's single wide run-down trailer.

They had completed recon on the trailer earlier and determined one pickup was parked on the small concrete parking pad. The five-man unit quietly crept up to and onto the wooden deck. One officer watched the single back door.

The lead officer had a clear protective shield, followed by four officers and a supervisor, Sgt Sparks.

Sgt Sparks nodded at the second officer, who stepped past the door and banged on it with his fist. "Odessa Police Department, search warrant, open the door." When no one answered, he repeated by knocking on the door and shouting for someone to come to the door. When no one came, Sgt Sparks motioned for the third officer, who held a large, solid, metal tub with handles used as a battering ram.

The officer stepped up and heaved the heavy ram against the thin metal trailer door which easily opened. He stepped aside as the others rushed into the single-wide trailer.

They immediately smelled the copper smell of blood mixed with decomposition. They located the two suspects after a quick search of the two-bedroom trailer. One was found headless in the shower, and the other was found in one of the bedrooms. He was on his back with his dead eyes open and staring. He had been cut from chin to groin, and his internal organs were missing. The other man's head was found propped up on the table with a butcher knife through his skull.

———

Elflein 4000
Buenos Aires, Argentina

THE NEXT SEVERAL days brought the same boredom for Sam and Wendi. Sam had even slipped out of one of the rear doors to go over the garden wall but never even got close due to numerous guards patrolling the grounds.

Wendi and Sam were sitting at the smaller table in the kitchen drinking coffee when Herman entered the room. "Good afternoon, I hope you are well?"

The two just stared at him.

"I have some good news. Another member of our organization has arrived." he announced proudly. A man entered behind Herman.

"Long time no see, Sam." said the man.

Sam sat, shocked for a moment, while Wendi looked back and forth in confusion between the two men. Realization dawned on Sam, who jumped to his feet and charged the man. "Steve, you're a lousy piece of crap!" he yelled. Sam punched Steve in the jaw, and when he fell, Sam jumped on him.

Before Sam could inflict any more injury on him, two guards immediately pulled Sam off.

Wendi stared, dumbfounded.

"You are a part of this nightmare!" shouted Sam as he was being restrained by the guards. "Four decent men have died."

Steve got to his feet and rubbed his jaw. "I didn't have a choice, Sam." he said apologetically.

"You always have a choice." snapped Sam. He jerked his arms loose but didn't try to attack Steve again.

"Gentlemen, gentlemen." said Herman. "Let's act like adults. Everyone, please, sit down."

Sam reluctantly sat back down, and Steve took a seat across the table. Wendi looked over at Sam.

"Who's he?" she asked.

Sam frowned. "He's one of my company's partners and was my best friend until now." Sam explained.

Steve looked away in embarrassment. "I swear, I didn't have a choice."

"He's right." said Herman, who had sat down at the table. "Mr. Peterson has a large amount of gambling debts that he owes. At last count, it was over a million dollars."

Sam sat and stared. "What? Gambling? My gawd, Steve, you owe that much?"

Steve blushed with embarrassment. "I have a gambling addiction. It's gotten out of hand."

Sam slammed his hand on the table. "You could've asked me for help. How were you ever going to pay that back? Does Tammy know?"

Steve shook his head. "Of course not. Tammy and the kids have no idea. I meant to stop, but I just thought if I tried one more time, I could fix it. Then I was contacted by the people I owed money to, they said a man wanted to cover my debts. I jumped at the idea. I swear, I didn't know anyone would be killed."

Sam held his head in his hands in disbelief. Wendi reached over and put her hand on his shoulder.

Herman smiled brightly. "We've covered his debts but at a cost. He signed over a part of his share of the company to us."

Sam's head snapped up and he glared at Steve, who wouldn't make eye contact.

"Don't blame your friend, he had no choice, he had to take this deal. The people he owes money to would have most likely killed him or made something horrible happen to his wife and children. This way, it's a win for us and for him." explained Herman.

Wendi finally felt bad for both men. "Do you know about Hitler?" she asked Steve.

Steve looked at her like she was talking nonsense. "Hitler?"

"Obviously not." said Wendi. "Your new associates have cloned Hitler, who is half demon. They're Nazis."

Steve looked back sadly, "What have I done."

―――――

J Double T Ranch
Sutton County, Texas

KNOWING that Jake was not going to take the doctor's suggestion and rest, Ellie got Jake to agree to not do any real strenuous work for a day or so. Jake was in the barn doing clean-up and inventory when his cellphone rang.

"Hey, Jake, this is Oscar." said Deputy Director Ruiz. "Are you taking it easy?"

Jake laughed. "Ellie and I compromised. I'm only allowed to do some light work. What's up?"

"I spoke to Director Chisom and it's a go for the raid on Hell's Corner. Will you be available to go?"

"Absolutely," replied Jake. "It's time to clean that rathole up. Who all is going?"

"Stephanie and Terrell, three half-demons, two FBI strike forces, and some National Guard troops if needed." said Deputy Director Ruiz. "I'll send transport for you this afternoon."

"I'll be ready." said Jake.

Now I have to tell Ellie.

He walked towards the house. Ellie had decided to stay home to keep an eye on Jake but was able to remotely log in and do some work.

Jake walked up behind her and stopped, sensing him standing there, she turned around. He stood there with his hat in his hand. "Ellie, I got a call from Oscar." he said softly.

"So, when do we leave for New Orleans?" she asked without hesitation.

Jake was shocked at her response. "How did you know?"

Ellie gave him a smirk. "As soon as I heard the name Tarnac, I knew we'd be going, and I'm surprised it took this long."

Jake gave a lopsided grin. "And you're not mad?"

Ellie smiled. "Nothing short of an apocalypse could keep you from going. I'll get our stuff packed."

"You don't have to go."

Ellie got up and took his hand. "First, whenever I get left behind, something bad happens. Second, as I've said before, where you go, I go. I know I can't go on the raid, so we'll take Roscoe, and I'll just hang around to be the cheering section."

Jake laughed and hugged her. "How could I have gotten so lucky."

Later that afternoon, as Jake sat their bags out front, he saw Pam's Explorer arrive. Jake sighed and shook his head.

Pam parked and hopped out of her SUV. "Howdy, Jake, so we're going back to New Orleans?"

Thirty minutes later, he heard a helicopter. The same black with no markings, small, twin turbine Agusta A 109 light utility copter that they've flown on before appeared and landed. Ellie and Pam came out with Roy.

"Y'all be careful." said Roy. "Ned and I'll keep the ranch safe while you're gone."

Ned was standing in the yard looking at the helicopter. "Those things are an abomination against nature." he grumbled.

Jake carried their bags to the helicopter while Ellie and Pam hugged Roy. "Thanks for your help."

Roy grinned. "Of course, now go save the world."

They walked over to the helicopter, ducked, and climbed aboard along with Roscoe. Within seconds they were airborne, headed towards New Orleans.

CHAPTER THIRTEEN

Elflein 4000
Buenos Aires, Argentina

SAM, Wendi, and Steve were summoned into the library for a meeting with Herman and Hitler. The three entered the library and took their seats, waiting for Herman and Hitler to arrive. Sam had still not spoken to Steve and chose to sit as far away from him as possible. Sam and Wendi sat on a luxurious Italian-made couch, while Steve sat in an overstuffed leather chair.

"Honest, Sam, I had no idea that anyone would get hurt. They just told me they wanted to use our company to do some drilling." explained Steve.

Sam glared at him. "It's not your company anymore, you gave them your share, remember?"

Steve hung his head.

"I can't believe you'd go in with Nazis and demons. You're an idiot."

"I didn't know they were Nazis." replied Steve trying to regain some semblance of respect. "What makes you believe demons are involved? If they even exist."

"I agree with Sam, you're an idiot!" snapped Wendi. "They ripped my car door off and carried me off. Sam has injuries to his shoulders from them dragging him away after they murdered your oil rig crew. And they have a Hitler clone that's half demon."

Steve shook his head. "I don't think he's a Hitler clone, maybe just a doppelganger or someone they made to look like Hitler."

At that moment, Herman and Hitler entered the room. "Thank you for meeting with us." said Herman.

"Like we had a choice." grumbled Sam.

Herman ignored the reply and sat at his desk. Hitler leaned against one of the bookcases. It was the first time Steve had seen the new Hitler, he was amazed at the resemblance.

"You two haven't met yet." said Herman. "Mr. Peterson, I'd like for you to meet Adolph Hitler II."

Steve continued to stare. "Is this for real?"

"Absolutely," said Herman. "Adolph is going to be our new Fuhrer."

Sam shook his head in frustration. "See, Steve, I told you."

"What do you want from us?" asked Wendi.

Herman sat back and smiled. "Why, Dr. Hamilton, I want your expertise."

"I'm a volcanologist, not an oil drilling expert."

"Exactly," said Herman with an even bigger smile. "Your expertise is essential to our plans."

"They just want to do some drilling." interrupted Steve.

Herman laughed loudly. "Mr. Peterson, my naïve colleague, not just drill but change the world."

"That monster I talked to said you were going to destroy the world and remake it." argued Wendi. "I won't be a part of it."

Herman leaned over his desk and made an evil grin. "Oh, you will, my dear. You have parents and relatives that would be harmed if you didn't. Imagine some of those so-called monsters visiting them."

Wendi jumped to her feet. "You wouldn't, you can't."

"Oh, yes I can, so sit down." snarled Herman.

Sam reached up, took Wendi's arm, and pulled her back onto the couch. Wendi put her face in her hands and began to cry. Hitler walked over and handed her a handkerchief.

"It won't come to that, just help us." he said.

Sam glared at Herman. "Where do you want us to drill, and what for?"

Herman sat back in his chair and put his hands behind his head. "First, I want you to drill in Costa Rica. What for, will be explained later."

"Steve, you are definitely an idiot." said Sam.

New Orleans FBI Office
1250 Poydras Street
New Orleans, Louisiana

FBI SPECIAL AGENT Thomas Kline had been in the FBI for over 15 years, and during that time, he had never encountered such a group that sat in the large conference room located at their office. Looking around the room, he saw the two FBI agents, Williams and Pyle from DC, Lt. Colonel Taft, FBI Special Agent Best from the special tactical units, Colonel Damore from the National Guard, and three of the strangest looking people he had ever laid eyes on. He'd heard that there were half-demons that were now agents, but he'd never seen them until now. One was a hairless woman with one yellow eye, a winged half-eagle-man with one yellow eye, and the largest ape he'd ever seen, also with one yellow eye. He had been given a file on the situation and what they wanted to do in the area known as Hell's Corner.

"Good morning, and welcome to New Orleans." he said. "I've read through the file, and my understanding is that our goal is to raid the notorious section they call Hell's Corner."

Agent Williams nodded. "That's right, the plan is to not only destroy that area once and for all, but to locate a demon named Tarnac. As you read in the file, we believe he's responsible for, or at least has knowledge of, their recent activity. We did have a lead on the two men that tried to run Jake and his wife off the road in Texas, but Odessa police found them dead in their trailer."

"Cleaning up loose ends." said Jake.

Agent Kline thumbed through the file. "So, how do you want this to go? You know the local law enforcement has tried many times to raid that place but never located them."

"Yes, we know that. The problem is that demons can make themselves invisible or transparent, so they can't be seen. Our remedy is Colonel Taft and our three agents who can see demons in whatever form or transparency they're in, meaning they can't hide."

Agent Kline looked over at the three half-demons. Eudora and Soaring Eagle nodded while Kong just stared at him from under his huge brow.

"Agent Pyle and I, Colonel Taft, and the three other agents will accompany Agent Best." explained Agent Williams.

Agent Best glanced over at Agent Williams. "I'll have two tactical units that will make the initial entry." said Agent Best. He'd been in a relationship with Agent Williams several years ago, he later led a raid on a demon's laboratory that ended up being a trap. Sadly, several agents had been killed. "The national guard will set up a perimeter and they have wrecking equipment on standby to level the place. Right now, I have agents doing surveillance. Strangely, they've reported that these creatures are visible, so we think that they disappear when they sense that law enforcement is coming. Thankfully they can't do that with Colonel Taft and the other agents."

"You make it sound easy." replied Agent Kline.

"It never is," said Agent Pyle. "Not with demons."

"I read that Colonel Taft and the three agents are the only ones that can kill demons."

"That's correct," answered Agent Best. "But we've determined that demons can't touch holy ground, like cemeteries, holy sites, and inside of churches. So, our lab developed bullets that have cemetery dirt embedded in it. It's toxic to demons, and my understanding is that it can at least incapacitate them, and if enough injury can be inflicted, it may kill them."

"Sounds like a plan, so when do we hit it?" asked Agent Kline.

"We think right before daybreak." replied Agent Williams.

———

Blake Hotel-Best Western Premier
500 St. Charles Ave.
New Orleans

PAM AND ELLIE sat drinking coffee in the café inside the hotel, not far from the Superdome and Jackson Square in the downtown area of New Orleans. After a day of shopping, they were ready for a break.

"This is a lot better than last time we were here." said Pam.

Ellie put down her coffee cup and chuckled. "That's an understatement. Last time it was just us and Jake trying to figure out how we were going to get into that cesspool. Now we have the FBI and national guard to help us."

"We were lucky to get out of there alive." said Pam. "If it wasn't for..." Pam hesitated, and her face saddened. "Mobak, if it wasn't for him, we wouldn't have gotten in."

Mobak had been a small demon that Jake kidnapped and forced him to help them get into the mansion. Jake had agreed to let him go rather than kill him after he'd gotten them in. During that short time, they had grown surprisingly fond of the tiny demon. After he had helped them inside, and as they left, Jake let him go. When the demon horde chased them and attacked, Mobak tried to help save Pam, resulting in him being critically injured. They brought the little demon back to their hotel, where Malachy met them. Mobak succumbed to his injuries, and Malachy subsequently buried him on Jake's property. There's a small headstone there that simply says, Mobak.

Ellie nodded. "He helped us in the end."

"I'm just glad they're going to put an end to that place." said Pam.

Interrupting their reminiscing, Jake walked up and sat down. "It's all set to go at daybreak."

Both women nodded.

"Where's Roscoe?"

"Oh, he's protecting the bed up in the room." said Ellie with a grin. She then reached over and put her hand on his arm. "Promise me everyone will be extra careful. We'll be praying for you."

"We will. We have enough help do the job this time. You keep Roscoe near you until we get back." replied Jake. He then picked up a menu and smiled. "So, what's for dinner?"

As they looked at the menu, Pam spoke up. "If it's at daybreak, I'll be asleep. A girl has to get her beauty sleep."

Ellie grinned and Jake rolled his eyes.

———

Elflein 4000
Buenos Aires, Argentina

SAM AND WENDI wandered around the beautifully manicured property under constant watch.

"How long do you think we've been here?" asked Wendi.

Sam shrugged his shoulders. "Several days, maybe a week. It's hard to tell."

"Surely the authorities are looking for us."

"Of course, they are." answered Sam. "Those monsters left four good men dead back in Texas. I'm sure the authorities are turning over every rock to find us. Didn't you say a coworker witnessed your kidnapping?"

Wendi nodded. "A research assistant, Tina, and we have surveillance cameras all around the building. I'm just concerned they're not looking in the right place. Who would think to look for us in Argentina?"

"We have to hang in there and hope they can find us. We also need to see if we can find a hole in their security and escape."

As they walked along, Steve walked up. "I've been looking for y'all."

Sam frowned. "We can't leave, so you didn't have to look too hard. We're prisoners here, unlike you."

"That's right," said Wendi enthusiastically. "You can leave. You can call the authorities."

Steve shook his head. "No, even though they paid off my debt, they'll kill my family if I warn anyone. I imagine they'd kill your families too."

Sam glared at Steve. "So, what do you want?"

"I wanted to say that Herman told me that once we are finished, they'll let us go."

Sam clenched his fists and turned to Steve. "Are you real? You really think after they kidnap us, force us to do whatever they want, that they'd just open the door and let us go?"

Steve stepped back. "Herman gave me his word."

"He. Is. A. Nazi!" yelled Sam which brought the guards walking closer.

"Shhh, not so loud." warned Wendi as she watched the guards.

Sam took a huge breath and let it out slowly. "Steve, I've known you since we were kids but never realized how stupid you can be."

Steve held up his hands. "But all they want to do is drill for oil and minerals."

Sam shook his head. "I don't believe it. They want something else. They don't need demons and Wendi if they just want to drill for oil in Costa Rica. Whatever they have planned can't be good, and then you'll be an international fugitive. At least we're captives and forced to help them."

"I'll just explain that I was blackmailed."

"We'll be dead," added Wendi. "They aren't going to let us live."

CHAPTER FOURTEEN

Hell's Corner
Louisiana

IN THE PREDAWN LIGHT, two FBI tactical units in Lenco BearCat G2 armored vehicles, three National Guard units in BATT UMG armored vehicles, two local ambulances, and two Orleans Parish deputy cars set up a half mile from the mansion. The odd group of human and half-demon FBI agents, National Guard Colonel Damore, Orleans Parish Lieutenant Landry, and Jake gathered around one of the parish vehicles.

Dressed in full black tactical FBI gear, Agent Best had a map of the area laid out on the hood. "Our surveillance units report that they haven't seen any activity in over an hour."

Jake, dressed in military tactical gear, shook his head. "That's not good. That means they've seen us, so they'll be expecting us."

"Great, so we're going in blind?" asked Agent Kline.

"Not entirely, as we said yesterday, we can see them as well as Jake." answered Eudora. She was also dressed in black tactical gear, not that she needed it, but because she thought it looked cool. "We can point them out as we go."

"But we can't hurt them until they materialize or reappear or whatever you call it?" asked Agent Best.

"Yes and no." replied Jake. "The four of us that can see demons all the time can harm them in whichever state they're in, meaning if we can see them, we can kill them. Soaring Eagle and I will be with one unit, and Eudora and Kong will be with the other unit. We can point them out and fire when or if we need to. We've learned that right before they appear, you can smell ashes and sulfur. The air seems to briefly shimmer, and then they'll solidify. They can't harm you until then, so it's not a great advantage, but it helps."

Agent Best nodded. "I made sure we only used agents that volunteered for this. They have the cemetery embedded rounds for their AR-15s and handguns."

"You also gave our troops the same rounds for our weapons and our 50 calibers on our armored vehicles." added Colonel Damore. "We also have the wrecking ball and bulldozers standing by."

"Excellent." said Agent Best. "Hopefully we won't need you until it's over, but be ready to come in just in case." He turned to Orleans Parish Lieutenant Archie Landry. "Lieutenant, we just need your people to keep a loose perimeter. You don't have the special rounds, so don't engage them unless you have to, it won't do any good."

Lieutenant Landry nodded. "We've tried many times but have never been able to drive these monsters out."

"We'll do everything we can to make that happen." said Agent Best.

Jake spoke up. "Let me reiterate that you can slow them down and possibly incapacitate these things. They're deadly, dangerous, and will enjoy killing you." he explained.

"So don't hesitate to shoot them, because they won't hesitate to rip you to shreds." added Agent Williams, who unconsciously touched the scars on her cheek.

"Besides eliminating this sewer of devils, our main goal is to locate a demon named Tarnac." said Jake. "His room was on the second floor of the mansion last time we were here, but no guarantees. As you saw in the file, he's a large demon that resembles a part-alligator part-crocodile creature. Our plan is to capture him, if possible, to find out if he knows why demons are kidnapping people. There are ghosts that inhabit the mansion, they can't harm you. Last time, they warned me, so maybe they can help us locate him."

"Ghosts and demons, who would've thought." commented Lt. Colonel Damore.

"Lots of fun for all." said Agent Kline.

Agent Best pointed to the map. "The mansion has a circular drive at the front. My unit will take the south entrance, and the other unit will take the north entrance. I'm not going to worry about the back because we don't care if they run out the back. Our goal is to secure the mansion and locate this croc demon, then Colonel Damore can tear it down. We are on channel two on the radios. My unit is unit one, and the other is unit two. Any questions?" asked Agent Best.

When no one replied, Agent Best folded the map. "Let's load up and get 'er done. We'll take the lead."

Jake, Agent Kline, Agent Best and his team loaded up in unit one. Soaring Eagle would fly. Agent Williams, Agent Pyle, Eudora, and their team loaded into unit two. Kong wouldn't fit inside so he decided to ride on top.

Without headlights, the two armored vehicles moved within a hundred yards of the mansion. A few dim candle lights could be seen flickering inside, but no movement could be seen.

"See anything?" asked Agent Best.

"Nothing but a few ghosts outside." replied Jake. "That makes me nervous. They know we're here. Do we abort?"

Agent Kline looked over at Agent Best.

"Negative." answered Agent Best. "But since they know we're coming, there's no need to be covert." Agent Best keyed his radio. "Nothing outside so far, so go, go, go."

They turned on the headlights and raced up and into the southern entrance. The other armored vehicle switched on their lights and drove into the northern entrance. Both vehicles stopped at each end of the mansion and the teams bailed out. They spread out and approached the mansion from two sides. Lights from rifle-mounted flashlights bounced everywhere as they ran, using anything for cover as they approached the dilapidated mansion.

Jake saw a confederate ghost nearby. "Where are the demons?"

The confederate officer dressed in full uniform, Sabre and all, just stared at him for a moment, then spoke. "Suh, I remember you. You're the man with the two prostitutes that fought the demons. You killed some of them."

"Yes," said Jake. "We've come to clean out this nest."

"Good for you, Suh, and looks like you've brought reinforcements," replied the ghost. "You're going to need them, I'm afraid they're inside, and they know you're coming. They won't let us inside, so I don't know where those devils are hiding."

"Thanks."

Agents Best and Kline had watched the brief conversation Jake was having with someone they couldn't see.

Jake turned to them. "A helpful confederate ghost said they're inside."

"Of course," said Agent Kline with a smirk. "Did the ghost say where?"

Jake shook his head. "No, the demons won't let them inside the mansion. They want the demons gone too."

Agent Best nodded and keyed his radio. "Ok people, we have info that they're inside and waiting for us so lock and load and keep your head on a swivel. You're free to engage if need be."

Soaring Eagle landed and approached. "I can't see anyone from the air, but I know they're here, I can sense them."

The two teams cautiously worked their way up to the main double doors. Even though the windows were boarded up, they took extra care not to stand directly in front of them. They could see candlelight emanating through the cracks between the boards, but saw no movement.

Agent Best motioned for one of the FBI agents to come forward with the large metal battering ram. Before the agent could get to the door, Kong reached out and put his massive hand in the way.

"No." said Kong in a deep, guttering voice, shocking them all as they had never heard him speak. The huge ape stepped around them and stood in front of the door.

"What's he doing?" asked Agent Best.

"No idea." answered Agent Williams.

The half-demon half-human ape raised his head, beat his chest, and let out a deafening roar. He rammed the double doors, ripping them completely off the hinges, sending them flying into the interior of the mansion.

"That's awesome." said Agent Pyle.

"Knock, knock." said Agent Kline.

"Go, go!" yelled Agent Best.

The FBI teams flooded into the entryway of the mansion, each team going in opposite directions, guns up, and sweeping the area.

"Clear." said Agent Best.

"Clear." said Agent Williams.

They continued throughout the first floor, clearing the entire first floor without any encounters. They converged on the large stairway that led to the second floor.

"Kong and I will go first." said Eudora.

"10-4." said Agent Best. "The rest of us will give you cover and follow."

Kong led the way up the stairs that creaked under his weight, with Eudora closely behind. Upon arriving on the second floor, they looked around, but the hallway was empty.

"I'm glad he's on our side." commented one of the agents.

The two teams carefully followed up the stairs to the second floor. Using hand signals, they split up and worked their way down the hall. They systematically cleared each room. When they reached the door where Jake had last encountered Tarnac, he halted.

"This is where he was last time." said Jake. He nodded to Kong, who used one hand and slammed the door open. They rushed in and kept close to the walls. The inside appeared to be empty.

"Anything?" asked Agent Best.

"Nothing." said Jake.

They slowly and carefully worked their way around the ballroom.

"This is disgusting." said one agent.

When they passed the corpse hanging by shackles, another agent had to stop and vomit. "Sorry, I've never seen anything like this before."

"No one's judging." said Agent Best.

They ended at the far end, where Tarnac's throne sat. They all stood and stared.

"Much of an ego?" said an agent sarcastically.

"This place definitely needs to be torn down." commented another agent.

Agent Best shined his light around, then keyed his radio. "Unit one is clear, nothing here."

"Unit two is clear also." said Agent Williams.

"Looks like everyone flew the coop." said Agent Kline.

"Now, let's check the third floor." said Agent Best.

"Be quiet." said Soaring Eagle sharply.

They all turned to him as he looked around, then up. "I hear faint scratching, and I can smell them." He pointed up at the ceiling. "Upstairs."

"Ok, people." said Agent Best. "We've got hostiles upstairs on the third floor. Even with Kong, let's try to go quietly and carefully."

"I can hear them now too." radioed Eudora.

As the teams worked their way back down the hall, they heard the increased sound of footsteps and scratching coming from the third floor.

"Sounds like they're coming down." said Agent Pyle.

"I have contact." said Agent Williams as several demons came storming down the stairs. She fired her AR-15 into them, resulting in screeches and screams. More demons of all sizes and shapes continued to rush down the stairs.

"Engage!" yelled Agent Best.

The agents began firing into the horde while Kong roared again. He grabbed two demons and slammed them together, crushing their skulls.

Amidst the sounds of gunfire, Eudora heard wood being broken and ripped. She spun around and realized some of the demons had ripped the floorboards up on the third floor and dropped down into the second-floor rooms. "They're coming through the ceiling, coming up behind us!" she yelled as she shot several demons that came out of the rooms armed with swords and broadaxes. Soaring Eagle fired into several demons until his rifle was empty. He picked up one of the demon's swords and kept fighting.

The FBI agents fired, reloaded, and fired more rounds. The demons screamed and yelled. The cemetery embedded rounds didn't kill them, but at least it kept them at bay. Jake and the half-demons were able to kill most of the abhorrent creatures, but they still kept coming.

"The croc demon's gone, head back down!" yelled Agent Best.

The two teams merged at the top of the stairs but were stopped by a horde of demons coming up the stairs armed to the teeth.

"Great, more uglies." remarked Agent Pyle.

"Where did they come from?" asked an agent.

"Most likely from a cellar." said Jake as he shot another creature that tried to fly into the group.

"We didn't find a cellar." replied Agent Best.

"The mansion must've had a hidden cellar." yelled Agent Pyle as he fired into several demons while dodging knives, claws, and swords.

One demon leapt and grabbed an agent. It plunged a large thin sword into the agent's chest. Eudora grabbed the greenish bug demon with one hand and snapped its neck with the other. The FBI agent collapsed on the ground. A huge, hippo-sized demon armed with a broadaxe backhanded another agent into the wall and stormed towards Kong. The two behemoths met on the landing. While they wrestled each other, Agents Williams and Kline helped up the agent who had been slammed against the wall. His left arm hung loosely.

"I think my shoulder's dislocated." he said.

Agent Pyle took his AR-15. "Use your handgun then."

Kong and the hippo demon collided with a wall which collapsed, resulting in their momentum carrying them into an adjacent room where they continued fighting.

Several agents had minor stab wounds and claw marks but kept shooting. Soaring Eagle hacked and swung the sword into the horde. Kong could be heard roaring from the room.

"Those two could destroy the building just from fighting each other." said Agent Williams.

Jake keyed his radio. "Colonel Damore, fire into the first floor, maybe that will clear them out enough."

"Roger that, with pleasure. Ok, troops, let's show those monsters a thing or two." said Colonel Damore.

The National Guard units raced up and into the driveway. Their gunners began firing the 50-caliber guns into the first floor. The other guardsmen fired their AR-15s. This resulted in screaming and screeching from inside as they hit more demons. It seemed to slow them down, but wasn't killing them.

"We still can't get through." said Agent Pyle.

"I'm out and switching to a handgun." said Agent Williams.

"Me too." said another agent.

"We're running out of ammo." said Agent Kline.

Kong stomped through the hole in the wall carrying the huge broadaxe with a smile on his huge face. The ape swung the axe, hacking away at demons that were climbing the walls and ceiling to get to them. Seeing Kong gave Jake an idea, he yelled into the ape's ear over the sounds of gunfire.

Kong nodded and bent down, which allowed Jake to climb onto his back. He charged down the hall toward the end of the hallway, chopping and slamming demons out of the way. When he reached the end of the hall, he used his broadaxe to smash a giant hole in the wall. He climbed through and dropped safely to the ground. Jake leapt off and ran around the side of the house towards the national guard units. He climbed up into the turret and told the gunner to move. The gunner gladly climbed out and Jake took his place. Jake made sure it was fully loaded, aimed for the first floor, and began pouring 50-caliber rounds through the walls and boarded-up windows. Since he was able to kill demons, the rounds were causing deadly results, rather than just injuring them. He emptied the magazine, fed another, and then poured round after round into the third floor resulting in screams of death and agony.

On the second floor, the agents obviously noticed Jake's departure but were too busy fighting off demons. A few moments later, the demons began retreating.

"They're leaving." said Agent Pyle.

"Jake is firing the big guns." said Agent Williams. "More effective."

As demons fled the mansion like rats from a sinking ship, Jake kept up the deadly assault.

"The demons are fleeing." radioed Agent Best.

"We don't see them." answered Colonel Damore.

"That's because they've gone invisible." said Jake. "But not from me."

The scene was surreal as Jake fired into what seemed like thin air, and immediately, demons appeared, writhing in pain or falling dead. The rest fled on foot or flew off.

One of the guardsmen suddenly pointed at a group of men. "Where did they come from?"

"Who are they?" said another soldier.

They saw a group of men in confederate uniforms yelling and cheering as the demons fled. Small fires had broken out inside the mansion from candles that had been knocked over.

Jake had stopped firing when he didn't see any more demons coming from the mansion. "Those are ghosts," explained Jake. "They must have decided to appear to you." Jake keyed his radio. "What's your status, units one and two?"

"The demons appear to have left." answered Agent Best. "We'll be coming out. A few wounded need help, but the place is secure."

About two minutes later, some of the FBI agents came out, some limping, some scratched, and one being carried. The national guard medics immediately began giving aid to them. Some remained to confirm the building was secure. Shots could be heard coming from inside as Eudora and Soaring Eagle located demons and ended their terror. Kong went back inside and could be heard roaring occasionally.

"Hang on to a couple of them," radioed Jake. "We can at least question them."

The minor injured were bandaged up, and one agent was seriously injured. He was taken by one of the ambulances to the hospital.

"Jake, we have two demons detained on the first floor." said Agent Pyle.

Jake entered what was left of the first floor and met with Eudora, Soaring Eagle, Kong, and the other FBI agents. So many rounds had been fired it was a miracle the mansion was still standing. Smoke began pouring out of the second story as the fire spread. They found the agents in what was left of the formal living room. Two demons sat on the floor, surrounded by FBI agents with guns aimed at them. One demon was a black spider-looking demon with several broken limbs. The other one was a dark-brown rat-looking demon with black leathery wings. Both had bullet wounds and had not been able to escape with the rest. They glared at the humans.

"Traitors!" screeched the rat demon at Eudora, Kong, and Soaring Eagle.

"You true-bloods hate us and left us for dead." snapped Eudora. "You're scum."

Jake stepped up. "We don't have time for this, the fire is spreading. Why are you kidnapping humans?"

The spider demon smiled. "We kidnap humans all the time and eat them."

Soaring Eagle stepped forward and raised his sword. Jake held his hand up. "Where is Tarnac."

"Who's Tarnac?" said the spider demon sarcastically.

Eudora pointed to Kong. "I'm sure he would love to play with you. Imagine him pulling your legs off one at a time."

The spider demon glared at her, but the rat demon glanced around frantically. "Ok, so what do we get if we tell you?"

"Shut up!" screeched the spider demon.

"Kong hates spiders," remarked Eudora with a smile. "He squashes them."

Jake glanced at Agent Kline. "Can we make a deal if his information is good?" asked Jake.

Agent Kline shrugged. "I'm sure we can make a deal."

"He's in Buenos Aires." said the rat demon. "He's..."

He was cut off by the spider demon, who plunged a spider claw through the demon's eye and into his brain. Kong promptly crushed the spider demon with his foot.

"He wasn't going to talk anyway." said Agent Williams dryly.

By then, the fire had spread down to the first floor. They all rushed back outside and met with the rest of the group. "Did you find out anything useful?" asked Colonel Damore.

"One demon told us that Tarnac went to Buenos Aires." explained Jake.

"He would've said more, but the other demon killed him, then Kong squashed the other demon like a bug." said Agent Pyle dryly.

"Good." said the colonel.

Agent Best pointed to the mansion, which was almost fully engulfed in flames. "Whatever doesn't burn down is all yours for demolition."

Lt. Colonel Damore looked at the fire-engulfed mansion. The third and second floors had collapsed. "There might not be anything to tear down." he joked.

———

Blake Hotel-Best Western Premier
500 St. Charles Ave.
New Orleans

ELLIE STEPPED out of the front doors of the hotel with Roscoe. Other guests and employees gave the huge wolf dog a wide berth as they turned and headed down the sidewalk towards the local dog park. They soon arrived and Roscoe ran around, sniffing everything he could. Ellie sat down on a bench and watched. A couple of other dogs approached the huge wolf dog but then decided not to, which made Ellie smile.

A dark-haired woman in a sweatshirt, jeans and bright tennis shoes sat down at the other end of the bench. A few minutes later,

Roscoe padded up but didn't come to Ellie, he went to the woman instead. She scratched him behind the ears and rubbed him.

"Good boy, Roscoe." the woman said.

Surprised that the woman somehow knew Roscoe, Ellie turned to the woman and her eyes widened. "Kiara?"

The heavenly being, Kiara, smiled. "Greetings from the Most High God." she said.

Ellie smiled, got up and hugged the angel. "It's great to see you. I haven't seen you since Berlin. I didn't recognize you right away, dressed like us."

"I didn't want to draw attention, so I'm in disguise." she said with a wink. They both laughed. "Malachy wanted me to keep an extra sharp eye on you and Pamela while Jake and the FBI are raiding that devil's den."

Kiara was an angel who, from time to time, protected Ellie and Pam from demons. She'd saved them at least twice, once in Arizona and the other in Berlin.

"Thank you for watching out for us," replied Ellie. "Pam will be relieved."

"By the way, their raid was a success in driving the fallen out, but Tarnac wasn't there. Turns out he's in Buenos Aires."

"Buenos Aires?"

Kiara nodded. "I'll be around." she said and disappeared.

Roscoe stared at the spot where she had been and barked.

Buenos Aires?

———

Hell's Corner
Louisiana

THEY CALLED the local fire department to put out what was now just a bonfire. The bulldozers stood by to put an end to the demon's lair.

When the fire department arrived, Lt. Landry drove up, parked, and got out. He walked over to the group and was given the update.

"Well, at least you know where to start looking." he said. "I'm glad this eyesore is finally gone." He looked over at the group of confederates. "Who's that?"

"Confederate ghosts." replied Jake. "For whatever reason, they decided to appear to everyone."

"You mean they've been here the whole time?"

Jake nodded.

"I know New Orleans is famous for being haunted, but I never actually saw any until now."

Jake and Lt. Landry walked over to the confederate ghosts.

"Suh, we are indebted to you and your people for ridding this area of those devils."

"You're welcome," said Jake. "It's sad the mansion ended up like this. The fire department will extinguish the fire and the bulldozers will cover it up."

The confederate officer nodded sadly. "We understand, but it was once a grand mansion." He looked at Lt. Landry closely. "Your name tag says Landry. You grow up around these parts?"

Lt. Landry nodded. "I was born and raised here."

The ghost turned and spoke over his shoulder. "Corporal Landry."

A confederate wearing corporal stripes who looked remarkably like Lt. Landry came forward. The two men looked at each other for a moment.

"My family history has Landry's that fought and died in the war." explained Lt. Landry. "Never thought I'd meet one."

The corporal ghost smiled. "It's good to know the family name is still around."

Jake and Lt. Landry then bid them goodbye.

By then, the fire was almost out and the bulldozers had begun their work.

Lt. Landry glanced back but didn't see the confederates. "I can't see them anymore."

"I can't either, I guess they're done." replied Jake.

CHAPTER FIFTEEN

Elflein 4000
Buenos Aires, Argentina

IT WAS EARLY when Sam and Wendi were summoned to the library. When they arrived, Peterson, Hitler, and Herman were waiting. Steve appeared solemn while Adolph smiled.

"Good morning." said Herman. "I hope our early morning meeting didn't cause any problems?"

"Like we have a choice." grumbled Sam. Wendi kept silent.

Herman ignored Sam's remark. "We have great news; the final member of our team has arrived so we can proceed."

Suddenly they were all assaulted by the horrible smell of ashes, sulfur, and decaying flesh. They heard scratching and turned at the sound to see a horrible creature standing there. Wendi drew back in shock, Sam stood in front of her to protect her. Adolph stared wide-eyed while Steve jumped to his feet and moved away.

The creature known as Tarnac stood and grinned.

New Orleans FBI Office
1250 Poydras Street
New Orleans, Louisiana

JAKE and the FBI agents met in their conference room once again for debriefing. Agent Pyle had a bandage on his upper arm from being clawed, and Agent Kline came in limping from a leg injury. The others had miraculously escaped with minor scratches and stab wounds. The only agent that had been seriously injured had gone into surgery at the local hospital and was expected to live. Kong, who was too big for the chairs, sat back on his haunches next to Eudora. He leaned the huge broadaxe that he had kept against the table. Soaring Eagle sat on the other side of Eudora, he had also kept the demon sword.

"I can't say this was a complete success." said Agent Kline. "We closed down that horror fest, but the demon you were looking for wasn't there."

"That's true," said Jake. "But we did get a lead on his location."

Agent Williams was nursing a cup of coffee and put it down. "It still doesn't tell us why they kidnapped the two people or if they're connected." she commented.

"It could be a coincidence that he decided to leave the country." said Agent Kline.

Agent Pyle shook his head. "No such thing as coincidence when dealing with these things."

"I agree," said Eudora. "The pure-bloods don't do things like this without a good reason."

"I'm surprised your angel friends didn't show up." said Agent Kline.

Jake shrugged. "They have their own agenda and plans. I'm just grateful when they do show up."

"I need everyone to email me their supplement report and I'll brief Deputy Director Ruiz." said Agent Williams. "We need to find a link to Buenos Aires."

"Ah, Buenos Aires." said Agent Pyle with a huge smile. "Beach and babes, I can hardly wait."

Agent Williams punched in his injured arm.

"Ow, beast."

Elflein 4000

Buenos Aires, Argentina

WHILE MOST OF the group in the library sat stunned, Herman smiled brightly. "Welcome, my friend." he said.

The reptile demon stomped over to Wendi with his tail swaying. "Well, Dr Hamilton, it's good to see you again."

Wendi didn't know whether to faint or throw up.

Sam glared at the demon. "Are you responsible for the deaths of my oil rig crew?"

Tarnac lifted his head and laughed, filling the room with the stench of decay. "Why yes, I am. It was a wonderful slaughter, wasn't it? I hope you enjoyed it."

Sam clenched his fists and swung at the demon, who easily blocked the blow and grabbed Sam around the neck, choking him.

"Ignorant human," he snarled. "If I didn't have use for you, I would eat you."

"This is not what we agreed upon." stammered Steve. "You said it was just drilling for oil, not having demons around."

Tarnac dropped Sam, who fell to the floor and grabbed his throat, gasping for breath. Tarnac then turned to Steve. "I need this human for his knowledge, but I only need you for access to your company accounts, dead or alive." Tarnac then stared at Hitler. "So, Degen was able to create a Frankenstein after all."

Adolph frowned. He'd been shocked that Wendi was right about demons, and even more shocked that the demon had yellow eyes, but wasn't going to let on. "I don't know who this Frankenstein person is, but I am Adolph Hitler II."

"I know that Degen and that woman had plans for you, but I'm not sure what use you will be to me."

"Please, let's not start this off wrong." said Herman. "Everyone can be of use, so let's get down to business."

Wendi looked over at Hitler, who continued to watch Tarnac. He then unconsciously reached up and touched his face near his yellow eye.

"What is it that you want from us?" demanded Sam after he regained his breath.

Herman reached in the box on his desk and removed another cigar which he lit. "That will be explained when the time comes, but for now, we have a work room in the basement set up for you." He looked at Wendi. "How would you set off a volcanic eruption?"

Wendi wasn't sure she heard him correctly. "What did you say?"

"I asked how would you cause a volcanic eruption?"

Wendi rubbed her temples with her fingertips. "Are you serious?"

Tarnac leaned over towards her. "Absolutely, and you will help us, or my minions will have a fun time with your family. I think your niece just started kindergarten."

Wendi stepped back wide-eyed and sat down on one of the couches. She put her hand to her mouth.

"Do I need to repeat myself?" asked Herman.

Wendi shook her head. "It all depends on the size of the volcano, if it's active and how far down the magma is."

"Excellent." said Herman. "Mr. Donaldson's rigs can drill to whatever depth we need."

"You want to drill so you can set off a volcano?" asked Sam.

Tarnac grinned, showing his sharp teeth. "That's exactly what we want."

Sam turned and glared at Steve, whose face had gone pale.

Herman stood up, smiled, and slapped his palm on the table. "So, it's settled. Now, we just need to plan a practice run. But let's have breakfast first."

———

Federal Bureau of Investigation

Office of Deputy Director of Paranormal Activities
935 Pennsylvania Avenue Northwest
Washington, D.C.

DIRECTOR CHISOM KNOCKED, then entered Deputy Director Ruiz's office and sat down in one of the chairs across from him. Deputy Director Ruiz had been typing on his laptop and looked up.

"Good morning, sir." said Deputy Director Ruiz.

"I hope so." he replied. The director held a coffee cup and then crossed his legs to make himself comfortable. "So, what's the news?"

Deputy Director Ruiz closed his laptop and sat back. "First, the two men that we believe attacked Jake and his wife were found dead in Odessa. It was a bloody mess. Our agents were successful in shutting down that hell hole in Louisiana. During the raid, it was accidentally set on fire and burned to the ground."

"Saves having to tear it down." commented Director Chisom.

Deputy Director Ruiz nodded. "That was my thought. We were lucky. Even though those monsters were waiting and tried to ambush them, they were able to accomplish the operation. There were a few minor injuries, and one agent was seriously injured but is expected to recover."

Director Chisom nodded. "That's good news."

"However, the demon named Tarnac was long gone."

Director Chisom sipped his coffee and then asked, "Do we know if he had anything to do with the kidnappings?"

Deputy Director Ruiz shrugged. "We don't have anything for sure. They were able to detain two injured demons. One was not talking, but the other said that Tarnac had gone to Buenos Aires."

"That's all he would say?"

"Well, the other demon killed him before he could tell us more." explained Deputy Director Ruiz. "Kong ended him."

Director Chisom smiled briefly. "I'm beginning to really like that ape. So where do we go from here?"

"All the agents are submitting their reports, but for now, we'll be looking for any connection between Buenos Aires and the captives. It's not much to go on, but we've had less."

"I don't suppose Taft's angel friends gave us anything?"

Deputy Director Ruiz shook his head.

Director Chisom got up and headed to the door. "I'll brief the president. Contact our office in Buenos Aires and get them briefed. We need to find these people as soon as we can, if they're still alive."

Blake Hotel-Best Western Premier
500 St. Charles Ave.
New Orleans

PAM WAS TYPING an email to her editor back in Texas on her laptop while Ellie paced the floor. "Jake should have been back by now." she said.

"Kiara told you that it was a success," said Pam. "Maybe they're just running behind."

As if on cue, the door opened and Jake entered. Ellie ran over and hugged, then kissed Jake. "I was getting worried."

Jake faked being shocked. "What? You were worried about little ol' me?"

Ellie frowned. "You know what I mean."

Jake smiled. "I'm just messing with you. We had to debrief at the FBI office after we left Hell's Corner, which is no longer there."

"Good." said Pam. "So, what happened?"

Jake and Ellie sat down on the sofa while Jake explained what happened during the raid and the subsequent fire.

"Maybe since the mansion's gone and the demons left, the ghosts didn't want to stay?" said Pam.

Ellie shrugged. "Who knows."

The room was suddenly filled with the presence of the angel, Malachy. "Greetings."

Jake got up and shook the huge angel's hand. "You look tired."

Malachy sighed. His tunic was torn and marred. He sat down in one of the overstuffed chairs and leaned his huge sword against the side of it. "We've been in almost constant battle with the fallen since you arrived in New Orleans. They didn't want you to find out anything about what's going on."

"You were there?" asked Jake. "I didn't see you or the demons fighting."

"You can see us when you're supposed to, but the Lord doesn't always allow even you to see some of the activity." explained Malachy. "We were nearby, but you were kept from seeing it."

"You said they were trying to keep us from finding out what's going on, did you mean about Buenos Aires?" asked Ellie.

Jake was surprised and looked over at Ellie. "How did you know about Buenos Aires?"

Ellie smiled brightly. "You're not the only one who has friends in high places. Kiara told me."

Malachy nodded. "As I said, the fallen were adamant about you not finding out anything, so just in case, I asked Kiara to watch over Ellie and Pamela."

"Y'all are great." said Pam.

"Thank you, we are pleased to serve the Lord our Master." replied Malachy. "The fallen are making big plans, so you need to be vigilant."

"So, do you get to talk to Jesus, you know, like in person?" asked Pam.

Malachy smiled and winked but didn't answer. "We will do our part to help. And good luck." He stood, picked up his sword and disappeared.

Ellie frowned at Pam. "You shouldn't have asked him that question."

"Why not? He's in heaven, so he must, right?" replied Pam.

Ellie then grinned. "Actually, I've always wanted to ask him that."

CHAPTER SIXTEEN

The White House
1600 Pennsylvania Avenue Northwest
Washington D.C.

DIRECTOR CHISOM ENTERED the oval office and shook hands with President Campbell. "Good afternoon, Bill, I hope you have some good news for me?" He motioned for Director Chisom to sit.

"Yes, sir." replied Director Chisom. "Hell's Corner was a partial success."

President Campbell sat behind his desk, wearing a white shirt and slacks, but his tie was undone. "Give me the good news first."

"The rundown mansion is no longer standing. During the raid, it caught fire and burned to the ground." explained Director Chisom.

"Good riddance." said the President.

Director Chisom looked at some of his notes. "Several of the agents received minor injuries, and one was serious, but he'll be fine."

"Excellent."

"The bad news is that they didn't find Tarnac there, he was gone. They did find out that he'd gone to Buenos Aires, but not why."

The President sat back. "Do we know if he's part of the kidnappings?"

Director Chison shook his head. "No, sir, but we're working all angles to see if there's a link."

"Anything on the men that attacked the Tafts?"

Director Chisom frowned. "Odessa PD found them dead, ripped to pieces."

The President shook his head in disgust. "They're thorough monsters, aren't they?"

"Yes, sir, they are."

The President stood up. "Ok, keep me informed. If I need to call the Argentina president, let me know."

"We're contacting the FBI field office in the Embassy in Buenos Aires to get them digging." replied Director Chisom before he left.

Elflein 4000
Buenos Aires, Argentina

THE BASEMENT AREA that Sam and Wendi were in had all the modern equipment for Wendi to work with. They had seismometers and seismographs that detect and record earthquakes, instruments that measure ground deformation, instruments that detect and measure volcanic gases, and instruments that determine how much lava is moving underground.

She sat on a stool and marveled at the array of expensive equipment. "This is cutting edge, state-of-the-art equipment." she said.

"Yup," said Sam. "Looks like they spared no expense to wreak havoc. So how do you make a volcano erupt?"

"It's all about pressure, or actually, a drop in pressure." explained Wendi. "It's like a bottle of champagne or soda with the top on. If the cork or lid is on, it's ok, but when the pressure builds and you release the cork, it comes gushing out. For volcanos, it's called lithostatic pressure, when the volcano's pressure is released, the magma, rock, ash, and gases explode out.

Another way is to add water. The magma would boil the water, which builds up pressure, causing it to erupt. The key is how much water to use, if you use too much water, it will drown out the magma. Too little water and it wouldn't build enough pressure to explode."

Sam shook his head. "Either way, it doesn't sound good. Why would these lunatics want to cause an eruption?"

Wendi shrugged. "Who knows with Nazis. Maybe they want to blackmail the world?"

"Maybe they just want to be destructive." suggested Sam. "If it's for blackmail, then the authorities could just protect the areas."

"Maybe," answered Wendi. "But there are too many volcanos to protect worldwide."

Sam paced back and forth. "This is insane. We can't let them do it."

"But they'll kill our families." said Wendi sadly.

They stopped talking at the sound of footsteps coming down the stairs. Herman entered the room carrying several files and waved his arms around. "How do you like your new lab?"

When neither Sam nor Wendi responded, he continued. "We don't wish to blackmail the world, we want to change the world, or at least most of it."

"You've been spying on us?" snapped Sam.

"Of course we have." Herman replied. He pointed to surveillance cameras mounted in each corner of the lab. "We also have listening devices installed."

Sam clenched his jaw. "You people are evil."

Herman sat down on one of the stools. "Evil is in the eye of the beholder. You call us evil, but after World War II, you took our scientists who helped develop the nuclear weapons that can plunge the world into a nuclear wasteland. America pushes their agenda on the world, or else you sanction them. Don't lecture me on evil, Mr. Donaldson."

"Yes, but it was to deter other countries or people like you from using it for world domination. Look what you tried to do in Berlin." replied Sam. "You still want to use death and destruction to spread your perfect Arian race and ideology. Then you annihilate anyone that doesn't meet your standards."

"Enough!" yelled Herman. "I will not argue politics with you. We also had research completed of our own on volcanos." He got up and dropped the file in front of Wendi. "I expect you to confirm that you agree with our findings and have a plan designed by the end of the day."

"That's impossible," complained Wendi. "It would take me at least a week."

"Two days." replied Herman. "Two days or your families suffer."

After Herman left, Wendi opened the file and looked through it. Sam came over and looked over her shoulder.

"What does he want to do?" he asked.

Wendi's looked up and wiped a tear from her eye. "He wants to cause a volcanic eruption in Latin America."

––––––––––––

Federal Bureau of Investigation
Office of Deputy Director of Paranormal Activities
935 Pennsylvania Avenue Northwest
Washington, D.C.

FOR SEVERAL DAYS, Agent Pyle and Williams had been going through any information they could find about Wendi and Sam that might help link them to Tarnac or Buenos Aires.

Agent Williams threw down some papers in disgust. "Nothing, not a peep on the Hamilton woman." she said.

"I know." replied Agent Pyle. He rubbed his eyes. "I've been over the Donaldson family financial records and phone records but turned up nothing."

"They have to be somewhere; we just have to find it."

"Were you ever able to talk to Donaldson's partners?"

"Yes and no." Agent Williams shuffled through some papers. "I talked to Benton and Stafford, who haven't heard anything either, but I can't get ahold of Peterson yet. They say he's out of the country on business."

Agent Pyle leaned back and folded his arms. "Convenient."

Agent Williams looked up. "What did you say?"

Agent Pyle raised his eyebrows. "I said that's convenient."

"Hmmmm, so Donaldson is kidnapped, and his best friend goes out of the country rather than stay home and be of help to the family." She sat back in her chair and rubbed her chin.

"You don't think he has anything to do with this?"

"I'm just saying it's strange that he goes out of the country after the kidnapping and we hear Tarnac went to Buenos Aries." she replied.

"That's stretching it a bit, isn't it?" said Agent Pyle.

"Maybe, but I think we should look into Mr. Peterson and see what he's been up to."

———

La Fortuna de San Carlos
Costa Rica

LA FORTUNA IS one of Costa Rica's most popular and talked about destinations. Located in the Northern Highlands of Costa Rica, the resort town is centered on a beautiful park and a large church. The main sight is Arenal, a volcano that stands tall at 5,358 feet, can be seen for miles around, and provides the backdrop for the town. The town hosts many restaurants, hotels, resorts, hot springs spas, tour operators, and shops. Lake Arenal is nearby and is the country's largest, with a surface that covers nearly 33 square miles.

The Anderson family had just returned from the hot springs and were riding back to their hotel in a local cab. They were admiring the beautiful scenery when suddenly, in the area between the volcano and the lake, a series of rapid explosions occurred, rocking the vehicle and the family of four.

Tom Anderson leaned forwarded towards the driver. "What was that?"

The driver shrugged his shoulders. "I don't know, Senior."

"What's going on, mom?" asked five-year-old Meredith Anderson.

Her mother, Rebecca Anderson, shook her head and held her daughter closer. "I don't know, honey." She looked over at her husband with wide eyes.

Their eight-year-old son, Jimmy, pointed to the volcano. "Is the volcano awake?"

"No." replied Juan, the driver. "It hasn't been active for several years."

"I think it is now." remarked Jimmy as he pointed to the volcano and ash and smoke began to pour out of the cone.

The ground began to rumble and it was difficult to keep the van going straight. More ash and rock exploded up into the atmosphere. Juan rushed to get them to the hotel while dodging people running in all directions. Rock and debris rained down on the town, causing more panic. Juan stopped in front of the hotel, and as the family fled into the hotel, a huge cloud of ash, rock, and toxic gas descended on the resort town.

J Double T Ranch
Sutton County, Texas

JAKE AND ELLIE returned to their ranch, and life had returned to normal. Ellie had her church responsibilities while Jake and Roy worked on the ranch.

Jake sat on his horse, Buck, and looked out across the vast west Texas scenery full of grasslands and stands of shin oak, juniper, and mesquite. He watched the cattle feed on the grassland and thought how different this was from his experience just days ago in New Orleans. He wished it could just stay like this and that he could forget about demons and monsters.

Roy rode up. "We should move them in a day or so, so they don't overgraze. It looks like it's going to be a hot summer."

Jake nodded. "Yeah, we need to be careful so we have enough to last the summer."

"Any word on the kidnapped folks or that alligator monster?"

Jake shook his head. "Nope, nothing so far, but I'm sure the FBI is doing everything they can. I was just thinking about how nice it would be if things just stayed like this."

Roy shifted his weight in the saddle. "Yep, me too."

Later that evening, Jake, Ellie, and Roy sat at the dinner table while Ned sat, smoking his pipe, in a chair in the nearby living room.

Ellie put her tea glass down. "There was a volcanic eruption in Costa Rica today."

Jake set down his fork and wiped his mouth. "That's not good. Don't volcanos erupt occasionally down there?"

"Yes, but the news is saying that it was dormant." explained Ellie. "That area is a popular resort area, so it was crowded with people. Witnesses reported hearing explosions near the volcano right before the eruption."

"Terrorists?" asked Roy.

"The news hasn't said anything about that yet. The sad news is that it happened so fast and because it was so crowded, people couldn't flee fast enough. They fear hundreds of people might be dead or injured."

"Explosions and a volcano eruption doesn't sound like an accident." commented Jake. "The woman that was kidnapped was a volcanologist."

"You think she has something to do with it?" asked Ellie.

"Could be a coincidence." commented Roy.

Jake shook his head. "Maybe, but that's a huge coincidence, and I'm not a big fan of coincidences."

Basement Laboratory
Elflein 4000
Buenos Aires, Argentina

WENDI SAT and wept while Sam held her tightly. After hearing the latest news from Costa Rica, she had broken down sobbing. Steve came down the stairs and attempted to walk over to them, but the stare Sam gave him stopped him. He went and sat on a stool across the room.

"I'm guessing, since we haven't seen you, that you went to Costa Rica to oversee the drilling?" said Sam. "I hope your gambling debts were worth it."

"I'm sorry, I didn't have a choice." Steve said softly.

"Save it!" snapped Sam.

"I didn't mean for this to happen." replied Steve in an attempt to save face.

"Too late for that."

"I had to." said Steve. "I ordered the equipment and hired local workers to drill the holes. We paid off some of the local authorities to look the other way. I thought they were just going to use it as a threat. I didn't think they'd do it."

"That's right, you didn't think." said Sam.

"Stop it." said Wendi. "I'm the one who's to blame. I confirmed the information on how to do it."

Sam squeezed her shoulders. "No, you're not to blame. They already had the information, so they would've done it anyway."

Hitler came down the stairs and entered the lab. He took in the tense scene and looked sadly at Wendi. "I'm sorry you're upset, but Herman said it was necessary."

Wendi looked up at him with tears flowing down her face. "You're sorry. You're part of this. These people were killed, murdered by your people."

Hitler stood with his hands clasped. "Herman said that sometimes people have to be sacrificed for the good of the cause."

Sam let go of Wendi and approached Hitler. "Don't you ever think for yourself? Did it ever occur to you that Herman could be brainwashing you?"

Hitler looked back and forth between the two, not sure what to say.

"You said demons didn't exist!" snapped Wendi. "But you saw

that monster, Tarnac. And he has yellow eyes just like your right eye. Didn't Herman say it was a chemical reaction from the DNA? Adolph, he's been lying to you."

"Herman wouldn't lie to me." replied Hitler.

Sam threw his hands up in the air in frustration and walked away from him.

The air suddenly filled with the smell of sulfur and ashes. Tarnac appeared and smiled brightly, showing his sharp teeth. "Wasn't the eruption fantastic? Dr. Hamilton's instructions confirmed what we already knew, and the drilling from your company allowing us to set the explosives was absolutely amazing. I can't be happier at the carnage and death. This is going exactly as I had planned. The next phase will be even more magnificent." said Tarnac, who then clomped up the stairs with his tail swishing behind him. Hitler obediently followed him.

"Who would have given them this information?" asked Sam.

Wendi wiped the tears from her eyes and picked up a piece of paper. "The file says that Dr. Hankersly was given a grant to do the study as hypothetical research. I've met him before, and I don't think he'd do it knowing they had plans to make it happen."

"So, why not just snatch him and use him?"

Wendi shrugged. "My guess is they wanted someone else to confirm his calculations."

"Seems they thought of everything, so why keep us?"

"I think they're just keeping us as insurance, to make sure it works. I'm worried about what the next phase is." said Wendi sadly.

CHAPTER SEVENTEEN

Federal Bureau of Investigation
Office of Deputy Director of Paranormal Activities
935 Pennsylvania Avenue Northwest
Washington, D.C.

DIRECTOR CHISOM once again knocked and entered Deputy Director Ruiz's office to find the deputy director, Agent Pyle, and Agent Williams waiting for him. Carrying his customary cup of coffee, he found a seat.

"Thank you for coming, sir." said Deputy Director Ruiz.

Director Chisom nodded. "From your phone call, it sounded like you might have some information for me."

"Yes, sir, we do." he said. "I'll let our lead agent explain it." He motioned to Agent Williams.

"Good to see you again, Agent Williams." said the director. "I see you still haven't maimed or killed Agent Pyle." he joked.

"Thank you, sir." answered Agent Williams with a smirk. "But the day is still young."

Agent Pyle rolled his eyes.

While most agents for the FBI didn't interact with the FBI

Director very often, these agents were an exception. When Deputy Director Ruiz was still a special agent, he and Agent Williams were partners. They worked closely with the director when they were trying to locate the president's daughter and put a stop to the demon, Ghazi. Since then, Agent Williams and Agent Pyle went on to help stop the Nazi's bomb-attempt in Berlin.

"So, what do you have for me?" the director asked.

Agent Williams began. "We've been trying without success to find any kind of link between the kidnappings and Tarnac. A few days ago, we noticed that one of Tex-Am co-owners, Steven Peterson, is out of the country."

"Why is that odd? I'm sure they drill in other countries."

"Steven Peterson and Sam Donaldson have been friends since they were children and are best friends." explained Agent Williams. "According to our research, Sam Donaldson is the brains behind the company, and Steven Peterson is more of the hands-on person."

"Go on."

"We've been so busy watching the Donaldson's records and activity that we didn't think to check Peterson since they were so close. Then we thought it was odd that when the oil company employees are killed and Donaldson gets kidnapped, rather than go to be with the families, Peterson suddenly leaves the country. If they were so close, why would he do that."

Director Chisom nodded. "I follow you, and I'm guessing you turned up something?"

Agent Williams nodded. "Yes, sir, we checked his financials and noticed that he has been spending a lot of money at casinos, a lot of money. Then we checked and found out that he flew to Buenos Aires soon after the kidnappings."

Director Chisom sat up straighter. "Buenos Aires?"

"Exactly, and while there, he was very active in ordering drilling supplies and equipment to be shipped there." Agent Williams further explained.

"Didn't you say Tarnac went to Buenos Aires?"

Deputy Director Ruiz nodded.

"It gets better, sir. We also found out that he had some drilling equipment delivered to Costa Rica and flew there a few days before the volcano erupted. We're trying to see if they were delivered to La Fortuna de San Carlos, but we can't get the locals to help. It's either they were paid off or because of the crisis there."

Director Chisom sat and thought for several moments. "So, we have a kidnapped victim's best friend leave the country right after the kidnapping and fly to Buenos Aires where we think a major demon lord went, his company's drilling equipment is sent there and to Costa Rica where he also goes, and a volcano suddenly erupts after a series of explosions. This friend is also spending a lot of money gambling at casinos. Any idea how much?"

"We figured about one million dollars." answered Agent Pyle.

Director Chisom raised his eyebrows in surprise. "Wow, that's a lot of money. Are you thinking blackmail?"

"Who knows, sir." said Deputy Director Ruiz.

Director Chisom stood up. "Ok, let's not do anything with his accounts. We don't want him to know we suspect him, but monitor his activity. Get ahold of the agents in the embassy and tell them. I'll brief the president. Get your team together and go to Buenos Aires."

"Ah, yes, Buenos Aires." said Agent Pyle happily. He then covered his injured arm and frowned at Agent Williams.

Elflein 4000
Buenos Aires, Argentina

WENDI WAS SITTING in the kitchen eating her lunch when Hitler came in and sat down. She looked up but didn't speak.

"You're angry with me?" asked Hitler.

Wendi put her sandwich down and stared at him. "Angry? You forced me to confirm how to cause a volcanic eruption, which you made happen, that caused hundreds of people to die, if not more."

Hitler sat for a moment. "I'm sorry for the loss of life. Herman said it was necessary to make the world safe."

"So, again, you're listening to Herman without checking for yourself. Is killing innocent people making the world safe?"

"I owe Herman my life." he said. "If he hadn't saved me, then who knows what would have happened to me."

"Did Herman tell you that?"

"Yes, of course." he replied.

Wendi thought for a moment. "The news never mentioned you in their reports about what happened in Berlin. What I read was that a group of Nazis tried to blow up the world leaders at an economic summit meeting but were stopped. From what I read and saw on the news, there were demons and something they call half-demons involved too. Herman never told you about the demons, did he? Did it ever occur to you that if the authorities had found you, they would have realized you were innocent?"

Hitler shook his head. "Herman must have had a reason for not telling me."

Wendi sighed in frustration. "Adolph, you're naïve, and Herman wants to keep you in the dark for his own agenda. Do you know what his plans are now?"

Hitler looked down and shifted in his chair. "Herman said something about setting off more eruptions in certain parts of the world to cleanse the world to make it safe."

Wendi put her head in her hands. "And kill more innocent people, and you're ok with this?"

"Herman said it's what's best."

Wendi stood up. "And if I don't fit into his plans, will I be killed to make the world safe?" She stormed out, leaving Hitler alone with his thoughts.

———

J Double T Ranch
Sutton County, Texas

JAKE HAD GOTTEN out of the shower and was getting dressed after a hard day of work on the ranch. He loved working his ranch and how it was growing. Soon he would have Roy hire another hand. He hated having to go off to deal with demons and leave Roy with the responsibilities, but he couldn't let these monsters run amuck. He heard the front door open, and Ellie came in. He dreaded telling her the news from Washington. She wandered back and found him in the bedroom.

"How was your day?" he asked.

"It was great, I talked to a couple who received salvation and want to join the church." she explained.

"That's wonderful." he replied.

Ellie stopped and looked at Jake. She put one hand on her hip. "Ok, Jacob Travis, I can tell from your voice that something's up."

Jake knew he was a goner when she used his middle name. He let out a long breath. "Oscar called earlier."

She smiled and nodded. "I figured it was something like that. So, when do we leave for Buenos Aires?"

Jake looked at her, grinned, and hugged her tight. "I have the best wife in the world."

She hugged him back and looked up into his rugged face. "And don't you ever forget it." she said with a smile.

"We'll be staying near the U.S. Embassy. Promise me that you won't get into trouble."

Ellie laughed. "What? Me? Perish the thought."

"I'm guessing that annoying person will go too." said Jake with a frown.

"Oh, I'm sure Pam will go. When do we leave?"

"We'll drive to Dyess Air Force Base in Abilene tomorrow and fly out. He said Terrell and Stephanie are already on their way there with the rest of their team."

———

Elflein 4000
Buenos Aires, Argentina

HERMAN SAT behind his desk in the library, going over the plans he'd made, when he smelled a familiar stench.

He looked up and saw Tarnac sitting in a chair.

"How are my plans going?" demanded Tarnac.

His plans? Thought Herman. "Everything is going as planned. In a day or so, we will be able to move everything to the base in Antarctica. Soon we can be secure there and begin causing eruptions at designated locations around the world to bring them to their knees."

What a gullible fool. You have no idea what I'm going to do. "Excellent, Herman, just as you planned." Tarnac got up to leave. "Now, I have some annoying business to take care of."

"Anything I can help with?" asked Herman.

Tarnac shook his hideous head. "No, just some pestering humans and half-demons that think they come down here and stop us."

Tarnac stomped out of the room. Herman lit another cigar and waved the smoke around with his hand to cover the stench. He thought soon he'd have no need for Tarnac.

CHAPTER EIGHTEEN

Airborne over South America

AFTER A BRIEF LAYOVER in Mexico City, the U.S. Air Force C-17 cargo aircraft, the largest military transport aircraft in the world, continued south with cargo bound for Argentina.

On board, the loadmaster sat in his seat and stared at the unusual occupants. He'd flown all over the world and transported all sorts of cargo and people, but nothing like this. The Army Lt. Colonel with the two women and the two human FBI agents weren't that unusual, but the huge wolf dog, the giant ape, the woman without hair and a half-eagle-man took the prize.

"Any idea how you're supposed to find Mr. Donaldson and Miss Hamilton or that monster Tarnac?" asked Ellie.

Jake pointed to Agent Williams, who appeared to be asleep. "Stephanie contacted the FBI agent in Buenos Aires who are supposed to help us. Specifically, we aren't sure exactly how to locate them."

"So, we're going to play by ear when you get there?" she said with a smirk.

Jake laughed. "I hope we can locate that Peterson guy, he might lead us to them or at least know where they are."

A few hours later, the flight crew announced they were descending to land at the Punta Indio Naval Air Base, just south of Buenos Aries. As they were beginning their descent, they all heard a sudden thump and looked at the loadmaster.

Staff Sergeant Nathan Potter looked around but shrugged. "No idea. Maybe we hit a bird?"

A few moments later, two more loud thumps were heard. "I don't like this." said the now fully awake Agent Williams.

They heard the screech of tearing metal, and the aircraft tilted to the side.

"What's going on?" asked Agent Pyle.

"The pilot says we've lost an engine." explained SSgt Potter. "He says there's some kind of creature flying next to us and it damaged the number one engine."

"Demons," said Jake. "They're trying to cause us to crash."

"Lower the ramp." said Soaring Eagle.

"Another one is attacking the number two engine." said SSgt Potter.

"Are we low enough that we don't need oxygen masks?" asked Agent Williams.

SSgt Potter nodded as he unplugged his headset.

"Now." demanded Soaring Eagle as he walked to the rear of the aircraft, past the large crates of cargo.

SSgt Potter rushed to the back, plugged his headset back in and hit the button to lower the loading ramp, resulting in a blast of air into the cargo bay. When the ramp was lowered enough for Soaring Eagle, he leapt out of the aircraft armed with his sword.

The pilot had been able to compensate for the loss of the engine and leveled the aircraft out. Jake released his seat belt and worked his way back to the ramp, followed by Roscoe.

"What are you doing?" yelled SSgt Potter so Jake could hear him over the wind.

Jake removed his Colt .45. "Just in case."

The aircraft continued their descent as Soaring Eagle and a demon flew by, wrestling and fighting with swords. Another demon suddenly landed on the ramp and was promptly shot by Jake. The demon's face showed shock at being injured and it fell out of the aircraft.

"Was that gunfire?" asked the pilot into SSgt Potter's headset.

"Yes, sir." answered SSgt Potter into his mic. "One of those creatures tried to come in through the ramp so Colonel Taft shot it."

Agents Pyle and Williams had made their way back to the rear of the aircraft.

"Do you see anymore?" yelled Agent Williams over the sound of the wind.

Jake shook his head.

Soaring Eagle fought the high wind but was able to land back on the ramp. "There were only two."

SSgt Potter motioned towards their seats. "Better get buckled in."

They all climbed around the cargo and back into their seats.

The C-17 Globemaster landed safely and taxied to a stop near a hangar where two white vans were parked.

The group unloaded with their gear and luggage, and then walked towards the vans.

SSgt Potter stood at the bottom of the ramp, stared at the damaged jet engine, and shook his head. "Wait til the rest of the squadron hears about this, they'll never believe it."

A dark-haired, middle-aged man approached the group. "Welcome to Argentina, I'm Special Agent Alex Contreras. I hope your flight was ok."

Agent Williams shook his hand. "I'm Special Agent Stephanie Williams. The flight was fine, the final descent was a little rough though." she said as she pointed to the damaged engine.

"Whoa," said Agent Contreras wide-eyed. "What happened?"

"Demons happened." said Agent Pyle.

"Aren't you the Terrell Pyle who played wide receiver for the Ravens?" asked Agent Contreras.

Agent Pyle nodded. "Yep, until my career-ending injury, but thanks for remembering. I still have at least one fan. Now I just get injured by demons and Agent Williams."

Agent Williams grinned. "He deserves it."

The rest of the group introduced themselves. Agent Contreras stared in amazement at the half demons. "I've heard about our new special agents but never thought I'd meet you." He turned to Jake, Ellie, and Pam. "And you must be the famous demon-hunter, his two female friends, and of course the wolf-dog."

Jake shook his head. He hated being called that.

Elflein 4000
Buenos Aires, Argentina

TARNAC STORMED DOWN THE HALL, his claws scratching the marble floors and his tail slamming into the walls. "Idiots!" he yelled. "Total idiots!"

Sam and Wendi heard the yelling and looked around the corner into the hallway from the living room. Herman came out of the library. "What's going on?" asked Herman.

Tarnac grabbed a large wooden cabinet, picked it up, and slammed it to the floor in anger. "I sent two idiots to kill that cowboy and his friends along with those FBI agents, and they couldn't even do that."

"What happened?"

Tarnac continued to pace the hallway. "I sent them on a simple task to destroy the jet engines on their aircraft so it would crash, and they failed!" yelled Tarnac as he stomped off.

Sam and Wendi went back into the living room. Sam grinned at Wendi. "He said FBI agents and some other people were flying here."

Wendi nodded. "Maybe that means they know where we are."

"I hope so," said Sam. "Why else would they make that monster so mad?"

U.S. Embassy
Av. Colombia 4300
Buenos Aires

THEY RODE along the coast in the two vans towards Buenos Aires while admiring the beauty of Argentina.

"Wow, it's so beautiful." said Pam. "Why is it we get to go to these wonderful places then end up running, screaming, and shooting demons?"

Jake frowned. Ellie smiled. "Hush, Pamela, don't jinx us."

"Look at the beaches," commented Agent Pyle. "And look at the babes on the beach." He suddenly grabbed his injured arm and looked at Agent Williams. "Don't you dare."

"Too bad you're here for business, lover boy." replied Agent Williams dryly.

Kong just grunted. He took up the whole back seat and had to duck his head so he didn't hit it on the roof of the van. Eudora smiled, reached back, and patted her big friend. Due to limited space, Soaring Eagle and Agent Contreras rode in the other van with the gear and luggage.

Agent Contreras turned to him. "Is this your first trip to this area?"

Soaring Eagle nodded. "Yes, we were created in Arizona. We went to the military base in Nevada and demanded to go to Berlin to help, but that's it.

Created? Thought Agent Contreras. He couldn't comprehend how these people felt about how they came to be, but he was impressed that they decided to help mankind who may or may not approve of them.

They traveled to Buenos Aires without incident. The vans took them to the Palmero and Oro Apartments, used primarily by embassy employees, about a quarter of a mile from the U.S Embassy. They unloaded their gear and suitcases and walked into the lobby where Agent Contreras handed out keys, as he had already booked their apartments prior to their arrival. Jake and Ellie were given their own room. Agent Williams, Pam and Eudora shared an apartment. Agent Pyle was lucky enough to get his own apartment. Kong and Soaring Eagle shared the last apartment.

They all trooped over to the elevator, where two embassy employees waited for the elevator. When the elevator door opened, they looked at the half-eagle-man and the huge ape and said they would wait for the next elevator. Kong and Soaring Eagle took up the whole elevator while the rest, suppressing smiles and snickers, also waited for the next one.

After depositing their gear and luggage, Pam and Ellie stayed in Ellie's room with Roscoe to get some rest. Kong and Soaring Eagle felt the small elevators were too confining, so they took the stairs while the others took the elevators back down to the lobby. To avoid any unusual attention, they rode in the vans to the U.S. Embassy, a modern multifloored office building surrounded by an iron fence. They processed through security, but Kong was too large to go through the metal detector. The Marines manning the metal detector decided not to object to his huge battle-axe and Soaring Eagles sword since, technically, they were FBI agents and let them go around. They were led past staring employees into a briefing room.

Once they all got seated, except for Kong, who was too big for any of the chairs, so he just waited behind the seated Eudora, his immense size still dwarfing her. Agent Contreras handed out some paperwork. "Here is the latest we have on Steven Peterson. After my conversation with Agent Pyle and Williams, I started checking and confirmed that he had arrived in Buenos Aires three days after the kidnappings. He then flew to Costa Rica four days later. He returned the day before the eruption. I spoke to Costa Rica's special investigators in La Fortuna, who are still sifting through the damage. They were able to confirm that the explosions were caused by someone drilling holes in specific locations, which were then packed with explosives that were detonated. The explosions caused the water to interact with the volcano's magma, which resulted in the eruption. Someone knew exactly how to do it to make it erupt."

"Someone like Dr. Hamilton." said Jake.

"Yes," answered Agent Contreras. "Sadly, the drilling equipment was destroyed by the explosions and magma, so we can't confirm it belonged to Tex-Am. They suspect local workers were used and they doubt they will ever be able to identify them."

They nodded in acknowledgement or shook their heads in frustration.

"Thanks, Alex, for checking into that." said Agent Williams. "Did you find out anything about Peterson's activities while he's been here?"

Agent Contreras looked through his paperwork until he found what he was looking for. "Yes, we were able to follow his credit card purchases. There's nothing unusual, just some normal purchases like delis, coffee shops, etc."

"Any idea where he's staying?" asked Jake.

Agent Contreras shook his head. "No."

"What about his phone records? We could see who he's been calling. We could figure out where he might be staying or who he's working with." suggested Agent Pyle.

"That's a good idea, Terrell," replied Agent Williams. "But I'm afraid we don't have time to wait. We were hoping the credit cards would be the easiest way to lead us to him. We would have to get a judge here to sign a search warrant that phone companies now require, rather than a subpoena, and then send it to a judge in the U.S. to approve it. Then we'd have to send the search warrant to the phone company and wait for the information, it would take weeks."

"Ok, so if this Tarnac character is here somewhere, can't you just follow some demons?" asked Agent Contreras.

Eudora spoke up. "We see demons everywhere. We wouldn't know which ones to follow, and it would take too long to follow them all if that was even possible."

"She's right," added Jake. "And if Tarnac is involved, I doubt trying to detain and question some of them would do any good. When we tried that in Texas and New Orleans, one demon killed the other to keep him quiet and another killed himself. They're more afraid of Tarnac than us."

"Wow, that sounds bizarre, even for demons." said Agent Contreras. "Did the other demon refuse to talk?"

"Kong squashed him." answered Agent Williams.

"Oh." said Agent Contreras as he looked over at Kong who just grinned.

"Peterson has to get around somehow, so can we check Uber or taxi companies to see if he uses them?" asked Agent Williams.

"I thought about that and checked the airport cameras, a dark-colored private vehicle met him at the airport and the cameras aren't good enough to give us a license plate."

Agent Williams sat back and threw her pen down in frustration. Agent Pyle sighed, got up, went to the sidebar, and got some coffee. Jake rubbed his eyes. Soaring Eagle tapped his pen on the table in thought.

"Any other ideas?" asked Agent Contreras.

The group sat sifting through paperwork for several minutes when the silence was suddenly broken by Kong's deep voice. "Check his credit cards to see if he frequents the same places at the same times, then follow him."

They all stared in awe. This was only the second time they had ever heard the giant ape speak.

"That's a great idea." said Agent Williams.

Eudora turned and smiled up at the big ape. He winked at her.

They all started looking through Peterson's credit card purchases.

"Look at this," said Agent Pyle. "On pages 15 and 18. He's gone to the same coffee shop."

"And on pages 20 and 22." added Jake.

"That's Café El Grande." said Agent Contreras. "It's a popular spot and has good coffee."

"And the times are between two and three almost every afternoon." said Soaring Eagle.

Agent Pyle motioned towards Kong. "I love this big guy."

Kong grunted.

Agent Williams smiled broadly. "Looks like our ape friend, I mean Agent Kong, found the kink."

"Now, we just have to set up surveillance and follow him." said Agent Contreras.

CHAPTER NINETEEN

Patio Bullrich
Posadas 1245, C1011 CABA
Buenos Aires

AFTER BEING COOPED up in their apartment while Jake met with the FBI about locating Peterson, Ellie and Pam threatened a mutiny when Jake returned if he didn't take them out. Jake called a taxi and they rode down the Avenida Del Liberator, passing the embassies of Peru, Italy, Poland, Spain, and many more. They arrived at one of the more modern and upscale malls, The Patio Bullrich. Jake insisted on bringing Roscoe but knew that most places frowned on pets in a mall, especially a huge half-wolf dog, so Jake had obtained a vest that identified him as a military police dog, and Jake wore a windbreaker that had US Embassy stenciled on it.

They entered the multilevel mall, and Jake followed Ellie and Pam from women's stores to fashion stores to shoe stores. He patiently waited near the doors, watching people as they stared at him in his jeans, windbreaker, cowboy boots, and Stetson hat. He had Roscoe on a leash, which was just for show as Roscoe was voice trained. Even so, people gave them both a wide birth.

Ellie and Pam came out carrying several bags. Ellie had noticed the looks they got as they walked around. "If you're trying to be incognito, it's not working." she said with a grin.

Jake frowned. "I'm not trying to, just keeping an eye on you two so you don't buy out the mall."

"I'm hungry." announced Pam.

"I can use something to eat after buying out all of the stores." added Ellie as she nudged Jake in the ribs with her elbow.

They decided to eat at Francesca's, located inside the mall. The restaurant had seating inside and out in the main atrium of the mall. The waiter sat them at a table out in the atrium in a corner so as not to scare off patrons.

They looked over the menu while Roscoe curled up on the floor next to Jake.

"So, when is this surveillance going to begin?" asked Pam.

Jake glanced around before answering. "I'm not sure this is the place to discuss this."

"C'mon Jake, don't be paranoid, no one's listening or cares. Besides, no one dares get close enough to hear for fear of being eaten alive."

Jake looked around and noticed that all the tables next to them were empty. He smiled, reached down, and rubbed Roscoe. "That's why I brought him. And to answer your question, Peterson frequents one certain café almost every day between certain hours, so I would imagine we'll set up a schedule to watch for him."

"If you're going to do it, you'll need to wear something less obvious." said Pam.

Ellie snickered. "She's right dear, you'll have to blend in better."

Jake faked being offended. "You mean these clothes don't make me look like a local? Ok, I'll make sure I change before we do."

"I'm not sure that will be enough." said Ellie smiling. "You're a head and shoulders taller than most people here."

"Maybe you can walk around on your knees." added Pam.

Jake huffed and lifted his menu up to block his face. The two women giggled.

They sat and enjoyed their dinner while Ellie and Pam discussed the items they had purchased and if they needed to buy anything else. Jake obviously didn't join in the discussion and quietly ate *pesca della giornata*—the Fish of the day with vegetables, mushroom pesto and salmoriglio sauce—while Ellie and Pam shared the *Salmone affumicato foglie verde*—which was Smoked salmon, green leaf mix, roasted onion, roasted tomato and lemon fennel. Jake sneaked Roscoe bits of his dinner and would feed him more when they got back to their rented apartment.

When they were finished, Pam sat back and sighed. "That was awesome. A lot better than the food they gave us on the military plane."

Ellie nodded. "Yes, it was fabulous."

The waiter returned to the table with the check and Jake's credit card, making sure he stood on the opposite side of the table from Roscoe.

He thanked them for coming when Roscoe growled. "Senior, what did I do?" asked the waiter.

Jake, suddenly alert, looked around. "You didn't do anything."

The waiter backed away as Roscoe stood up and growled even more. The waiter sniffed the air, frowned, and looked around. Something caught Jake's eye and he looked up at the next level of the mall, he smelled ashes and sulfur at about the same time.

A huge, eight-foot-tall creature, black and red in color, leapt over the railing and landed on some of the tables, crushing them and knocking some of the guests out of their chairs. The waiter was frozen in fear.

The thing didn't have a weapon but was covered in armor and it had four huge arms with razor-sharp claws. Three horns protruded from his head as he roared and turned towards them. As customers fled in terror, Jake jumped to his feet, drew his Colt 45 from under his windbreaker and shoved the waiter out of the way.

"Call for help, I'll find y'all later." Jake said to Ellie and Pam, who had already gotten to their feet and were running from the area.

Jake fired twice into the torso of the behemoth, which had no effect. *Bulletproof armor*, thought Jake. Before he could fire another time, the creature picked up a table and threw it at Jake, who dodged it. Roscoe leapt and bit into one of the creature's huge legs. The creature swatted Roscoe away.

"Go with Ellie." ordered Jake.

Roscoe hesitated, but then took off in the direction of Ellie and Pam.

Ellie and Pam ran into a woman's clothing store, followed by Roscoe. Ellie dialed on her phone, and it rang twice.

"Agent Williams." said the familiar voice.

"Stephanie, we're being attacked by demons at the Bullrich mall." said Ellie.

"On our way." snapped Agent Williams.

———

THE FBI AGENTS were all in the briefing room going over maps and plans for the surveillance.

"The Taft's are being attacked at a mall called Bullrich."

Agent Contreras pointed to the mall on the map they had laid out on the table. "It's not too far from here."

Soaring Eagle ran to the window, opened it, and flew out. The rest ran outside, and while the three human FBI agents dashed to Agent Contreras' car, Eudora climbed on Kong's back. Kong leapt over the metal perimeter fencing and raced down the street. Once in the car, the three agents sped after them, hoping they would be there in time.

———

JAKE TOOK aim at the monster's head but was stopped by another smaller demon that collided with him. He was knocked to the ground, and his gun slid out of reach. The other demon cackled, but his laughter was cut short by a mall security guard who fired a two-pronged taser into the demon. The taser shot electricity into the spotted leopard-looking demon. The demon only hissed at the mild irritant of being tased and drove his sword through the security guard's torso, killing him. As the demon pulled the sword out,

Malachy appeared and engaged him. The two fought with swords like two knights from medieval times.

———

ALONG WITH ELLIE AND PAM, numerous people had also taken refuge inside the store. Several people hid behind the counter, while some hid in the dressing rooms. No sooner had they entered the store, two demons followed them inside. One was a large locust-looking demon, while the other was a smaller furry thing with two sets of eyes. Roscoe growled and barked at the demons who just laughed insidiously. The furry demon reached out for Pam, but Roscoe bit into its arm. The demon jerked back but Roscoe held on. The locust demon tried to reach Ellie, who had found an empty clothes rack and swung it back and forth at the thing. Pam grabbed a pole used to take down clothes off the wall and began hitting the creature. The thing opened its mouth and emitted a strange stringy weblike green substance that wrapped around Ellie's waist. It started pulling her nearer.

"Locusts can't do that!" yelled Pam.

"This one can." replied Ellie as she struggled against the string-like web.

Pam struck the creature over and over with the pole without success.

———

THE HUGE RED demon grabbed Jake by the leg and pulled him toward him. Jake frantically tried to reach his gun. The monster squeezed, causing one of his claws to pierce through Jake's boot into his calf. Jake kicked the devil's arm several times, but it was no use. The thing lifted Jake up into the air by his leg while Jake kicked and punched it. The huge demon raised one of his four clawed hands to impale Jake when a flurry of feathers rushed by him. Soaring Eagle grabbed the thing's arm and sliced off its hand with his sword, causing the thing to screech, shattering glass nearby. The demon grabbed Soaring Eagle's arm to stop him from stabbing him and tried to use the fourth arm to slash him, but Soaring Eagle grabbed that arm. It became a contest of strength between the demon and half-demon while Jake hung upside down in the grasp of the third arm.

The creature slung Jake around towards Soaring Eagle and they both collided, causing them to fall to the ground, stunned. The demon gave them a triumphant smile when they heard a challenging roar echo throughout the mall. Before the demon could turn, Kong swung his mighty battle axe and buried it in the creature's spinal cord. The thing fell to the ground while Jake and Soaring Eagle got to their feet.

Ellie, thought Jake. He ran in their direction, followed by Soaring Eagle and Kong, while Malachy and the other demon continued to battle.

———

THE FURRY DEMON grabbed Roscoe by the neck, ripped him from his arm, and slung Roscoe across the store into a rack of clothes. The creature turned to attack the two women when Eudora leapt onto his back, put her gun to his head and pulled the trigger. The creature collapsed and immediately started decomposing.

Pam grabbed Ellie and it became a tug of war that they were losing as the creature pulled Ellie closer and closer. A thin golden sword suddenly severed the stringy web-like cord. Kiara stepped in front of the two women and began slashing and hacking at the locust demon.

Eudora fired several shots into the locust demon, causing it to stumble back. Kiara jumped and spun in the air like a ballerina, beheading the monster with a single fluid motion. The creature fell back onto a rack of expensive leather coats.

Kiara landed and turned to the two women. "Are you okay?"

Ellie and Pam nodded.

Jake, Soaring Eagle, and Kong arrived at the entrance to the store and saw Ellie, Pam, and Eudora helping the other people past the decomposing monsters and out of the store.

"Are y'all ok?" asked Jake.

"Yes," answered Ellie. "Kiara, Eudora, and Roscoe came to our rescue."

They looked and saw Kiara still inside the store. She waved and disappeared. Jake rubbed Roscoe's head. "Good boy."

Pam turned to Eudora, raised her hand and said, "High-five." Eudora looked quizzically at her so Pam reached over and raised her hand. Pam slapped her hand in the typical high-five gesture and said, "Girl Power."

Eudora smiled brightly.

Malachy came up behind them, holding his sword. Jake turned to him. "Thank you again, my friend."

Malachy nodded and disappeared.

———

THE FBI AGENTS arrived at the mall and rushed inside. They followed the smell through the mall to the restaurant where the two demons were decomposing.

"Whoa, that's a big pile of... of decomposing demon." commented Agent Pyle.

Agent Williams looked around at the broken tables and chairs.

Agent Contreras noticed the top half of the security guard's body covered with a tarp. "We have at least one casualty."

"Oh no." said Agent Pyle sadly. "I really hate demons."

"Stand in line." replied Agent Williams.

Kong came lumbering back.

"Is everyone ok? Where are they?" asked Agent Williams.

Kong grunted and pointed towards the women's store.

The agents ran down to the store, where the rest were trying to calm frightened customers in front of the store.

Agent Contreras went into the store where the other two deceased demons were. He held his hand over his mouth. "Do they always do this?"

Agent Pyle and Williams followed him in. "Yep," said Agent Pyle. "They decompose rapidly after they die."

Agent Contreras stared at them. "This one looks like a giant bug."

"They come in all sizes and shapes," added Agent Williams. "And they all have claws and sharp teeth." She pointed to the scars on her cheek.

Agent Contreras nodded. "I wondered about your, you know, scars, but I didn't want to pry. I've never seen one, alive that is."

"This and the attack on the aircraft confirms we're on the right track." said Agent Williams.

Kong returned from the restaurant area carrying his broadaxe, along with the armor he'd taken off the large demon. With a few minor adjustments, it would fit him.

The Buenos Aires police and Embassy Marines arrived on the scene. Ambulances were called to treat a few minor injuries that occurred when people fled, and Jake's puncture wound was bandaged. The only fatality was the unfortunate security guard. Buenos Aires investigators arrived and spoke to everyone involved in the incident. There was little question as to what had happened with several piles of demons rotting and stinking up the mall. Security cameras also confirmed their sequence of events.

———

Elflein 4000
Buenos Aires, Argentina

SAM WAS in his room when he heard Tarnac yelling, so he poked his head into the hallway. He could hear Tarnac ranting in the library.

"I'm surrounded by idiots!" yelled Tarnac.

Herman sat quietly.

"What does it take to get rid of these worthless humans? I sent four minions this time, and even they failed."

"I saw on the news that they had some help. There were some

people that helped, what they're calling half-demon FBI agents." explained Herman.

"Those worthless half-breed abominations that Degen created? They're just working for the humans to try to be accepted."

"Apparently so, but not to worry, our plans have been set, so within a few days, we'll be gone from here." explained Herman.

Tarnac's yellow eyes glowed with anger. "That cowboy stopped Ghazi and Degen. I will not allow him and his friends to interfere with our plans."

Herman nodded. "I'm aware of that, but they have no clue where we are, and they can't possibly know where we're going."

"If they do, it'll be their frozen tomb." snarled Tarnac.

Sam thought for a moment. It sounded to him like the FBI was actively looking for them, but when they leave, the FBI will never find them. He needed to find a way to warn them.

Palmero and Oro Apartments
Buenos Aires

IT WAS late at night when Ellie awoke and realized Jake was not in bed. She found him in the living room, sitting on the couch and sipping a cup of coffee. Ellie snuggled up next to him on the couch. "Why can't you sleep?" she asked.

"What's wrong?"

Jake let out a heavy sigh. "We've been blessed to have Malachy and Kiara, who have saved our lives numerous times." explained Jake. "They've shown up to help many times but then not at other times. I think of all the people that've lost their lives trying to help us, like Lt Begget and the doctor in Arizona, those soldiers in Nevada helping us look for the nuclear bomb, and earlier this evening at the mall with the security guard. Malachy arrived but not soon enough to save the unfortunate man who was just doing his job and trying to help. When it was over, Malachy didn't say anything, he just left."

Ellie sat for a moment and rubbed his shoulder. "We don't exactly know how angels work. We know that some angels protect us, some reveal things to us and some minister to us. God uses angels as He uses us. He doesn't need us or angels to accomplish His purposes, but chooses to. We have the assurance from God that we are His children through faith in Christ, that He works all things together for good. Jesus will never leave us or forsake us. Yahweh is an omniscient, omnipotent, all-loving God.

"The Bible doesn't state exactly that there are guardian angels assigned for every single person, but that doesn't mean they aren't. You were specifically chosen to stop these demons, and I feel Malachy's purpose is to help stop these demons too and help look out for us."

Jake nodded.

"As far as Malachy not staying around, I think because of what's going on right now, he's busy fighting unseen battles, and we should be thankful he showed up to help."

"Yes, of course," said Jake. "I just feel for them."

"I understand," replied Ellie. "None of us have a guarantee of how long we live on this earth. All I can say is that it was their time. God is in control and either allows things to happen, or makes things happen. Just like I said to that young man in Utah, God didn't cause the death of his friends, a deranged half-bear demon did. Heaven is a much better place for us, but until that time comes, we do God's will. In this case, it's stopping these demons from whatever they're planning, and getting those two people back."

Jake stared at his lovely wife, kissed her, and then smirked. "Was that from one of your sermons?"

Ellie rolled her eyes and got up. "C'mon, let's go to bed."

CHAPTER TWENTY

Café El Grande
Buenos Aires

EUDORA SAT AT THE CAFÉ, wearing a brunette wig, sunglasses, spotted blue and white shirt, and slacks. She sipped tea and ate provoleta with Agent Contreras, who was dressed in a light-yellow shirt and jeans. They had been watching for Steve Peterson for over an hour.

"He didn't show yesterday, do you think he will today?" she asked.

Agent Contreras shrugged his shoulders. "I don't know. His habit has been to come every couple of days. I hope what happened at the mall didn't change his habits."

"Without him, we'd have to start over."

"I'm afraid you're right."

They ate in silence for a few minutes.

"So, what made you decide to join the FBI?" asked Agent Contreras.

Eudora put down her fork. "I want to make a difference. The Nazis created that lab in Arizona to do DNA testing and experiments. They were trying to create the perfect cross between a demon and Hitler, with perhaps some animal DNA mixed in. Some of the experiments went badly, and some did not. The ones that weren't dangerous were sent to Nevada to dig a tunnel to the nuclear bomb that didn't detonate years ago during testing and had been left buried. They used kidnapped women as surrogates to make us, but many didn't live through it.

"They only referred to us with numbers, not names. It was like we were just animals to be experimented on. We decided that we weren't animals and gave ourselves names. When the full-bloods found the bomb, they caved in the tunnel and trapped the ones digging. The Nazis planned to kill all the women and us at the lab when they left Arizona, but we stopped them. Afterwards, we went back and helped dig out the ones that had been left behind. Most had died, but a few lived, so we went to live in the isolated areas on the Navajo reservation. Most stayed, but some of us wanted to help stop the demons and Nazis from ever doing this again. Even though we may have some demon and animal DNA, we are still part human, and so we went to the military base near where they found the bomb and demanded that they allow us to help. At first, they didn't want us, but there was a man named Colonel Price there that had worked with Jake. He convinced them to let us help and flew us to Berlin, where we helped stop their plan. The FBI then recruited us to be part of their special unit, so here we are."

Agent Contreras nodded and smiled. "I'd heard bits of it, but most was classified. We appreciate that you joined us, we can't do it without your help. You've been a huge asset and essential members of the FBI." He then frowned. "Did you say that they were trying to make another Hitler?"

"Yes, and they did."

Agent Contreras' mouth dropped open. "For real?"

Eudora nodded. "The Nazis were able to get him out of their hidden bunker in Berlin, and so far, we haven't been able to find him."

Agent Contreras shook his head. "Just what this world needs, another Hitler."

Eudora pointed to a man walking up. "There's Peterson."

Agent Contreras turned and saw Steven Peterson sit down several tables over, so he picked up his phone and called Agent Williams, who was sitting in a car down the street with agent Pyle.

"Peterson's here." he said when she answered.

"Ok," replied Agent Williams. "We'll be waiting." She hung up.

———

THIRTY MINUTES LATER, Peterson paid for his lunch and then walked down the street. Agent Contreras called and said that he was on the move. They followed him discreetly for two blocks but stopped when a dark black vehicle pulled up and stopped. Peterson got in, and it drove off. Agent Contreras gave Agents Williams and Pyle the vehicle info.

They followed the black vehicle through the area and into a wealthy residential neighborhood. They pulled over and parked when the car pulled into a gated residence. After waiting fifteen minutes, they felt this was where he was staying.

"Bingo." said Agent Williams.

"Do you think the two kidnapped people are in there?" asked Agent Pyle.

"I'd bet your badge on it." replied Agent Williams.

"Me too, no, wait, what? My badge."

Agent Williams smiled and called Agent Contreras to give him the info.

———

The White House
1600 Pennsylvania Avenue Northwest
Washington D.C.

DIRECTOR CHISOM ENTERED the oval office where the President, William Campbell, and Secretary of State, Phil Jennings, waited.

The President smiled. "Good morning, Bill, sounds like your agents had some excitement."

"Yes, sir, I think we're making progress." said Director Chisom.

"If progress means shooting and killing demons in a crowded mall… I heard about it this morning from Ambassador Withers in Buenos Aires." replied President Campbell.

Director Chisom cringed inwardly. "Colonel Taft, his wife, and her friend were ambushed by some of those heathens. Unfortunately, a security guard tried to help and was killed. From the report, some of their angel friends, as well as our half-demon agents, helped stop the demons. We're obviously making them nervous, so we believe that we're getting closer."

The President nodded. "I agree. General Littlestone advised me the other day that demons attacked their aircraft when they were trying to land."

"Are you getting closer to finding the kidnapped victims?" asked Secretary of State, Phil Jennings.

"We hope so. We do know that one of Donaldson's co-owners, Steven Peterson, flew to Buenos Aires and Costa Rica. We believe their company is responsible for drilling the holes for the explosives in Costa Rica that caused the eruption. However, information is still sporadic there." explained Director Chisom. "We aren't sure if he is part of this nightmare or just a pawn."

The President sat for a few moments in thought. "I read that report, the death toll is in the hundreds so far and may increase. So many lives were lost in Costa Rica. If you're right and these people caused it, we need to stop this soon."

"Our FBI agents set up surveillance at a local café in Buenos Aires where Peterson goes frequently and followed him to a residence in a wealthy neighborhood. We hope Donaldson and Hamilton are there, but if not, we'll detain Peterson and find out if he knows where they are." explained Director Chisom.

"Good, thank you, Bill." said the President. "I'll call the ambassador and tell him we're on it but with no specific details. So, our main priority is to find Peterson, and then if I need to, I can call

President Cardozo and see if he will help expedite anything we need."

———————

U.S. Embassy
Av. Colombia 4300
Buenos Aires

JAKE and the FBI agents met once again in the conference room. As soon as everyone was settled, Agent Contreras began. "As you all know, we have succeeded in locating Peterson in a wealthy neighborhood here in Buenos Aires. Our plan is to raid the mansion, but due to its location, we felt it was proper to ask for some local assistance. Apparently, you people carry some weight because the request for assistance came directly from the White House to Argentina President Cardozo." Agent Contreras pointed to a new person in the meeting, "This is INTERPOL's National Central Bureau Agent Hector Peralta. He's a member of the Policía Federal Argentina and has helped us before in investigations into organized crime, drug and human trafficking, and terrorism."

PFA Agent Peralta was in his thirties, black hair with a beard. He was wearing black military clothing that had PFA-INTERPOL stenciled on the back of his jacket. "Gracias, I'm honored to be of assistance to the famous demon hunters. From what I've been told and seen on TV, your visit has been less than hospitable. I will do everything I can to help find your kidnapped victims."

"Thanks, Hector." said Agent Contreras. "He has two agents stationed down the street keeping an eye on the residence while we determine how we want to proceed."

"What do we know about the residents there?" asked Jake.

Agent Contreras opened a file. "We may be opening up a can of worms. The records show that it's the residence of a Herman Schmidt, but that's all it showed, so we had to dig deeper. What we've found is not good and adds to our belief that Donaldson and Hamilton are there. Schmidt shows to be involved in investment companies, banking, the stock market, and has millions. When we dig further, it goes off into shell companies."

"Sounds shady." said Agent Pyle.

"Exactly." replied Agent Contreras. "Agent Peralta checked with some of his sources, and it appears that Schmidt delves in the black market."

"This just gets better and better." said Agent Williams.

"From what we've been told, his money is old money, from Germany."

"Germany?" asked Eudora.

Agent Contreras nodded. "Yep, and I know what you're thinking."

"Nazis." said Jake.

"Correct." answered Agent Contreras. "After World War II, the Argentina President was thought to have aided as many as 5,000 Nazis in escaping Germany and coming here. Over the years, we've been able to locate some, but many are still here using fake names and have descendants that we believe are carrying on their Nazi dreams. Their money has bought many a politician."

"Oh, great, Nazis again." said Agent Pyle.

"C'mon, Terrell, you love Nazis." Said Agent Williams. "So how does this affect us getting into the mansion?"

"We know that time is of the essence in the case of the kidnapped victims." answered Agent Contreras. "We believe but can't definitely prove that Peterson helped cause the volcanic eruption. No one wants more lives lost if they do this somewhere else, but we need to be careful which judge we take our information to. Some might be in Schmidt's or others' pockets."

"How long will it take?" asked Jake.

"If I can get all the documents together and the search warrant written, I can get Hector to get it signed after we make sure the judge isn't in their debt. I'm hoping for the end of the day at the latest."

"That will give me time to get a team together to help with the raid." added Agent Peralta.

Elflein 4000
Buenos Aires, Argentina

WENDI WAS USHERED into the library by one of the guards. Herman Schmidt, Adolph Hitler II, Steve, and Sam were already in the room. When she glanced at Sam, she was shocked at his appearance. His left eye was swollen shut and his lip was split. He had numerous bruises on his face and arms. She rushed over and sat on a couch next to him.

"Sam, what happened?" she asked.

"What happened, Dr. Hamilton," interrupted Herman, "Is that Mr. Donaldson tried to leave a message as to where we are going. He had to pay the price."

Wendi glared at him, "You people are animals."

Sam tried to smile but winced because of his injured lip. "Don't worry about it, I've had worse when I worked the oil fields."

The room filled with the familiar stench and Tarnac walked in with several disgusting demons. "Is everything ready for our departure?"

"But of course," replied Schmidt. "I was just about to inform our guests that we will be leaving today. Mr. Peterson has been extra helpful in having the equipment shipped to Ushuaia, where we will arrive later."

Sam looked over at Steve, who wouldn't make eye contact. "You're going to ruin our company, you snake." He jumped up and tried to swing a fist at his partner, but one of the demons slammed Sam to the floor.

Steve tried to help Sam up but was shoved away. "Don't touch me." snapped Sam as he got to his feet and sat back on the couch.

Tarnac smiled widely, showing his sharp teeth. "I just love watching two old friends fight, makes me happy."

"Was all this necessary?" asked Hitler. "Did you think they wouldn't try to escape or warn someone?"

Herman stood up from his seat behind the desk. "These people are nothing!" he yelled. "They are for our use, Adolph. They don't have our beliefs or heritage. We are wasting time. Your winter gear has already been loaded on our transport. We will be leaving shortly."

Wendi looked at Hitler. "Happy now?"

CHAPTER TWENTY-ONE

Elflein 4000
Buenos Aires, Argentina

IT WAS WELL past midnight when Agent Contreras radioed the two PFA agents doing surveillance on the property but received no answer.

Agents Contreras, Pyle, and Williams rode in a Ford F150 crew cab pickup to their location. As Agent Contreras walked up to the four-door sedan, he shined his light on the vehicle and immediately noticed blood spatter on the windows, so he drew his handgun. Seeing him suddenly draw his weapon, Agents Williams and Pyle leapt out of the pickup and drew their weapons. They approached carefully as backup for Agent Contreras and saw the front passenger side door was gone, it had been ripped off. He hesitated but looked inside, knowing what he would find. The PFA agents were dead, their bodies ripped to pieces. Agent Contreras turned away and gagged. His shoulders sagged as the FBI agents approached.

"I knew both of them personally," said Agent Contreras sadly. "One even had a wife and two children."

"I'm sorry." said Agent Williams.

"They knew we were watching." said Agent Pyle.

———

ALL THE GEOF, FBI Agents, PFA agents, and Jake wore the standard tactical gear, armed with an assault rifle and handgun. Each had a throat mic and earpiece to keep in contact. Agent Contreras activated his throat mic. "Juan and Freddy are dead. Looks like demons killed them. They know we've been watching."

"Acknowledged." answered PFA Agent Peralta. He sat with Jake inside a BDX, a Belgium-made assault vehicle used for these types of operations. He looked at Jake, who shook his head sadly.

Agent Peralta frowned. "Let's do this."

The Federal Operations Special Group, also called the *Grupo Especial de Operaciones Federales* (GEOF), and the specialized tactical unit of the Policía Federal Argentina drove up in the BDX to the front gate of the mansion. They were followed by the half-demons, who rode in a black Iveco Daily, Italian-made, large, light commercial van. Eudora sat in the passenger seat with a GEOF driver while Soaring Eagle and Kong were cramped in the back. The first thing they noticed was the gate was wide open.

"The gate's open." radioed Agent Peralta.

"We will be there in 30 seconds." answered Agent Contreras.

"I'll check the area from the air." said Soaring Eagle as he opened the back of the van. He flew off into the dark night while Kong climbed out and walked around to Eudora's side of the van. He was wearing his armor and carrying his Broadaxe.

As soon as the agents in the F150 pickup arrived, the driver of the BDX drove rapidly up the drive to the large portico at the front, with Kong lumbering alongside. Agent Contreras parked the F150, and they exited the truck with guns in hand.

"I don't see any activity, demon or otherwise." said Soaring Eagle using his throat mic.

The team deployed rapidly out of the back of the BDX and took up defensive positions around the front. They approached the front doors. Jake looked back at Kong. "Do you want to knock?" he asked with a smirk.

Kong grinned, stepped up to the doors, swung his battle axe, and tore the doors from the hinges. The agents rushed into the mansion that was dark and quiet.

"It's quiet." said Agent Pyle.

"Almost too quiet." said Agent Williams.

"You just had to say that, didn't you."

"Use your night vision goggles." said Agent Peralta.

They all turned on the night vision attached to their helmets.

Jake looked around. "I don't see any demons."

"We don't either." added Eudora.

"We'll clear the east side." said Agent Peralta. "The rest of you check the westside."

"Affirmative." answered Agent Contreras.

The two groups split up and searched the entire first floor. Both groups reported in that it was empty. It was as if they had just left.

"There's a basement door here in the back hallway," said Jake. "We'll check it out."

"You know the monsters are always waiting in the basement." said Agent Pyle.

Agent Williams rolled her eyes. "Sissy."

"Just saying. You go first."

Jake opened the door and looked at the narrow walls and the steps leading down. "Perhaps Kong should stay up here. I don't know if he would fit."

"Kong and I will stay up here to cover your back." said Eudora.

Jake led the group down the stairs and found the room empty except for tables and trash. They turned off their night vision and used their flashlights to look around.

"Looks like they had some sort of working lab here." said Agent Pyle.

"See if they left anything we can use." said Agent Contreras.

The tables were bare, so they checked the trash cans. Agent Pyle held up a crumpled piece of paper. "Looks like some kind of math calculations."

"Nothing in the other trash that helps." said Jake.

Agent Contreras walked over and looked at the paper. "Seems to me that this is more like physics. My brother is a science teacher. Let me call him."

"It's after midnight." said Jake.

"He's my brother, he'll get over it." Agent Contreras called and, after a few rings, spoke to his brother in Spanish for a few moments, then hung up. "I owe him a case of beer, but he said those are equations for injecting something in the ground. A lot of pressure."

"Probably how they set off the eruption." said Agent Williams. "It doesn't tell us anything about where they are though?"

Agent Contreras shook his head.

———

THE GEOF TEAM had systematically been searching the second floor but didn't locate anyone. They had a few bedrooms left. They opened one of them to find a man tied to a chair with duct tape over his mouth. Agent Peralta walked towards the man who was frantically shaking his head. "It's ok, your safe now." he said. "Are you Mr. Donaldson?"

The man violently shook his head.

Soaring Eagle landed on the second-floor balcony. He looked in and saw the man. "That's Peterson."

Agent Peralta reached for the duct tape on his mouth. From Soaring Eagle's angle at the balcony door, he saw the explosives attached to the back of the chair.

"Bomb!" yelled Soaring Eagle.

Agent Peralta ripped the tape off Peterson's mouth as Soaring Eagle yelled.

"Run!" yelled Peterson.

Agent Peralta looked behind him and saw the explosives. Too late, he saw the motion detector on the wall. He looked down at the timer counting down from 5.

"Get out, go!" yelled Agent Peralta to his men, who turned and fled out the door.

Soaring Eagle dove back out through the balcony door, and as he took flight, he heard Peterson yell, "Antarctica."

Agent Peralta tried to pull the ropes off Peterson. "No, too late. Run." said Peterson as the bomb exploded.

———

IN THE BASEMENT, they all heard in their earpieces Soaring Eagle yell and Agent Peralta telling them to get out, followed by an explosion. The building shook, but fortunately, they were far enough away from the blast that they were just shaken but not injured.

Above them, Kong and Eudora also heard the warning. Kong pushed Eudora to the ground and bent his huge body over her as the bomb went off, resulting in parts of the ceiling falling on the ape.

The GEOF agents who had been stationed on the outside perimeter raced inside as Soaring Eagle landed and followed. He had a few feathers singed, but he was unharmed.

The group from the basement raced up the stairs, but the door was blocked with debris from the explosion.

The stairway leading upstairs was heavily damaged, so Soaring Eagle flew up to the second level to check on the others.

Kong raised up and knocked the pieces of the ceiling that had fallen on him away. Eudora patted him and smiled. "Thanks."

Kong grunted and shoved debris away from the basement door to allow the others to enter.

"Are y'all ok?" asked Jake.

Kong and Eudora nodded.

"Is everyone ok?" asked Agent Contreras using his throat mic.

No one answered from upstairs as the agents from outside came down the hall.

"The eagle-man went upstairs to check." said one of the GEOF agents.

They all rushed around to the bottom of the stairs. Most of the staircase was missing, but a small section was still attached so Agent Pyle started going up.

"No, Terrell, it might not hold you." said Agent Williams.

Agent Pyle ignored her and carefully worked his way up towards the top but midway, the stairs started creaking and shifting. As a part of the stairs gave way, he leapt the last few feet to the top. He disappeared down a hallway through the smoke and dust.

"Do you see anyone?" asked Agent Contreras.

"Stand by, too much smoke and dust." replied Agent Pyle between coughs.

"Soaring Eagle?"

"I found two injured." Soaring Eagle replied.

Eudora turned to Kong. "Throw me."

Kong hesitated but then grabbed her and tossed her through the air up onto the second floor. She landed, slid on the marble floor, got to her feet, and disappeared into the smoke and dust.

A few moments later, Agent Pyle and Eudora appeared, helping one of the GEOF agents who was limping badly. Kong motioned for him to jump to him.

"Seriously?" said the GEOF agent.

"Yep." said Agent Pyle.

"It'll be ok." said Eudora.

They helped the GEOF agent to the edge, he jumped off and landed in Kong's arms.

"*Gracias, mi amigo.*" said the agent.

Soaring Eagle came out of the smoke carrying an agent in each arm. He flew down to the first level. One man was cut, bruised, and shaken up but alive. The other man was unconscious. He laid the unconscious man on a couch.

"What about the rest?" asked Agent Contreras.

Soaring Eagle shook his head sadly.

They all looked at Agent Pyle, who was coughing from the smoke. He shook his head. "So, how do we get down?"

"Easy." answered Eudora, who then pushed Agent Pyle off the landing and he was caught by Kong.

Eudora then jumped safely into Kong's arms.

Jake kicked some of the debris in anger. "These men gave their lives for nothing."

Agent Contreras cursed while he helped one of the agents towards the door.

"It was not all in vain." announced Soaring Eagle.

They all stopped what they were doing and looked at him.

"Right before the explosion, Peterson said one word, Antarctica."

CHAPTER TWENTY-TWO

Private Jet
Airborne over southern Argentina

HERMAN SAT in one of the cushioned seats and looked at his cellphone. He lit up a cigar and blew smoke into the air. "Excellent." he said out loud to himself.

Sam and Wendi sat across from him and looked up at his remark.

"My plan went off without a problem."

"What plan?" asked Wendi.

Herman smiled. "We left a bomb and Mr. Peterson for the authorities to find when they raided the house. My cellphone notified me that the bomb detonated."

Sam stiffened. "You didn't let Steve go?"

"Of course not," said Herman. "He was our bait for them. Since we have his portion of your company and his usefulness was coming to an end, I used him one last time."

Sam sat, shocked. Even though he was mad at Steve, he was still his friend. Sam lunged over the aisle and punched Herman. He kept hitting him with his fists until the security men pulled Sam off. One hit Sam in the head with a rifle, and then they kicked him while he was on the ground. Herman got to his feet and ordered them to stop. He wiped the blood from his nose.

"You're lucky I still have use for you." snarled Herman.

Wendi helped Sam up and into a seat. Blood ran down his head.

Herman frowned. "Dr. Hamilton, get something to stop the bleeding. I don't want any on my seats. One seat costs more than you make in a year."

Wendi glared at him but went to the wet bar and got some towels and ice. She wrapped the ice in a towel and put it to his head. She dabbed away the blood. "I'm so sorry." she said.

"He did it to himself, but he was still my friend." said Sam.

"How touching." said Herman. "Now you know if you don't do as I say, I will not hesitate to kill you and your entire family." He looked for his cigar, but it had been crushed. "Barbarians, you ruined an excellent Cuban cigar." He brought out another one and lit it.

Hitler sat a few seats down but didn't say anything.

Elflein 4000
Buenos Aires, Argentina

THE AREA WAS FILLED with ambulances, fire personnel, and more PFA agents. Crime scene tape had been stretched around the mansion as they began the gruesome task of photographing the damage and the dead. Fortunately, Soaring Eagle's warning had saved most of the GEOF agents. Agent Peralta and two other agents had been killed by the blast. The injured had been taken to the hospital. Agent Pyle had been given oxygen by the paramedics but refused to go to the hospital.

The group stood around the BDX vehicle.

"I'm sorry about your loss." said Jake.

Agent Williams and Pyle also gave him their condolences.

Agent Contreras nodded somberly. "Gracias, had it not been for Soaring Eagle, it would have been worse."

Soaring Eagle nodded. "We're a team, we look out for each other."

"Are you sure that was Peterson?" asked Agent Williams.

"Yes," replied Soaring Eagle. "I recognized him from the photos in the file."

"They'll have to confirm it through DNA. I'm sure there isn't much left to identify."

"And you're sure he said Antarctica?" asked Agent Pyle.

Soaring Eagle nodded.

"Why would they go to a frozen continent?" asked Agent Contreras.

"I don't know." answered Agent Williams.

"If they did, it was part of their plan. We need to try to make sure that's where they went." said Jake.

"And we need more help." added Agent Pyle.

———

Palmero and Oro Apartments
Buenos Aires

PAM AND ELLIE kept themselves busy while waiting for news. Pam was at the table on her laptop cruising her social media when she saw a news break concerning Buenos Aires, so she clicked on it. "Oh, crap."

Ellie was sitting on the couch and had her Bible and study guide on her lap. At Pam's outburst, she put it down and walked over to the table. "What's up?"

Pam pointed to the news article. It showed the headlines about a possible terrorist bombing at a wealthy residence during a raid that had several fatalities. The clip showed a mansion partially in ruins with smoke pouring out. She saw PFA and GEOF officials coming and going. One shot showed the BDX assault vehicle.

Ellie put her hand to her mouth. "Oh, no."

The next clip focused on the three half-demons, Jake, and

Agents Williams and Pyle talking to them. It was only a brief five-second clip but enough to make her breathe a huge sigh of relief.

"I guess things didn't go as planned." said Pam.

"I feel for those who were killed." said Ellie.

Pam nodded. "It's so sad. It's a dangerous business when dealing with demons."

"And Nazis."

"They're both nasty monsters." said Pam with a frown.

Roscoe was asleep on the rug when his head jerked up and he growled. The two women looked over at him.

Roscoe got up and walked towards the balcony glass doors. He started barking. Ellie walked quickly into the bedroom and returned momentarily, shoving something into her waist. Pam had gotten up and was trying to see out of the glass doors without getting too close.

Ellie grabbed her arm and pulled her farther away as a demon appeared on the balcony. It was only six feet tall, but black as midnight, with cracks in his skin that glowed red, and a thin black tail. He folded his black leathery wings behind him and stared through the glass with glowing yellow eyes.

"Time to leave." said Ellie.

The two women ran to the door as they heard glass breaking and Roscoe barking. Pam jerked the door open and raced into the hallway with Ellie behind her.

"Roscoe, come on." she yelled back.

Roscoe ran out behind them and Ellie slammed the door closed. They ran towards the elevator when the door exploded outwards into the hallway. The heathen scrambled into the hallway and looked both ways as they reached the elevator. Pam pushed the elevator button several times.

"It's not going to get here in time." said Ellie. "Head to the stairs."

They dashed around the corner and entered the stairwell. They ran down a flight of stairs and then they heard the thing in the stairwell.

"I'm cominggg." he said in a nerve-grating voice, followed by a high pierced laugh.

Roscoe stopped and growled.

"No, boy, come on." said Ellie as they continued down the stairs to the first level. Pam threw the metal door open, and they entered the lobby. She tried to shut the door, but the creature slammed into it, knocking her back against the wall. Ellie stopped, helped Pam up, and ran towards the front of the lobby with the demon close behind. Suddenly, the elevator dinged, and a young man stepped off. His eyes widened in fright and he tried to go back into the elevator, but the doors closed.

"Run!" yelled Ellie.

Before the man could react, the demon grabbed him by the throat and lifted him off the ground. Roscoe barked and growled. The two women stopped and Ellie reached under her shirt, pulled one of Jake's Colt 45's from her waist, and pointed it at the monster.

"Let him go." she said.

The creature laughed in another ear-splitting tone. "Drop your gun, or I will kill this worthless bag of air."

Ellie kept her gun aimed at the thing.

The demon squeezed harder and the young man's face began to turn red. Ellie began to falter.

"Don't do it." said Pam.

The man's face was turning redder from the pressure.

"Ok, stop, don't hurt him." said Ellie. She tossed the gun aside. "Now, let him go."

The creature smiled, showing a double row of razor-sharp teeth. "Weak woman. You care too much." The demon reached out for Ellie when Roscoe leapt, biting down on the creature's arm. He roared. Ellie dove to the ground, grabbed the gun, rolled over and pointed it at the devil.

The demon opened his mouth wide to engulf Roscoe's head.

"Hey," said Ellie. "Eat this." She pulled the trigger. The round entered the monster's mouth and exited the back of his head, splattering demon blood and brain matter everywhere. He dropped Roscoe and the young man, then grabbed his head in agony. Smoke came from inside his head as the toxic cemetery-round burned. He fell to his knees when the wound wouldn't heal over quickly. Ellie got to her feet and fired two more rounds into his head. The demon jerked back from the force and fell to the ground. His metabolism was trying to heal around the toxic dust.

Pam stared at Ellie, who pointed the gun at the creature as he was writhing on the ground. "Nice shooting Anne Oakley."

"Jake's been making me practice just in case." Ellie explained.

The young man regained his breath and ran, screaming, out of the building. Roscoe growled at the demon.

Ellie aimed the gun once more and fired twice more into the demon's skull. The creature's head exploded and was just a blob of skin and bone. The creature's body still tried to heal around what was left of his skull. He wasn't dead, but he wasn't a threat anymore. They heard sirens.

Elflein 4000
Buenos Aires, Argentina

JAKE HUNG up his cellphone again. Agent Williams looked over and saw his concerned look. "Everything ok?" she asked.

Jake shook his head. "Ellie and Pam aren't answering their phones."

Agent Pyle walked up. "What's going on? We're about to leave."

"Jake can't reach Ellie or Pam." said Agent Williams.

"Maybe it's nothing. Maybe they're in the bathroom."

"Together?" said Agent Williams. "Seriously, Terrell."

"I've called several times." said Jake.

Agent Contreras rushed up to them. "I just received a call from the embassy. Shots have been fired at the apartments where your wife and friend are at. The caller was a man who said a monster attacked him."

They dashed towards the F150 pickup. Jake saw Eudora about to get into the van. Kong and Soaring Eagle were already in the back.

"Eudora," he yelled. "Ellie and Pam are in trouble at the apartments."

Eudora ran to the back of the van and opened it. She said something to them, and Soaring Eagle leapt out and into the air. "We'll meet you there."

———

Palmero and Oro Apartments
Buenos Aires

SOARING Eagle arrived first and landed at the entrance to the apartments. The Buenos Aries police and embassy marines were already on the scene. Two Buenos Aires officers pulled their handguns, thinking he was another demon. An Embassy Marine standing nearby told them to stand down and explained he was one of the good guys.

Soaring Eagle raced by them and into the lobby to find Pam, Ellie, and Roscoe standing off to one side with two more US marines. He then saw the demon on the ground.

"Are you okay?" he asked them.

Ellie nodded. "Yes, thanks, we're fine."

Pam motioned to Ellie and then pointed at the demon on the ground. "Calamity Jane here shot that thing full of holes."

"Nice shooting." said Soaring Eagle with a grin. He went over to the creature and examined him. Most of his skull and brain were gone, but he technically wasn't dead yet.

Moments later, the rest of the team arrived and ran inside. Jake ran up to Ellie and hugged her. "I was concerned about y'all."

"Yes, honey, we're fine." said Ellie. She motioned to the marine standing near her. He held Jake's Colt 45. "I used your gun."

"Yep, she's a dead-eye shot." said Pam.

Jake smiled. "See, I told you those practice lessons would pay off."

They walked over to where the rest were looking at the demon. Kong nudged it with his foot and grunted.

Agent Williams knelt and looked closer. "Most of its head is gone, but it's not decomposing."

"So, it's not dead?" commented Agent Pyle.

"Apparently not." she replied.

Jake bent down and looked at the demon. Normally, besides Jake, if a human shoots a demon, it will rejuvenate the injury, but the shrapnel from the cemetery-dirt-round spread when it struck bone, preventing it from completely repairing the injury. The demon's skin had healed as much as it could, but most of his skull and brain matter were gone.

"How in the world is that thing still alive?" asked Agent Contreras.

Jake shrugged. "I don't know."

"What do we do with it?"

"Put it out of its misery." said Jake. He looked at Soaring Eagle and nodded.

Soaring Eagle pulled his sword and decapitated the monster.

Orion Oil Jettey
Dockside Warehouse
Ushuaia, Argentina

SAM AND WENDI were brought aboard a large cargo ship that was docked at the commercial dock. The several-thousand-foot pier extended from the shore that allowed cruise ships, container ships, and other commercial ships to dock. The temperature was drastically different from Buenos Aries, as the temperature in Ushuaia rarely rose above 65 degrees, and mostly stayed in the 30's. They had been given their polar gear and locked in one of the small quarters. Sam looked out the window at the busy dock, a cruise ship, and the beautiful snowcapped mountains in the background.

"I feel so helpless." said Sam. "We're only feet from a cruise ship and thousands of people, but we can't do anything."

Wendi sat on one of the bunks with her knees drawn up. "I know. If we tried anything, they'd kill us."

Sam shook his head. "No, they need us, but they'd kill our families. All we can do is wait for an opportunity to escape or warn someone."

———

U.S. Embassy
Av. Colombia 4300
Buenos Aires

THE FBI TEAM, Jake, Ellie, and Pam sat in the briefing room. The table was cluttered with files, papers, and empty to-go lunches.

"So, I called Director Chisom earlier and gave him the update." explained Agent Williams. "He spoke to the President about the updates. The Argentina President and our Ambassador are not too happy about what happened at the mall, the mansion, and now the apartments. They want us gone."

"Don't they get it?" said Agent Pyle angrily. "These are monsters and Nazis."

"Politics." said Agent Contreras.

Agent Williams nodded. "Yep, but the President supports us and knows the score."

"So, where do we go from here?" asked Jake.

"We checked, Schmidt has a private jet," explained Agent Contreras. "I checked, and his jet left yesterday. Their flight plan showed they flew to Ushuaia."

"Where's that?" asked Ellie.

"It's Argentina's farthest southern port."

"And the closest to Antarctica?" asked Agent Pyle.

Agent Contreras nodded.

"What is Antarctica?" asked Eudora. "We're still learning about this world."

"Sorry, we sometimes forget." said Agent Williams.

"I thought we all might want to know, so I got together some info." said Agent Contreras. "Antarctica is the fifth largest continent out of seven, and larger than most countries. It's at the bottom of the earth. It's about five million square miles of rock, ice, and snow. Average temperatures range from -2 to -50 degrees on a good day."

"So, not a warm and pleasant place." said Eudora.

"No, it's not." said Agent Pyle. "So, how do we find them in five million square miles?"

"Director Chisom has decided to send us to Ushuaia." said Agent Williams. She motioned at Agent Pyle. "As Terrell said earlier, we need more help. Some special forces are being sent there too. They'll bring us our cold weather gear and equipment. We're to meet with them, and they have some information about how to locate Schmidt."

"How do we get there?" asked Jake.

Agent Williams nodded. "The aircraft that brought us here remained for repairs and will fly us to the naval base there."

"I hope we don't have any more trouble on the flight like last time." said Agent Pyle.

"What's the fun in that?" asked Agent Williams.

CHAPTER TWENTY-THREE

Punta Indio Naval Air Base
South of Buenos Aires

THE TEAM ARRIVED at the naval base's tarmac in two white vans. The C-17 Globemaster was already in preflight with the engines warming. SSgt Potter stood at the top of the rear ramp that he'd lowered to accommodate Kong since he was too large to enter through the side door.

"Welcome back," he said. "We repaired the damage, so let's not change that."

The group laughed and loaded their gear into the aircraft.

"We hope we don't have any unwanted boarders either so keep your fingers crossed." said Jake.

The huge aircraft taxied and soon became airborne for their three-and-a-half-hour flight to Ushuaia.

———

Southern Ocean
North of Antarctica

THE CARGO SHIP plowed through the rough seas of the Drake Passage on their two-day trip to Antarctica. The Drake Passage is the waterway that connects the Atlantic and Pacific oceans between South America and Antarctica. It was known for its turbulent seas.

Wendi was wrapped in a blanket on her bunk, seasick from the rough waters. Sam sat in a chair next to a small desk in the cramped quarters, reading an outdated magazine left on the table. The door opened, and Hitler entered.

"The accommodations are not ideal, but I hope you're not too uncomfortable." he said.

Sam looked up and snorted. "Wendi's seasick, as if you care."

Hitler came over to her bunk and reached out for her, but she rolled over away from him. He hung his head and turned back to the door. "I'm sorry, I'll have someone bring her some Dramamine to help." he said as he left.

When he left, Wendi rolled back over and looked at Sam.

"I think he likes you." said Sam to lighten the mood.

In response, Wendi threw up in the trash can next to the bed.

———

Admiral Berisso Integrated Naval Base
Ushuaia

THE C-17 LANDED at the Admiral Berisso Integrated Naval base, also known as the Ushuaia Naval base. The aircraft taxied to a large hanger, where the team were ushered into a metal building next to the hanger by armed Argentina naval personnel.

They were provided several cots and supplies for while they waited for the special ops troops to arrive from the U.S.

"I get the feeling they don't want us here." commented Agent Pyle. "They weren't like this in Buenos Aires."

"That was before we wrecked their mall and raided a mansion that was blown up." said Jake.

"Good point. Hey, we didn't blow up that house, the Nazis did."

"Doesn't matter," said Agent Contreras. "We caused them political issues and unwanted attention. The sooner we're gone, the happier they'll be."

They all made themselves comfortable. Kong pushed two cots together and laid down, almost collapsing them. He was soon snoring. Roscoe curled up under the cot.

"I hope those cots don't give out." said Ellie.

Jake laughed. "I'm sure he'll be fine."

"Alex, you don't have to come with us." said Eudora. "You did your job back in Buenos Aires. We can take it from here."

Agent Contreras shook his head. "I know, but these monsters killed people under my watch. I owe them."

"We understand," said Jake. "Sadly, when we deal with demons, people get hurt. I'm sorry for your loss. We'll make them pay."

"Gracias, so what're we going to do with Mrs. Taft and Miss Martin?"

"I want to put them both on a plane headed back home." answered Jake receiving a frown from Ellie. "But I know that's not going to happen."

"You got that right." said Pam.

"Our experience has shown that these demons will attack them if we don't keep them close." explained Agent Williams. "They've attacked them in D.C., Berlin, kidnapped them in Arizona, and attacked them in their apartment in Buenos Aires when we thought they were safe. They're better off with us so we can keep an eye on them."

"I see, so they try to hit the weak link?" said Agent Contreras.

"Weak link?" said Pam. "Who's weak? Hey, we ran over a demon in Florida, blew up a demon in Virginia, and Ellie shot that demon full of holes back at the apartment building."

"And destroyed part of a hotel in Virginia." added Jake with a grin. "They also damaged a famous cemetery in Berlin. The German Chancellor told them not to come back."

Ellie punched him in the ribs. "He did not."

"You go girls." said Eudora.

"We have about eleven hours until the special ops team gets here so we might as well take Kong's advice and get some rest." said Agent Williams.

"I'm hungry." said Pam.

"Maybe we should just feed the demons to her and save the bullets." said Jake.

"Rude."

———

ELEVEN AND A HALF HOURS LATER, an LC-130 landed at the naval airbase and parked next to the C-17. The doors opened, and troops began disembarking. The special ops force all wore the same white severe cold combat clothing without designations. Jake knew they were a collection of the best personnel from the Navy SEALS, Army Rangers, and Marines.

Several men approached the building where the rest waited. Jake recognized the man leading them, walked quickly up to him, and saluted him.

"General Price, we didn't expect you to join the fun."

General Price smiled and shook Jake's hand. "I wouldn't miss this for the world. We have unfinished business with these Nazis."

"Agreed." said Eudora.

General Price looked over at her. "I heard that you joined the FBI. It's good to see you again, along with your two other friends."

"They called you general. When I met you in Nevada, they called you Colonel." said Eudora.

"Somebody thought I needed to be promoted."

Soaring Eagle nodded to the general, and Kong just grunted.

Agents Pyle and Williams also shook the general's hand. General Price looked over at Agent Pyle. "Last time I saw you, you had been beaten up by a little demon." he joked.

"Awe, general, that's cold. He was a really big demon, and I was tied up." said Agent Pyle.

The group laughed.

As the rest of the special ops group entered, the general motioned to them. "Some of your old compadres came along too. You remember Lt. Colonel Wilkins and Sgt O'Rork?"

"Of course." said Jake as he shook his hand. "Congrats on your promotion."

"Same to you, Lt. Colonel Taft." said Colonel Wilkins.

General Price approached Ellie and Pam, who hugged him. "It's good to see you and your trusty sidekick. I heard you're still causing trouble, even here."

Ellie smiled. "The demons started it."

"I'm sure they did, and I heard you took care of it."

"So, where's Agent Williams?" yelled a familiar voice.

They all turned to see a six-foot-three, muscled, tattooed man with a crew cut approach.

"And you remember Corporal Horatio Smith?" asked Colonel Wilkins.

"Colonel, did you have to use my real name?" asked the man.

"Tank?" said Agent Williams. "I figured they would've kicked you out by now."

Tank roared with laughter. "Now, darlin', I'm the best they have."

Agent Williams punched him in the stomach, which had little to no effect. "I've told you not to call me that, Horatio."

Agent Pyle leaned over to Agent Contreras. "I think they like each other."

"Who could tell?" answered Agent Contreras with a grin.

"Where's Sergeant G?" asked Jake.

"He's holding the fort back in Nevada." replied the general. "We have two new additions to our group." He motioned to a six-foot-tall, fit black woman. "This is Gunnery Sgt Carlton; we call her Gunny."

Gunnery Sgt Carlton smiled and shook Jake's hand.

General Price pointed to another shorter Hispanic female. "And this is our sniper, Corporal Moreno."

Corporal Moreno smiled and nodded.

General Price motioned to the other troops approaching. "We brought twenty hand-picked men. Gunny will command one group, and O'Rork will head up the other. Follow me and I'll show you what we have for this mission."

"While you kids go look at your toys, Pam and I will wait inside." said Ellie.

———

THEY FOLLOWED the general into the cargo bay of the LC-130. Inside were pallets of weapons and supplies, but the main cargo held two large, white in color, squarish vehicles with snow treads. The general pointed to the vehicles.

"These are the newest cold-weather vehicles." he explained. "It's an Oshkosh Defense and BAE System made for us as a Cold Weather All-Terrain Vehicle (CATV). The front vehicle is powered by a 6-cylinder, 325-horsepower engine. It will carry our troops and a payload. As you see in the front is a V-shaped hull to deflect mine blasts and armor that can stop 7.62-millimeter bullets. It pulls a rear chassis that can hold troops and gear. This makes it more flexible on rough terrain."

They all walked around the vehicle and admired the new military vehicle.

"They'll get us there with no problems." He walked over to a pallet and unhooked the straps. He unlocked the hasps on one of the crates and lifted out an odd-looking shotgun with a drum magazine. The general smiled. "This is an AA12. Some of you may not have ever seen one. This shotgun fires 300 rounds per minute from an 8-round magazine or a 32-round drum magazine."

He handed the weapon to Jake who smiled. "I used one occasionally. They can do a lot of damage in a short time." Jake handed it around to the rest of the group to examine it.

"And I have an extra surprise." added General Price. "They fire an explosive round that has cemetery dirt."

"I'm in love." said Jake.

"We also have plenty of cemetery rounds for the ARs and handguns. Corporal Moreno is also a demolitions expert. We have whatever we need to blow open anything if need be. It also has cemetery dirt embedded in the explosives just in case."

"Looks like you came extra prepared." said Agent Williams.

"We've learned a lot since Nevada, so we want to be ready." answered the general. "We'll meet inside in ten and I'll give you what we know and our game plan."

———

EXACTLY TEN MINUTES LATER, the group met in a large room that had been set up as a briefing room. General Price stepped up to a large LED screen at the front of the room and began. Behind him was a map of Antarctica displayed on the screen. "This is what we know so far, back in 1939, a German expedition went to Antarctica on the ship MS Schwenland. Their purpose was to claim an area now known as Dronning Maud Land to protect the German whaling industry. However, the Norwegians had already claimed that section of Antarctica, so we believe the Germans moved to the Pacific side of the continent.

"There was information that a Nazi Antarctic base called "New Berchtesgaden" had been built in 1939.

"We believe this base was expanded during the war and supplied by submarine deliveries. It's believed the British attempted to destroy this base in 1945, but since they deny it, the exact location of the base is unknown."

General Price then pressed a handheld remote device and a satellite photo of Antarctica appeared. "As you can see, this is a photo of Antarctica taken by a satellite. We requested an infrared scan, and this is what we found." He clicked the device and another infrared photo of Antarctica appeared. He pointed to a section on the southwestern part of Antarctica. "This is the area called Marle Byrd Land." He then zoomed in on a smaller area. "There's a series of buildings that show up that are not reported by any known country, and it appears to be active." He zoomed in further on the photo, which showed a cargo ship docked at a man-made dock. "This ship appears to be unloading cargo, so we did a reverse time-lapse and traced it back to the docks at Ushuaia. The ship is the Silver Valkyrie which sailed from Ushuaia under the Grenadines flag bound for the Marshall Islands."

"So, it got lost and ended up at an unknown dock in Antarctica?" asked Agent Pyle sarcastically.

"Yes, and this area coincides with the information we have on any German bases in Antarctica."

"So, what's the plan, sir?" asked Jake.

General Price sat the remote down and took a sip of coffee. "We plan to go crash their party. We have the US Coast Guard Polar Sun headed to Antarctica as we speak to assist us. Even if it was here, going by ship wouldn't work because we have no way of offloading the CATVs and gear without a dock. Obviously, we can't use theirs, so our plan is to use the LC-130 with skis to land a few miles away and drive in. Once we arrive, my hope is to gain entry without causing an alarm and ultimately rescue the kidnapped people and secure the base."

"But why Antarctica?" asked Agent Contreras. "It's so remote."

"Exactly, and because it's so remote, I'm sure they believe they can come and go without suspicion."

"So, when do we leave?" asked Colonel Wilkins.

"I know it's short notice, but we need to be airborne in four hours. The weather shows a front moving across there and I don't want to be caught in it. We have your cold weather gear onboard. We even had some specially designed weather gear for our eagle friend. We weren't sure if he could tolerate the cold otherwise."

Soaring Eagle shrugged. "I don't know. I'm sure my demon DNA would, but not sure about my human part."

General Price nodded towards Kong. "We have super large gear for Kong."

Kong patted his armor. "This is all I need."

The general stared. "I didn't think he could talk."

"He's the strong silent type." said Eudora with a grin.

New Berchtesgaden
Antarctica

AFTER DOCKING, Wendi and Sam were escorted up on deck and had their first experience with the arctic cold. They'd been given cold weather gear, but it still didn't prepare them for the intense cold. As soon as they stepped out, the frigid air seemed to cut through them despite their winter gear. Wendi and Sam stared out at the vast white frozen continent.

"It's amazing," said Wendi. "It's beautiful, even with these evil people here."

"It's an ugly frozen wasteland." said Sam sarcastically.

They were led down the gangplank and onto the dock. They followed the rest to a series of metal Quonset hut buildings. The insides were warmer, but only barely above freezing. The interior held tables and chairs, a few cots, and radio equipment, but not much more.

"This is it?" asked Sam.

As if answering his question, Herman entered wearing a smile. He lifted his goggles up. "Welcome to our new home."

The look on Sam and Wendi's faces told him they thought he was crazy.

"No, no, these are just the buildings we use when we dock and unload supplies. The main base is several miles away. Follow me."

He led them back outside and around the back to a large garage with the doors open, where numerous snowcats sat idling. Once everyone was aboard, the caravan began driving towards a large ridge of ice and snow.

The inside of the snowcats were warm but rattled and bounced as they plowed through the snow. Two hours later, they arrived at a tall ridge of ice where a huge tunnel had been carved out of the ice. They drove into the tunnel for another half mile but stopped at a large metal door. The snowcats sat idle for a few moments before the large doors began to creak and slide back. They continued down the tunnel and into a large garage parking area. The snowcats parked and unloaded the occupants. The walls of ice were a beautiful blue and green color, lit up by electrical lights. The beauty was stained by the presence of numerous hideous demons in the area.

They followed the group to the far end of the garage, to another large set of closed metal doors. They passed through a smaller set of doors off to the side, down another tunnel and into a huge multi-level complex. The complex was circular, with a large open area in the middle that went down several floors. Tunnels led off the ring to unknown rooms.

"Isn't this wonderful?" asked Herman, accompanied by Hitler. "It wasn't like this when it was first built, but since the 1940's, it's been expanded and improved. We have living quarters, a cafeteria, work rooms, all the modern conveniences. We have generators hidden on the surface that provides us with power."

Sam and Wendi looked down over the railing.

"This reminds me of pictures of a missile silo." commented Sam.

"Excellent observation, Mr. Donaldson. In the 60's this was going to be a nuclear missile silo, but that idea was abandoned. Now, it's our home base of operations, where we will bring the world to its knees."

"This is insane." said Sam.

"What are those demons building?" asked Wendi. She pointed to a large group of demons building a platform with a tall derrick at the bottom of the silo.

"What?" Herman looked over the edge, frowned, and turned to several of his men. "Take these two to their rooms."

As Sam and Wendi were escorted down a tunnel, they looked back to see Herman yelling and waving at one of the workers while Hitler looked over the edge at the platform. They were led to one of the living quarters, which consisted of four bunks, lockers for their gear, a table in the middle with chairs, and an adjacent bathroom.

"Did you notice that Herman wasn't happy about what was going on? Sounds like trouble in paradise." said Wendi as she took off her jacket and placed it on the back of a chair.

Sam nodded. "That was a drilling platform."

Wendi froze. "A drilling platform? Here?"

"That's what it was, and Hitler looked clueless."

"He's just a pawn." said Wendi. "Herman's just using him for whatever he has planned."

"I have a bad feeling about this." said Sam.

Airborne
South Pacific Ocean

THEY WERE three hours into their six-hour flight to Antarctica. The LC-130 aircraft's heaters barely kept the cold out, and the web seating was far from comfortable. The turbulence from the incoming storm made the ride feel like a roller coaster. Despite the bumpy ride, the military personnel and FBI agents seemed to be able to sleep.

"How can they sleep in this thing?" asked Pam. "My teeth fillings are going to come out from this rattling, and I'm freezing."

Ellie smiled. "I guess they get used to it."

Jake laughed. "Why don't you climb into one of the CATVs? It might be warmer and more comfortable."

"Excellent." said Pam. She got up and worked her way to one of CATVs tied down to the cargo bay. She opened one of the doors and climbed in. She opened it a moment later. "It's warmer in here."

Ellie got up and joined her inside the vehicle. Jake chuckled to himself, closed his eyes, and fell asleep.

New Berchtesgaden
Antarctica

AFTER EATING A RATHER tasty meal in the cafeteria, they were led to a large work room where they smelled Tarnac before they saw him. He waved around the room at all the equipment that had been brought from Buenos Aires.

"Your equipment has been set up for you." he said. "Now that you're here, you can begin confirming the calculations your colleagues did for my plan."

"To cause eruptions at locations around the world so the Nazis can take over?" asked Wendi sarcastically.

The croc demon thought for a moment and then laughed, emitting a horrible stench of decay. "No, of course not."

"Isn't that what Herman wants to do? Asked Sam.

Tarnac stepped forward and grinned, showing his sharp teeth. "That's Schmidt's plan, I have much bigger plans."

"Like the drilling platform here?"

Tarnac turned towards the door, his tail banging into the tables. "The drilling platform here is my plan, not that idiot Schmidt's. He is of no consequence. The file on the desk tells you what I need."

After Tarnac left, Wendi picked up the file and browsed through it. Her face turned pale, and she suddenly had to sit down.

"What's wrong?" asked Sam.

Wendi looked terrified when she looked up at Sam. "He wants to set off massive volcanic eruptions here in Antarctica."

———

Marle Byrd Land
Antarctica

JAKE BANGED on the door of the CATV and opened it. "Time to wake up, time for the briefing."

Ellie and Pam had been able to sleep in the slightly warmer interior of the CATV. They climbed down and returned to their seats as General Price stood in the middle of the cargo bay and began his mission briefing.

"We're about 45 minutes from the LZ." He turned to Pam, Ellie, and the FBI agents. "That's military jargon for landing zone." he said with a smirk. "We need to be ready once the skids hit the snow. You've been handpicked to go on this mission. You've all seen combat in Iraq and Afghanistan, and some of you have fought these demons before. For those that haven't, let me reiterate that these monsters will kill you, rip you to shreds, and enjoy eating you. Sgt O'Rork was nearly killed by a scorpion demon and has the scars to prove it. Agent Williams has some scars from her adventures, and Agent Pyle was swallowed by a giant snake."

"And it took a week to get rid of the smell." said Agent Pyle.

The comment brought some chuckles.

"They come in all sizes and shapes." continued the general. "Colonel Taft, and the three FBI agents that some of you have been staring at during the flight, are the only ones that can see demons even when they're invisible. I know some of you have never seen anyone like our FBI friends, but I can assure you from experience, they're some of our best. So, please don't shoot them by mistake."

Kong grunted, causing numerous snickers.

"Also, Colonel Taft and the three FBI agents are the only ones that can kill demons. But each of you have been given special rounds for your weapons. Normally demons will heal up immediately when shot, but Holy ground as well as Holy water are toxic to demons, so each round has cemetery dirt embedded in it. We can slow them down and inflict severe damage with these rounds. Thanks to Mrs. Taft, who recently shot one in the head enough times, we learned that it didn't die but was totally incapacitated. So, if possible, aim for the head."

"General, how can we shoot them if we can't see them?" asked one of the men.

"Good question." replied the general. "As I said, Colonel Taft and the three FBI agents can see them when they're invisible. Demons can't hurt you while they're invisible and must solidify to do any harm, but those four can harm them when they're invisible. We think it's because the three FBI agents have partial demon DNA, and Colonel Taft's abilities were given to him from God. Right before they appear, the air will appear to shimmer, and of course, you'll get the stench of ash, decaying flesh and sulfur. That will give you a split-second warning, so be ready.

"In Nevada, we used the designations DH1-Demon Hunters 1, and DH2- Demon Hunters 2, so we'll use them again. I'll be DH1 and in the front CATV with Sgt O'Rork and his team, Agents Eudora, Contreras, and Kong, if we can fit him inside."

The comment brought snickers and chuckles.

"Colonel Wilkins will be DH2 and in the rear CATV with Gunny and her team, Colonel Taft, Mrs. Taft, Miss Martin, Agents Pyle, Williams, and Soaring Eagle."

"Yeah baby, me and Agent Williams together again, booyah." said Tank.

Agent Williams rolled her eyes amidst the grins and laughs.

"Stow it, Corporal." snapped the general. "Sadly, we don't know what type of force we'll meet when we arrive, human or otherwise. As I said before, our goal is to rescue the two kidnapped people and secure the site, if possible. If not, we get them out and then we can send in more forces if needed."

"Why not just drop a MOAB on them, sir?" asked Corporal Moreno.

General Price laughed. "I know you like blowing things up, corporal, but dropping a "mother of all bombs" in Antarctica would not be looked upon favorably by the international community. As it is, this is a covert ops mission because sending armed forces into Antarctica is frowned upon. That's why, rather than the navy, we have the coast guard coming to assist us. No one would notice a coast guard ship, but sending a naval destroyer might cause problems.

"I know you've had cold weather training, but remember to cover up. Any exposed skin will freeze within mere minutes. When we land and they open the rear, we'll exit and then bring the CATVs out. There's a storm moving in, so don't wander off, we need to move quickly, and I don't want anyone lost in the snow."

The meeting ended and they began getting their weather gear and weapons ready for landing.

Jake handed Ellie and Pam a Glock 9mm handgun with a holster. "As the general said, we're not sure what we'll find there, so attach these to your belts just in case. My hope is that you can stay in the CATV, but this will be a fluid operation, and anything can happen. It works the same as the Colt 45, but not as much kick." He looked at Pam. "I've had Ellie practicing, but do you know how to use one of these?"

Pam smiled, slammed a loaded magazine into the Glock, and

racked it. "Remember, cowboy, I grew up on a ranch with three brothers, I can shoot anything."

Jake nodded. They returned to their seats, and ten minutes later, the aircraft made a safe landing in the snow. The loadmaster lowered the rear ramp, and they felt the blast of arctic air. The teams unloaded into the snow and split into their assigned teams on either side as the CATVs were driven out.

Ellie looked out at the vast white frozen world of Antarctica. "Wow, I never dreamed I'd ever see this."

"Me either," said Pam. "Even with my goggles, I think my eyeballs are frozen."

Ellie laughed. "Now you can say you've been to Antarctica."

"Yeah, great, put on my gravestone, Pamela Martin, the frozen Texas girl. And I can't tell who's who. We all look alike in our little white snowman suits."

At that moment, in everyone's earpiece, they heard General Price's voice. "Alright, DH1 in the front and DH2 in the back. Let's roll."

"I want to sit next to Agent Williams." said Tank.

"Can I shoot him and leave him here?" asked Agent Williams.

They all loaded up in the CATVs, even Kong, and they began driving towards the Nazis' base and the deadly unknown that might be waiting.

CHAPTER TWENTY-FOUR

New Berchtesgaden
Antarctica

WENDI AND SAM were looking over the papers and files left for them in the work room. Sam went over the drilling equipment paperwork he'd been given while Wendi looked over the file Tarnac had left for her.

Sam got up and walked over to a coffee pot and poured himself a cup. "According to these manifests, they have enough drilling equipment for thirteen sites."

Wendi nodded. "Yes, and from the maps in this file, they've already placed the drilling equipment at eleven sites, twelve, counting this one."

Sam frowned. "So, they're just waiting on you to confirm their calculations?"

Wendi nodded sadly.

"Can you delay it?"

"I can try." answered Wendi. "I can tell them my calculations don't match Dr. Hankersly's, but what would be the purpose if they do it now or later?"

Sam shrugged. "I don't know. I'm just hoping someone knows where we are and will come to stop them."

Wendi shook her head. "Sam, no one knows we're here. They'd never look for us here."

"So, what would happen if the Nazis and demons were successful?"

Wendi sat back and rubbed her eyes. "It would be the end of the world as we know it. We don't know the exact number of volcanoes in Antarctica, but a recent study found over 138 volcanoes in West Antarctica alone. Many of the active volcanoes are right here in Marie Byrd Land."

"Geesh, either the Nazis already knew that or just dumb luck." commented Sam.

"Probably just dumb luck. My guess is they realized it recently and hatched this ludicrous plan." She pointed to a map of Antarctica on the table that had twelve red Xs marked on it.

"Antarctica is sitting on top of a huge volcanic ridge. These red Xs on the map indicate the drilling rigs. The explosions would start a chain reaction that would release heat, causing massive caverns in the ice, creating huge amounts of meltwater, and that just gets it started. It would be a domino effect. As the explosions decrease the pressure that keeps the volcanos in check, the magma would find a way out, causing an eruption. The twelve explosions and subsequent eruptions would wake up over a hundred more volcanoes and destabilize the entire continent. When they blow their tops, more ice will melt, causing more of the Antarctic ice to slide into the ocean."

Sam's mouth dropped open.

"And it only gets worse. As Antarctica's ice melts, the sea level around the world would rise over 200 feet, flooding all coastal cities and destroying any wildlife habitats there. It would also affect the weather, causing hurricanes and violent storms that would contaminate the soil with salt."

Sam stumbled over and sat in a chair.

"And that's not even talking about the air." continued Wendi. "These eruptions would release more toxic greenhouse gases than we saw with the eruption in Costa Rica. They'd spew out chemicals that would eat a hole in the ozone layer."

Sam's face took on a puzzled look. "You said they have twelve sites set up here to trigger eruptions?"

Wendi nodded.

Sam picked up the paperwork and started going through it. "I saw an order for thirteen rigs."

Wendi shrugged. "Maybe they want to have an extra?"

Sam shook his head. "That would be dumb." He kept searching until he found a piece of paper he had overlooked. He read it and looked up at her. "This one was shipped to Wyoming. Why would they do that?"

Wendi covered her mouth.

"What?"

"Yellowstone National Park. He wants to cause the super volcano to erupt."

"And that's really bad?"

"Imagine an eruption that would destroy most of the state, send ash into the air that would cover the Midwest in six feet of ash, not including the toxic gases." explained Wendi. "It would cause the temperature to drop, a new ice age. That and with the eruptions here, it would destroy life as we know it."

Sam felt sick, leaned over, and put his head in his hands. "We can't let this happen."

"If we don't, they'll kill us and our families, and do it anyways." said Wendi.

"So, if we help, we cause massive death and destruction, including our families, but if we don't, they kill us and our families and cause massive death and destruction." said Sam.

"I'm afraid so." said Wendi.

————

Nazi Dock
Marie Byrd Land

THE TWO CATVS arrived within a few hundred yards of the dock and Quonset huts. General Price used his binoculars and scanned the area.

"DH1 to DH2, I don't see any activity around the buildings or ship." said the general.

"Roger," replied Colonel Wilkins. "Those buildings won't hold all the supplies that a cargo ship can hold. They must still be aboard."

"I agree," answered the general. "I don't like this, but we have to find out if they're on board."

"We'd be sitting ducks on the dock if they're waiting for us."

"Suggestions?" asked General Price.

"I have a suggestion," said Soaring Eagle. "I can fly over the ship and land. I can also see if there's any activity or demons."

"Are you sure you can stand the cold?" asked Colonel Wilkins.

"Yes, the cold weather gear has kept me warm, and the cold doesn't seem to affect my wings."

"Go ahead, but be careful, the winds are picking up due to the incoming storm." said the general. "While you do that, I want DH1 to check the buildings for occupants. Kong needs to stay here for now, a giant armored ape would be spotted right away. I'm hoping they wouldn't expect anyone to come from the land side."

Soaring Eagle climbed out of the rear CATV and took to the air while the team led by O'Rork in DH1 filed out, spread out, and cautiously approached the buildings.

"I don't see any demons around." said Eudora.

"Check the smaller buildings first." said General Price.

O'Rork's twelve-person team, along with Agent Contreras and Eudora, spilt up and entered several of the smaller buildings. After clearing each building, they radioed in that no one was occupying the buildings.

"We did see one odd thing." said O'Rork. "There was a radio system in one of them that was totally destroyed."

"I copy." said the general.

"Head to that large building and we'll clear it." said O'Rork.

———

DH1 ARRIVED and formed up on the large building. It had a large overhead door and two smaller doors. "Looks like a garage." said Sgt O'Rork.

Sgt O'Rork pulled on the door, and they rushed in, but the garage was empty.

"All clear, general." said O'Rork.

"From the equipment in this building, it held vehicles, probably snowcats." said O'Rork.

"So, it's possible they went somewhere in the snowcats." said Colonel Wilkins.

"Possibly," answered General Price. "But we still have to check out the ship to be sure."

"Why would they leave everything unlocked?" asked Tank from inside DH2.

Everyone turned and stared at him. Agent Williams slapped the back of his helmet. "Because there aren't any thieves roaming Antarctica, idiot."

"She does that to me too." said Agent Pyle.

———

SOARING Eagle circled the ship twice before landing on the main deck at mid-ship. "No one in sight."

"Roger." said General Price.

"I'll check the bridge."

Soaring Eagle flew up the bridge castle near the stern to the landing outside of the bridge, and a quick look inside the window showed it was empty. He opened the door, stepped in, and looked around at the vacant bridge. All the equipment had been smashed and was inoperative. "Not a soul on the bridge, and all of the equipment has been smashed to pieces."

"That's odd." radioed Colonel Wilkins.

———

"O'RORK, take your men and set up a perimeter near the dock for cover." said General Price. "Colonel Wilkins, Gunny, take DH2 and Kong to the ship."

Jake turned to Ellie and Pam. "Stay warm and keep an eye on General Price. Roscoe, stay with Ellie."

The doors to the front CATV vehicles opened and the group unloaded and rendezvoused with DH1.

"Anything?" asked Gunny.

O'Rork shook his head.

"Ok, I want DH2 with me along with Agents Eudora and Kong. Tank, take point." said the colonel.

With Tank in the lead the team cautiously made their way down the dock and up the gangplank. When they reached the main deck, they automatically spread out. Soaring Eagle waved from the bridge railing.

"Moreno, I want you up on the landing by the bridge with your sniper rifle." said Colonel Wilkins.

Corporal Moreno nodded and ran into the main structure and up the interior stairwell to the landing where Soaring Eagle waited. "I've got a clear view from up here. It was strange, I didn't see or hear anyone inside."

"Alright, I want half to search the stern and half to the bow. Heads on a swivel." ordered the colonel.

DH2 split up and Agents Williams, Pyle, Kong, and Eudora worked their way across the cargo area with half the team. The main cargo doors were shut. They reached the forecastle at the front of the ship but didn't see anyone.

———

THE OTHER HALF began working their way through the main structure above the main deck. They checked the crew quarters, galley, and small storage rooms but found no one.

"Hey, Colonel, come look at the radio room." said Tank.

Gunny, Colonel Wilkins, and Jake went to the radio room. It had been smashed and damaged beyond repair.

"Why would they wreck their own radio?" asked Gunny.

Jake took a closer look at the ruined equipment. "See those scratches and marks. Those were made by demons. They destroyed the radio."

"Why would they do that?"

Jake shrugged. "I don't know."

Colonel Wilkins touched his throat mic. "General, it looks like the ship's radio has been destroyed by demons. Something's not right here."

"Acknowledged," answered the general. "The radios in the building and ship had been destroyed. Watch your backs, keep alert, something's amiss."

"We need to check the cargo holds. Start at each end and work your way to the middle." ordered Colonel Wilkins.

As the two teams began to descend the stairs to the cargo holds, Gunny stopped and held up a fist. They all stopped and dropped to a knee. She pointed to the stairs.

"There's blood on the stairs leading down to the hold." she said.

Colonel Wilkins nodded and radioed, "We have signs of blood leading to the cargo hold."

"Got it, or roger, or whatever you say." replied Agent Pyle.

Agent Williams rolled her eyes. "I can't bring you anywhere."

The two groups arrived at the outer cargo holds and entered. Both outer holds were empty.

"Nothing here, but I see blood smears leading to the next hold." radioed Colonel Wilkins.

"Same here." replied Agent Williams.

"I'm afraid of what we'll find." said Eudora.

Kong grunted. "I smell blood, lots of blood, and sulfur."

"Colonel," radioed Agent Williams. "Kong smells a lot of blood and sulfur."

"Roger," replied Colonel Wilkins. "Everyone be ready."

Colonel Wilkins entered another hold, but it was also empty. "This one's empty with lots of blood on the deck floor. If I'm guessing right, that leaves only one."

With guns up, aimed, and ready, both teams entered the

remaining cargo hold from opposite ends. They immediately froze at the sight that would come only from a horror movie. Blood was smeared everywhere, and body parts covered part of the floor. At least forty demons congregated in the middle of the hold, feasting on what used to be the ship's crew.

At the team's arrival, the demons looked up. Their faces covered in blood, some holding limbs ripped from bodies, and others eating out of skulls.

Kong squeezed through the hatch, stepped forward, roared, and pounded his chest.

"Engage!" yelled Colonel Wilkins into his throat mic. "Watch out for crossfire."

The two groups began firing into the horde of demons who screeched and growled. Demons leapt at them and wore shot. They screamed even more as the cemetery rounds caused injuries, but the demons still lived. One demon was able to get to the controls and activated the above cargohold doors. As the door began to swivel up and outward, several flew up to escape.

As one demon flew out of the hold, Soaring Eagle took to the air and fought with it. Corporal Moreno shot one with her high-powered rifle with its explosive rounds. The demon fell to the deck, and she followed up with a shot to the head. Another flew out and met the same fate.

"DH1, get up there and assist them." ordered General Price.

O'Rork and DH1 rushed down the dock and up the gangplank to the deck. They automatically spread out and began firing at any demons that flew out of the hold.

———

BELOW, Kong was wading through the demons, hacking, and clubbing as many as he could with his broadaxe. The rest of DH2 fired, reloaded, and fired. Jake and Eudora killed as many as they could, but one crablike demon grabbed one of the DH2 members and snapped his head off. Kong subsequently beheaded it with his broadax. Another member was stabbed through the chest while several were clawed.

"Everyone go back into the other holds." yelled Jake into his throat mic.

The team backed into the holds on either side.

"Eudora, use a grenade." radioed Jake as he grabbed a grenade.

"A what?" replied Eudora.

Agent Pyle handed her one of his grenades. "Pull this pin, you have about ten seconds to throw it at them before it explodes."

Eudora nodded. She pulled the pin on the grenade handed to her. At the same time, Jake pulled the pin on his grenade and they threw them into the hold.

Colonel Wilkins slammed the oval-shaped hatch door and spun the wheel, locking the door. Agent Pyle did the same on the other side, and seconds later they heard the explosions. Debris and body parts, both human and demon, blew out of the open hold and onto the deck.

"Moreno, do you see anyone alive inside?" asked Colonel Wilkins.

"Negative, sir." she said from the bridge landing.

O'Rork and his team looked into the open cargo hold. "I don't see anything either." he said.

Soaring Eagle, who had killed the demon he encountered landed back on the main deck. "I don't see anything moving."

"Stand by and be ready." order Colonel Wilkins. He spun the wheel on the hatch door and opened it. He stepped in followed by Jake. Nothing appeared to be moving.

"See any demons we can't?" asked the colonel.

Jake shook his head.

"Good thinking, using grenades, since whatever you and Agent Eudora use can kill them."

"Sitrep." said General Price.

"All the demons have been eliminated, sir." replied Colonel Wilkins. "It appears the whole ship's crew is dead. We have one fatality and one seriously injured. The rest have minor cuts and scrapes."

"Acknowledged, get everyone back to the CATVs."

———

THIRTY MINUTES LATER, after loading the deceased soldier into the CATV and attending to the wounded, the teams met inside the garage.

"This is a twist of events." said General Price. "We arrive here to find that the demons disabled all the radios and the ship's bridge equipment, and killed the crew."

"We thought they were working together." said Agent Williams.

"Apparently not," said Jake. "Maybe the demons have changed their plans?"

"That's a distinct possibility, but it doesn't change our mission." replied the general.

"When I flew over, I saw the tracks of large vehicles heading southeast." said Soaring Eagle.

"That has to be the snowcats." said Colonel Wilkins.

General Price nodded. "I agree, and we need to follow those ASAP before the storm covers them up. Mount up."

———

New Berchtesgaden
Antarctica

HERMAN, followed by Hitler, entered the old silo's control room. Tarnac stood at the window, looking down into the silo where the drilling rig was being set up. Herman's face was red with anger.

"Why are they still building this rig inside the silo?" demanded Herman. "I was told they were just prepping it to be shipped to another location, but it's almost complete. Now we have to disassemble it to ship it out."

Tarnac turned and shook his reptilian head. "It's not moving."

Herman stormed over to Tarnac. "It has no purpose then; we need it to cause eruptions to bring the world to its knees."

Tarnac threw his head back and laughed loudly. "I'm not going to bring the world to its knees, I'm going to destroy it and remake it in lord Satan's image."

Herman stared at the demon for a moment before realization hit him. "You don't want to dominate the human world; you want to exterminate them?"

Tarnac gave him an evil smile. "Exactly."

"You can't do that." said Herman.

Tarnac reached out and grabbed Herman by the throat and lifted him off the ground. "You're a stupid, pitiful human, I can do whatever I want."

Herman's face began turning red and he glanced at Hitler who stood, shocked.

Tarnac squeezed until he heard a crack, Herman's neck snapped, killing him. He dropped him to the floor and looked over at Hitler. "You're now in charge of the men. I will let you live for now, halfbreed, unless you give me trouble."

Hitler nodded and vomited onto the floor.

———

Southeastern Antarctica

THE DRIVE across the frozen tundra was monotonous. Some tried to rest, some rechecked their weapons, and others talked or just sat quietly.

Ellie had her head on Jake's shoulder, she tried to rest but couldn't. "What do you think we'll find when we get there?"

"I don't know." answered Jake. "We know there will be Nazis and demons. Since WW2 they've had time to prepare. Like I said earlier, it'll be a fluid situation. It'll be fine."

Pam heard them and leaned over. "He means we're just going to wing it."

"Can I kick her out?" asked Jake with a frown.

Ellie giggled.

Across from Agents Pyle and Williams, Gunny said, "So, I heard you were a famous football star."

"Don't say famous," said Agent Williams. "His head's big enough already."

Agent Pyle smiled. "She's just jealous. You can call me Terrell, and yes, I played for the Ravens for three years before I got hurt."

"So, Terrell, why didn't you just take your money and do something other than chase demons?" asked Gunny.

Agent Pyle's face took on a serious look. "After getting hurt, I knew I couldn't play football anymore, and I started thinking about my future. I wanted to do something important, so I joined the FBI. After a few years, I decided to join the paranormal unit and here I am."

"I'm sure your wife worries about you?"

"I'm not married." replied Agent Pyle.

Gunny smiled.

Agent Williams rolled her eyes. "No woman could stand to be around him that long."

"Hey," said Agent Pyle. "I'd be a great catch."

"For a demon to catch and eat." replied Agent Williams with a smirk.

"I'm not talking to you anymore."

"Promise?"

Gunny laughed.

"You can catch me, Agent Williams." said Tank who was sitting next to her.

Agent Williams frowned and shook her head. "Look what you started, Terrell." She looked over at Eudora, who sat next to the cramped Kong as he sat stoically. "So, what do you do for fun?"

Eudora thought for a moment. "I've never had time to do anything else other than my job."

"Well, all work and no play is bad for you. Maybe when we're done, I can show you the sights and entertainment of Buenos Aires."

Kong leaned forward and stared at Agent Contreras whose eyes widened. "Um, Kong can come too." said Agent Contreras.

Eudora smiled. "I think that would a great idea."

At that moment the CATV suddenly shifted, startling everyone.

"Looks like the storm is here." radioed General Price.

THE STORM HAD HIT an hour into their drive and quickly covered the snowcat tracks. From then on, they didn't know if they were still going in the right direction as the wind and snow turned everything white.

"Any idea if we're going in the right direction?" radioed Colonel Wilkins from the rear CATV. They had to keep a dangerously close distance to keep the front CATV in sight. "The storm is interfering with our GPS."

"I know." replied General Price. "All we can do is keep heading in the direction we think is right."

THIRTY MINUTES LATER THEY STOPPED. General Price cursed and slammed his fist on the dash. "We could be going in circles."

The rear CATV was able to stop before colliding with the other. "What's wrong?" radioed Colonel Wilkins.

"Without the tracks or a reliable GPS, we're lost." replied the general.

"Can we wait out the storm?" radioed Jake.

The general looked down at his fuel gauge. "I don't know. It depends on how long the storm lasts. We have extra gasoline, but it could be hours or even days before it blows over. We'll need fuel to get back, so we'll sit for a while and see if the storm subsides."

TWO HOURS later the storm had not lessened, and it had gotten dark. They'd braved the storm and refueled the vehicles. General Price looked out the window of the CATV but only saw darkness beyond the snow blowing in front of the headlights.

"General," radioed Colonel Wilkins. "Maybe we can abandon one of the CATVs and cram as much as we can into one. Then when the storm blows over we can radio the coast guard."

"I don't know if we would all fit in one, but that might be a last resort." answered the general. "Raise the armor on the windows and see if you can see any landmarks. But don't leave them open too long or you'll lose our heat."

Both sides of the rear chassis have armored windows that can be opened to allow the occupants to fire their weapons if need be. When both teams opened the windows, they were met by a frigid blast of air.

The troops on the wind side of the vehicles looked out but quickly shut them when all they saw was blackness.

The others on the alee side were able to keep their windows open longer but also only saw darkness.

"General," radioed Colonel Wilkins. "Nothing back here, just darkness."

"Same here." replied the frustrated general.

AS TANK WAS CLOSING the window, he caught a brief glimpse of light. He blinked, looked again, and saw a light in the distance. "Uh, colonel, I might be imagining it, but I see a light."

"Are you sure, Tank?" asked the colonel. "Why would a light be out here in the middle of nowhere in a storm?"

Agent Pyle reopened their window and saw the light and it was getting brighter. Agent Williams looked out also and confirmed it. "Colonel, there's a light getting brighter on the left side."

Everyone on the left side of the vehicle opened their windows, and despite the cold, stared at the light that was getting brighter as it approached.

"General," radioed Colonel Wilkins, "There's a light on the left side of us."

GENERAL PRICE LEANED past the driver and saw the light. "Alright, people, let's be ready in case whoever this is, is not friendly." he radioed back.

Weapons were aimed out the windows at the light. As the light came closer, they could tell it had a humanoid form.

"Looks almost human." said Agent Contreras from the front vehicle.

"I can almost make out what it is." radioed one of the soldiers. "It's tall, like a giant, and wearing white."

"A yeti with a lantern?" asked Tank sarcastically.

Agent Pyle stared at the form as it became clearer. He smiled suddenly and turned to Jake. "It's Malachy."

Jake stepped over to that side of the vehicle and looked out the small window. He grinned. "It sure is Malachy."

"It's Malachy." radioed Jake to the front vehicle.

Malachy glowed with a bright aura. He waved his arm and pointed, indicating he wanted them to follow.

General Price slapped the driver on the shoulder and smiled brightly. "Follow that angel."

The occupants of both CATVs cheered and clapped. Kong smiled and grunted.

The drivers turned the CATVs and began following the glowing Malachy as he led them through the darkness.

"Colonel Taft," radioed the general. "Thanks for having friends in high places."

Jake was still smiling and looked at Ellie who was grinning. "Don't thank me, thank God," answered Jake. "And of course, Malachy."

"Is that really an angel?" asked Gunny.

"Isn't he the one that helped us in Buenos Aries?" asked Agent Contreras.

"Yep," said Agent Williams. "He tries to keep Jake and Terrell out of trouble."

FOR THE NEXT hour and a half, they followed the heavenly being. Malachy suddenly stopped, gave a salute, and disappeared.

"I guess we're here." radioed Colonel Wilkins.

"Apparently," answered General Price. "But where is here."

The general squinted through the front windshield and could barely make out a huge ridge of ice. The driver of the rear CATV drove up next to his.

"Let's take it slow and easy," radioed the general. "Those ridges sometimes have crevasses. I hate to come this far and drive off into one."

They slowly drove forward side by side. After ten minutes they stopped and looked through the windshield as their headlights lit up a large tunnel carved out of the ice ridge.

"I don't see a welcome sign, but I think this is the place." radioed Colonel Wilkins from the front seat of his CATV.

"Looks like it." replied General Price. "Let's see who's home. Slow and easy."

The two CATVs entered the darkened tunnel.

———

New Berchtesgaden
Antarctica

WENDI AND SAM had been trying to work as slowly as possible in the fading hopes that someone knew where they were. Sam shook his head in frustration.

"All of the rigs are set up and the holes are drilled." he said. "All they need are the explosives to be sent down and detonated."

Wendi put down her pencil and shook her head sadly.

"How is it supposed to happen, just one big boom?"

"No, it has to be a sequential series of explosions to cause the chain reaction." explained Wendi. "Do they have to do it from each drilling site?"

Sam shook his head. "No, they can have them all set up to be set off from one location, probably here."

"So, a push of a button and it's over?" asked Wendi.

Before Sam had a chance to answer they were interrupted when Hitler came into the room.

"Adolph," said Wendi. "You're so pale. What's wrong."

Hitler sat down on one of the stools. "Herman's dead."

Sam looked over at Wendi who just shrugged. "I can't say I'm sad, but what happened?"

"Tarnac killed him." answered Hitler. "He was arguing with him about the drilling rig here in the silo, and Tarnac just killed him."

"I'm sorry." said Wendi. "I know you liked him."

Hitler rubbed his forehead. "He took me in and treated me like a son. But now, I'm not sure if I agree with what he was doing. He made it sound so correct and noble. It's so confusing."

Wendi got up, walked over to him, and put her hand on his shoulder. "I can only imagine coming into this world the way you did and only being told limited information."

Hitler looked up at her and nodded. "Thank you. Tarnac put me in charge. He expects me to be the same Hitler from back then, but just because I have DNA that makes me look like him doesn't mean I'm the same. I have my own thoughts and goals."

"And what're your goals?" asked Sam.

Hitler shook his head sadly. "I don't know. Herman made it all so simple. He said the world was bad and what he was doing would make it pure and right. I'm not sure causing volcanic eruptions around the world and killing millions is making things pure and right."

"Do you know what Tarnac wants?" asked Sam.

"Yes, I do now." said Hitler with a nod. "He wants to exterminate the human race."

"That's right." said Wendi. "He wants to cause massive eruptions here and in the United States that will destroy life as we know it, including us."

"But why?"

"Because he's a lousy, stinking demon." answered Sam.

"I don't know what Herman told you, Adolph, about who these creatures are." said Wendi. "They're angels that rebelled against our

God and were kicked out of heaven. They hate humans because God loves us. They want to destroy us to get revenge on God."

"Heaven? Herman said that this God of yours was worshipped by a corrupt race called the Jews. He said the demons were helping us save mankind from them and their allies."

Sam shook his head. "Sounds like typical Nazi propaganda."

"I told you before that the Nazis and Herman believe that anyone other than his race is inferior and either needs to be killed or controlled. The original Adolph Hitler started a world war out of greed and lust for power. He rounded up millions of Jews and put them in camps. He then killed, tortured, and experimented on them, men, women, and children. As I said, our God loves everyone. I know it's hard to just believe us, but check for yourself. We need your help to stop this."

Hitler got up and headed to the door. "I don't know what to do. I need to think."

After he left, Sam looked over at Wendi. "Maybe he'll see the light and help us."

"Even if he does and tries to help, what can he do?" asked Wendi. "Tarnac would just kill him too."

———

DH1 AND DH2 came to a curve in the tunnel and stopped.

"O'Rork, send a scout to see what's around the curve." radioed the general.

O'Rork sent two from the DH1 group, they disappeared around the curve and returned moments later.

"There's a huge metal door about two hundred yards down the tunnel, sir." radioed the female soldier. "There's also a surveillance camera mounted above it."

"I copy," replied the general. "Moreno, I want you to take out that camera."

"Yes, sir." radioed Corporal Moreno. She climbed out along with two others from DH2 and proceeded down the tunnel. A few moments later they heard a single shot.

"Camera's out." reported Corporal Moreno.

"Roger that, let's move in." radioed General Price.

The group moved up to the large metal doors and stopped. Both groups unloaded from the CATVs and took up positions, around the doors. There was no keypad or device to open the door.

"Do we blow the door?" asked Colonel Wilkins.

General Price shook his head. "I don't want the noise to alert them, but I don't see any other way."

"Someone is going to come check why the camera's out." said Jake.

"We could move back and ambush them when they come out." suggested Gunny.

"That would make noise." said the general.

From the back, they heard Kong's deep voice. "I have an idea." He walked up to the doors and stopped. He grabbed his broadaxe, flipped it around backwards and leapt into the air. He plunged the spear point attached to the end of the handle into the ice, hung on it for a moment, then swung up and sat perched on it like a tree limb. He grinned.

General Price smiled. "And when they come to check on the camera, Kong will greet them. Good plan."

"I told you I love that ape." said Agent Pyle.

Agent Williams rolled her eyes and Eudora grinned.

"Everyone back inside except for four personnel to give Kong some cover fire if needed. Try not to be seen." ordered General Price.

———

ONCE BACK ON BOARD, they backed the CATVs around the curve and out of sight. They didn't have to wait long when the massive doors creaked open. Two armed men casually walked out and looked up at the camera. They stared at the destroyed camera with a puzzled look. Movement caught their eye and their puzzled faces turned to terror when they saw a huge ape perched above the doors. Before they could react, Kong dropped down on them and slammed their heads together, killing them.

"Clear." radioed Kong. He jumped back up and jerked the axe from the ice.

The four soldiers came out of their hiding positions and covered the door while the rest drove up.

"Looks like a huge garage." radioed General Price as he stared through the windshield. "Check inside for more cameras and then proceed."

The four soldiers entered and looked around but didn't find any cameras. Once the CATVs were inside the garage, both teams exited the vehicles. The temperature was considerably warmer.

"Impressive." said Colonel Wilkins.

"This could hold a lot of hay." said Jake sarcastically.

Five snowcats were parked in the garage, along with numerous large, flat sleds used to pull equipment.

"They could move a lot of stuff with those things." said Tank.

"They've been busy beavers." said Pam.

Colonel Wilkins and Jake walked over to the other side of the garage where the second set of doors were. They saw a small box attached to the wall that appeared to be simple open and close buttons. The normal size side door didn't appear to have a locking mechanism.

"Besides the camera, they don't seem concerned about security." commented the colonel.

"I doubt they're worried about getting visitors." replied Jake.

They returned to middle of the garage and briefed the general.

"Ok, I want a small recon team to go through the side door and see what's on the other side." said General Price. "In case they meet with resistance, I want the rest of you set up to make an entry through the big doors."

Once everyone was set, Gunny, Tank, Moreno, and two others lined up by the door. Gunny quietly opened the door and they moved inside quietly. The tunnel continued for another hundred yards.

"The tunnel continues on this side." radioed Gunny using her mike and earpiece. We're going down further."

Without waiting for a reply, they stayed to the sides of the tunnel and worked their way to the light at the end.

They peeked around the edges of the tunnel at the circular landing that surrounded the silo. The landing was empty, so Gunny crawled over to the railing and looked down into the silo. She saw the drilling rig with demons and men working around it. "Holy cow," she said. "General," she radioed. "You're not going to believe what's in here."

CHAPTER TWENTY-FIVE

TARNAC, with his tail swaying back and forth, entered the control room and saw Hitler sitting at a desk looking at a computer. When Hitler smelled the noxious odor, he knew one of the demons had entered, so he clicked off the computer.

"What are you doing?" demanded Tarnac.

Hitler turned to him and smiled. "I'm just checking to make sure everything is on the right track."

Tarnac grumbled and stomped over to a large panel that displayed a large touch screen. The display showed the thirteen drill sites, but each had a red-light indicator.

"When will these be operational?" snarled Tarnac.

Hitler shrugged. "Dr. Hamilton and Mr. Donaldson are doing some last-minute checks on the system."

Tarnac slammed his clawed fist on the table. "I want them operational now."

"If the sequence is not set right the rigs will not explode properly and it won't work." explained Hitler.

"Make sure of it." snapped Tarnac as he stomped out.

Hitler frowned and shook his head. He turned back to the

computer and continued to read the historical accounts of World War II.

———

WENDI SAT and stared at the computer screen. Sam walked over and sat down next to her.

"What are you thinking?" he asked.

Wendi's eyes filled with tears. "I can't do this, Sam, I can't help them do this. Even if it costs ours and our family's lives."

Sam nodded. "I know, I've thought about it too. I've delayed it as long as I could in hopes that someone will come help."

Wendi nodded and wiped the tears from her eyes. "I know, but if we refuse, they will do it."

Sam stormed across the room and kicked a metal trash can in frustration.

———

THE SCOUT TEAM returned and explained to General Price and the rest what they saw. Gunny advised that the temperature was warm enough inside to remove their winter gear.

"That doesn't make sense," said Colonel Wilkins. "Why build a drilling rig here? It would cause an eruption here and kill them all."

General Price shook his head. "I don't know." He looked at Jake. "Any ideas?"

"No sir, with demons and Nazis you just never know."

"Maybe they're planning to abandon the base here and let it explode causing an eruption here like they did in Costa Rica." said Agent Williams.

The general shook his head. "How would they escape? They killed the ship's crew and disabled the ship. Unless they have other means, they're stuck here."

"Maybe the demons don't want them to escape." said Eudora.

"You may be right," said the general. "These monsters may have altered the Nazis' plans, but regardless of which plan, we have a job to do. We need to locate the two kidnapped people first and then either secure this site —"

"Or blow it up." said Corporal Moreno.

"If we have to."

"General, I see one armed guard walking towards us." radioed one of the team members watching the tunnel.

"He's probably checking on the other two." said Jake.

"Good, wait until he enters the garage, then grab him. Maybe he'll tell us where the two people are and what's going on."

———

THE ARMED GUARD looked bored as he strolled towards the tunnel door. His rifle was slung over his shoulder, and he wanted to get to the garage so he could smoke a cigarette. He could then look for the two that didn't report back about the camera problem. He casually opened the door, entered the garage, and froze when he saw several rifles pointed at his face.

———

HITLER ENTERED the workroom and saw Wendi and Sam working. "Tarnac sent me to find out what's keeping his plan from being operational."

Wendi shrugged. "These calculations have to be exact, or it won't work."

Hitler gave her a sly smile. "That's the lie I told Tarnac. So, what's the truth."

Wendi looked over at Sam who nodded. "The truth is we're trying to delay it as long as possible."

"Why?"

"Because we don't want to destroy the world so Tarnac, his buddy Satan, and those despicable creatures will be happy." said Sam.

"Adolph, you know he'll kill you too." said Wendi.

The young Hitler nodded. "I know. I've been doing some

research into this man called Hitler and the Nazis. I don't like what I saw. It's obvious now that Herman was lying and telling me only what he wanted me to know."

"So, help us stop this." pleaded Sam.

"I can't."

"Why not?" asked Wendi.

"I was just Herman's puppet. I don't even know if his men will even listen, much less help me. I'm sorry, I will try to delay Tarnac if I can, but I can't do anything more." Hitler turned and left the room.

———

THE NOW UNARMED guard named Stephen didn't get his cigarette break, instead, he sat sullenly with his wrists zip tied.

"He refuses to tell us anything except his name." said Colonel Wilkins.

"We don't have time for this." replied General Price. He thought for a moment and grinned. "Eudora, do you think you and Kong can convince him to talk?"

Eudora nodded. "We can give it a try." She walked around to where Stephen sat on the ground. She bent down and smiled.

"I'm Eudora." she said.

Stephen sneered at her when he saw her one yellow eye. "I've worked around demons. You half-breeds don't scare me. The demons say you're scum."

Eudora smiled. "Absolutely, Stephen, and demons know what true scum are. I hope they're paying you enough?"

Stephen lifted his chin and stuck out his chest. "The money is not that important. I serve the Fourth Reich."

"Of course, you do." she replied still smiling. "Have you met my friend Kong?"

Stephen glared at her.

"Hey, Kong, come say hello to Stephen."

She turned and pointed to Kong who lumbered around one of CATVs. Stephen stared at the armor-wearing ape in defiance. "The demons are more frightening."

"Do you think the demons are your friends?" she asked.

"They support our cause."

"Did you know that the demons killed and ate the ship's crew, destroyed their radio, and disabled the ship?"

"You lie." snapped Stephen.

Kong bent down and growled.

"Now, Stephen," said Eudora in a soft voice. "We're in a tiny bit of a hurry, so we'd like to know where the two kidnapped people are and how many of you there are."

Stephen glared but remained silent.

Eudora smiled again and pointed to Kong. "My friend Kong likes to pull people's arms off. But before that, he usually pulls their ears and noses off first."

Stephen's face paled, but he remained quiet.

"Then he pulls their legs off and uses their torso as a punching bag."

Stephen's eyes widened.

Kong bent down, his massive body dwarfing Stephen. He reached over and grabbed an ear and started pulling. Stephen bit his lip but finally, the pain was too much.

"Ok, ok, stop." he said.

Kong let go and sat back, pouting.

"Now look what you did." said Eudora with a frown. "Kong really wanted to add your ear to his collection."

"The two Americans are on the level below us," said Stephen. "They're in a workroom."

"Any guards in the workroom?" asked General Price.

Stephen shook his head.

"Do they have a command post or main room?"

"The control room is the level below that."

"How many men are there?"

"We have 40 armed men plus at least a hundred or more of Tarnac's demons." replied Stephen. "You don't stand a chance."

"Do you know what the drilling rig is for?"

Stephen shrugged. "They just said to help build it."

"Well, genius, I'm sure they plan to lower explosives down and

detonate them like they did in Costa Rica. It'll cause a volcanic eruption that will kill us all." explained the general.

Stephen thought for a moment and began looking around in a
panic. "No, no, I can't stay here. You've got to help me. I don't want
to die."

"Not even for the Fourth Reich?" asked Eudora.

"Get him out of my sight." ordered General Price.

They jerked Stephen to his feet while he begged them to
help him.

"And keep him quiet." said the general.

Once Stephen was out of sight, General Price turned to his
group. "Shed your winter gear. Gunny says it's warm enough inside,
but put your gear into the CATVs for when we need to leave. We
may have to leave in a hurry. I want DH1 on one side of the tunnel
and DH2 on the other. Colonel Wilkins, I want your team to secure
the two kidnappees while DH1 will work our way down to their
control room and see if we can disrupt their little plan. I want
Moreno to find a high spot with her fancy rifle."

"General," said Colonel Price. "For safety reasons, maybe you
should stay with the vehicles."

General Price smiled. "And miss all the fun, Phil? I still owe them
from Berlin and Nevada. Leave four people here to guard the
CATVs. I also need Kong to stay at the tunnel entrance. He would
be too easily spotted and can back us up when we need it."

Jake turned to Ellie and Pam. "Stay here and guard the CATVs
too with Roscoe."

"You mean stay here out of harm's way?" asked Ellie with a
smirk. She kissed Jake. "Be careful, I won't be there to protect you."

Jake grinned and walked off to join DH2.

"Is this when the screaming, running, and shooting starts?"
asked Pam.

Ellie rolled her eyes.

The two teams filed out through the side door and lined up on
either side of the tunnel. Colonel Wilkins and his team moved out
into the circular landing and quickly moved down to an alcove that
had a door. Gunny opened the door which led to a stairwell. She

motioned to Tank who nodded and slipped down the stairs while the remainder of the team followed.

General Price and his team went in the opposite direction and followed the landing around to another door that led to a stairway. The general had noticed that most of the activity was on the levels below them, mainly working on the platform.

———

TARNAC STORMED INTO THE WORKROOM, followed by Hitler. "Is the system operational yet?"

Sam frowned. "Yes."

Tarnac grinned. "Excellent, so how does it work?"

"The computers here are linked to a computer downstairs." explained Sam as he pointed to a computer on the table. "All you need to do is push the enter button and it will activate the explosives in sequence."

"Amazing." said Tarnac. He turned and stomped out the door, leaving Hitler.

"So, it's going to happen?" asked Hitler.

"Oh, it will happen, no thanks to you." replied Sam.

———

DH1 PASSED the workroom level and was halfway to the third level control room when two armed guards came into the stairway. They stopped and stared before realizing what was happening. By the time they had brought their weapons up , O'Rork shot both men.

———

"SO, IT'S ALL OVER WITH?" asked Hitler with a sad look.

"Yes, it's all over for mankind." said Sam.

They were interrupted when they heard gunfire and yelling. Hitler turned and ran from the room. Sam looked at Wendi whose eye widened.

They heard more gunshots.

"That's automatic weapons," said Sam. "We need to hide."

DH2 HAD REACHED the second level and were approaching the workroom when they heard the gunfire.

"We've lost our element of surprise." said Colonel Wilkins.

"Yep, we need to move faster." said Jake.

Suddenly the door to the workroom opened and a man who looked like a young Hitler came out and ran in the opposite direction without seeing them.

"I guess we know where the half-demon Hitler went." said Agent Williams.

GENERAL PRICE'S team tried to enter the control room's landing but were met by more gunfire.

"We can't get to the control room." radioed the general.

"Roger that." answered Colonel Wilkins. "Jake, take Thompson, Davidson, and the agents to the control room if you can."

Jake nodded and turned back into the stairwell followed by Thompson, Davidson, and Agents Williams and Pyle. Soaring Eagle stepped over to the railing and looked down. He saw a horde of demons and men racing up from below. "We're about to have company." He stepped off, drew his sword, and flew into a group of demons flying up the silo.

ELLIE AND PAM heard the gunshots and the four soldiers with them took up defensive positions to guard the side door.

"I told you so." said Pam.

KONG WAS STANDING in the tunnel at the entrance to the landing when he heard the shots. He stepped out onto the landing and looked down at the demons climbing and flying up the sides of the silo towards them. He roared, pounded his chest, and climbed over the railing. He dropped two levels down and hung on to the railing as the demons arrived. With one arm he swung his battle axe decapitating two demons.

———

COLONEL WILKINS and his team arrived at the workroom door when three armed guards came out of one of the tunnels. His team opened fire on the guards, killing two, but one of the soldiers, Corporal Reynolds, was shot in the chest. The remaining guard's head suddenly jerked back from a bullet fired from above.

"Thanks, Moreno." radioed the colonel. "Grab Reynolds and bring him inside."

They grabbed the injured corporal and pulled him into the work room. Colonel Wilkins looked around but didn't see anyone. "We're with the United States Armed Forces, are Sam Donaldson and Dr. Hamilton here?"

From behind a counter Sam and Wendi looked up. They stood up and smiled.

"Thank God." said Wendi with tears welling up in her eyes.

Sam hugged Wendi. "I told you someone would come."

"I'm Colonel Wilkins." said the colonel. "We need to go."

"Gladly." said Sam.

They looked down at Corporal Reynolds, he was dead.

Sam picked up his assault rifle.

"Do you know how to use that?" asked Gunny.

Sam nodded. "I served in the Texas National Guard."

They rushed out onto the landing.

"Let's get to the tunnel." ordered the colonel. "General, we have Hamilton and Donaldson. We're on our way to the tunnel." he radioed.

"Excellent." answered the general.

———

DH1 HAD RETREATED up the stairwell towards the top landing. Agent Contreras looked out over the stairwell railing.

"General," he said. "There are demons coming up the stairwell."

General Price looked over the side, saw the demons, and fired his assault rifle down into them. The rest fired down at the heathens who were quickly filling up the stairwell.

"There are too many." yelled O'Rork over the sound of gunfire.

Eudora turned to him. "Give me one of those hand bombs."

O'Rork cocked his head to the side then realized what she meant. He grabbed a grenade and handed it to her. She pulled the pin, waited a few seconds, and dropped in down the stairwell.

"Grenade, take cover!" yelled O'Rork.

Everyone ducked against the walls of the stairwell and covered their ears as the grenade exploded two levels down. They all looked over the side at the mass of dead and dying demons.

"Good call." said General Price.

———

DEMONS BEGAN FLYING into the tunnel entrance. They reached the side door, landed, and easily crushed the door. As they flowed into the garage, the four troopers, along with Pam and Ellie, opened fire on the devils. The injured demons had caused a pile-up at the door, which slowed them down until the large metal doors began to open.

"They're opening the doors!" yelled one of the soldiers.

"This is bad!" yelled Pam.

———

JAKE and his group heard the grenade explode in the stairwell.

"Sounds like they have their hands full." said Agent Williams. They were approximately twenty feet from the control room when demons began climbing over the railing.

"Ah, crap." said Agent Pyle who began firing at the demons with his AA12. The rest fired into the ever-increasing number of demons.

———

THE LAST MEMBER of DH1 had entered the top landing, but before slamming the door closed, O'Rork handed Eudora another "hand bomb".

"Work your magic." he said.

"Gladly." replied Eudora. She pulled the pin and rolled the grenade along the floor of the stairwell where it fell over the edge. Sgt O'Rork slammed the door and yelled once again, "Grenade!"

A few seconds later they heard the explosion, but the metal door kept the concussion in the stairwell.

General Price looked towards the tunnel which was quickly filling with demons. "Phil, they're trying to get into the garage." he radioed.

Colonel Price and DH2 had just exited the stairwell on the opposite side of the circular landing.

"We'll work our way there." radioed the colonel.

"That guard said there were only a hundred or so demons. There's way more." said Gunny.

"He lied." said the general.

"What? A Nazi lying?" said Tank sarcastically.

———

ON THE LEVEL BELOW, Jake's small team were fighting demons and Nazi guards.

"Try and hold them while I get into the control room."

"Hurry!" yelled Thompson, who was killed an instant later by a Nazi's bullet.

Jake dashed to the door of the control room, entered, and saw Tarnac standing at a computer monitor and a large screen TV.

"Stop, Tarnac, it's over." said Jake.

Tarnac spun around. "You!"

"Give up."

Tarnac laughed, held his clawed hand over the computer keyboard, and hit the enter button. "This world will be over." When nothing happened, he frowned and hit the enter button again.

Jake, armed with the AA12 auto shotgun fired an explosive round into the computer, obliterating it. Tarnac opened his croc-like mouth, roared, and charged. Jake fired another explosive round which struck Tarnac in the arm and blew his left arm off. Tarnac yelled in pain and grabbed Jake's right arm and twisted it, breaking his arm. Jake groaned and dropped the gun. Tarnac spun his tail around, hitting Jake in the side. Jake was knocked to the floor and felt a snap, along with a sharp pain in his ribs.

Tarnac stepped back and grabbed his large sword, which he had leaned against the computer console. Using his one remaining arm, he prepared to thrust the sword into Jake, but Hitler suddenly stepped in the way. Tarnac pierced Hitler through the torso. Jake leaned over, grabbed the shotgun with his left hand, and fired an explosive round up into Tarnac's head, which exploded. The headless croc demon released the sword and sunk to the floor.

I told you if I ever saw you again, I'd kill you.

Despite the pain, Jake rose to his feet and stumbled over to Hitler. The sword still protruded from his torso. He was on his knees, the hilt of the sword touching the ground, holding him upright. Jake bent down and placed a hand on his shoulder.

"Take it easy, I'll get help." Jake said as blood began to pool around Hitler.

Hitler shook his head. "No, it's too late."

"It's never too late, we can get you some medical help."

"I should never have existed." said Hitler. He fumbled with his words. "Tell… Wendi… I tried… to… help."

"I will." replied Jake.

Hitler leaned forward, breathed a heavy sigh, and died.

ELLIE, Pam, Roscoe, and only one soldier, Petty Officer 3rd Class Lawson, remained defending the garage. Pam and Ellie had emptied their handguns and were using the assault rifles of the three soldiers that were killed. Roscoe barked and attacked any demon that got near them.

"We need backup." said Pam into her throat mic.

"Coming." radioed a deep voice.

They looked up and saw Kong fighting his way to them, but before he reached them a huge buffalo-like demon with wings collided with Kong. In the entrance, the two huge creatures battled.

———

AGENTS WILLIAMS, Pyle, and Private Davidson continued to fire at the demons. One of the demons picked up a Nazi's rifle and began shooting at them.

"Wait, can they do that?" yelled Agent Pyle. "I thought they only used swords and stuff."

"I guess they can." answered Agent Williams.

"That's against the rules." replied Agent Pyle sarcastically.

At that moment a round from the demon's rifle struck Agent Williams in the chest and she slumped back.

"Noooo!" yelled Agent Pyle. He grabbed Agent Williams and leaned her against the wall while Private Davidson gave them cover fire.

"It'll be ok, Stephanie." said Agent Pyle. She gritted her teeth while Agent Pyle ripped her protective vest open and revealed a bullet wound through her chest. He grabbed his small medical kit each member carried attached to their waist, tore open the package of clotting agent, and sprinkled it on the wound. He could hear her wheezing and knew she had an open chest wound. He opened a plastic covering, which he placed over the wound to seal the escaping air. Her breathing returned to semi-normal, but her heart rate was slowing.

"Don't you die on me!" yelled Agent Pyle.

She tried to smile but her face was losing color and her lips were turning blue.

Private Davidson took a round to the throat and collapsed. Demons closed in. Suddenly, several of them died as rounds exploded in them. Agent Pyle looked up as Jake stumbled up and knelt. He handed the shotgun to Agent Pyle.

"My arm is broken and so are my ribs. It's hard for me to shoot. I think you can use this better." said Jake.

Agent Pyle took the shotgun, yelled in anger as loud as he could, and with a shotgun in each hand began firing exploding rounds into the demons.

———

COLONEL WILKINS' group with Tank, Gunny, and Moreno among them, were trying to reach the tunnel through the horde of demons.

"We have to get to the tunnel." said Colonel Wilkins.

They were close to the tunnel entrance, but unable to enter because of the demons. Several more soldiers went down, injured or killed. A huge demon with a long sword swiped at Colonel Wilkins, who shot it in the head, but not before the abomination severed his right leg off at the knee. Colonel Wilkins fell to the ground.

"Gunny!" he yelled over the sound of the gunfire.

Gunny turned and saw the wounded colonel. She grabbed her med kit from her waist and removed a tourniquet which she placed above his knee. She tightened it until the blood flow ceased. She grabbed a marker from her vest and quickly wrote the time on his pants leg.

"Tank!" she yelled. "We have to get the colonel through to the garage, he's wounded."

Colonel Wilkins picked up his assault rifle, shifted his weight, and kept firing until it clicked empty. He threw it down, pulled his handgun, and shot a demon through the open mouth.

———

GENERAL PRICE and his group were trying to punch a hole in the demon horde.

"I need some help getting through." radioed the general.

———

KONG WAS STILL FIGHTING with the buffalo demon when several demons leapt onto his back and tried to claw through his armor. Soaring Eagle flew up behind the buffalo demon and buried his sword through its skull. The behemoth collapsed, which gave Kong the opportunity to grab the demons off his back and crushed them.

With Kong and Soaring Eagle leading the way, General Price and his group fought through and into the garage. He saw Ellie, Pam, and Petty Officer Lawson alive and armed with assault rifles.

"I'm glad to see you, general." said Ellie.

"We weren't sure how long we could've held them off." added Pam.

The lull was short-lived as more demons came down the tunnel.

"Set up a defense to help DH2 get here." yelled the general.

———

EUDORA APPROACHED ELLIE AND PAM. "Get in the vehicle and we'll try to hold them off."

Ellie gave her a determined look. "No way, you saved us in Arizona and Argentina. We're not hiding, we're standing with you."

"I'm with her." added Pam.

Eudora smiled. "Girl Power."

———

DH2 ARRIVED at the entrance to the tunnel and with DH1's help, they caught the demons in a crossfire long enough for them to get into the garage. Tank carried Colonel Wilkins in a typical fireman's carry while the colonel shot at the demons.

"Glad you were able to join the show, Phil." said General Price. He noticed his missing leg. "Get him over by the CATV."

The demons renewed their attack. Unless the cemetery rounds inflicted serious injury or Eudora, Kong, or Soaring Eagle injured them, most of the demons were still able to continue attacking. They were rapidly running out of ammo, and most were down to their handguns when a bright flash flew over their heads, followed by another flash, and another. One of the flashes stopped and landed in front of them, they realized it was an angel. He raised a curved ram's horn to his lips and blew a long, loud, deep sound. More and more angels flew into the garage and engaged the demons. Many more flew by and into the silo.

Ellie and Pam smiled.

"Well, I'll be." said Tank.

"Are those what I think they are?" asked Moreno.

"Just like the one that guided us here." said Gunny.

———

JAKE PICKED off demon after demon with his Colt 45 while keeping an eye on Agent Williams. Her eyes were closed, and her face was getting ashen. "I don't think she can last much longer." he said.

"She has too." said Agent Pyle.

Jake reached over and squeezed her arm. "Hang in there Stephanie."

When his Colt 45 ran out, he grabbed his K-Bar knife and prepared to go hand to hand when he heard the ram's horn bellow.

"What's that?" asked Agent Pyle.

"That's a Shofar, a ram's horn, which means the cavalry has arrived." Jake said with a grin.

A huge shadow came over Jake and he brought his knife around, thinking it was a demon, but instead, he saw a familiar face.

"Malachy." said Jake.

The heavenly angel bent down and looked at Agent Williams.

"I'll take her." he said softly. He picked her up, which caused Agent Williams to groan and open her eyes.

"It's about time." she said weakly.

Malachy smiled down at her. "Hang on."

Agent Pyle looked over and saw the huge angel holding Agent Williams. Malachy looked at him, nodded, and disappeared.

Jake got to his feet as hundreds and hundreds of heavenly beings overtook the demons. "Head to the tunnel."

———

AS QUICKLY AS IT STARTED, the army of angels ended the demon's attack. DH1 and DH2 cheered. One familiar angel landed beside Ellie, Pam, and Eudora.

"Kiara." said Ellie.

Kiara smiled. "We thought you could use a hand."

"I thought we were doing ok." said Pam sarcastically.

"Seriously?" smirked Eudora.

Kong lumbered over and grunted.

"You're welcome." said Kiara. She smiled and disappeared.

———

AS SOON AS it was safe, the army of angels disappeared.

Jake and Agent Pyle slowly worked their way past the mounds of rapidly decaying demons. When Ellie saw him, she ran up, hugged him, and received a grunt in response. She then realized that his arm was injured.

"Oh, Jake, honey. I'm so sorry. You're injured." she said.

"It's just a broken arm, and maybe a broken rib or two." Jake said with a pained smile.

"Just?"

Roscoe, cut and scraped, came up and sat down. Jake leaned over and rubbed his head. "Good boy, you kept them safe."

"Hey, we kept him safe." said Pam arrogantly.

Jake grunted.

"Where's Stephanie?" yelled Tank as he came over to Jake.

"She was seriously injured, Tank. Malachy took her." explained Jake.

"Who's he?" demanded Tank.

"The angel that guided us here through the snow." answered Jake.

"Where did he take her?"

"Somewhere safe I'm sure of it."

———

O'RORK CAME over to Colonel Wilkins, who was sitting against the wheel of one of the vehicles. Being one of the team's medics, he looked at the injury and time written on his pants. "You have about ten minutes before we loosen the tourniquet for a minute to give the good tissue left some blood. I'll tighten it back up, but it's going to hurt. Do you want some pain meds?"

Colonel Wilkins shook his head.

O'Rork then put Jake's arm in a sling to help keep it still. The injured were loaded into one of the CATVs with half of the team, and they immediately drove towards the surface. Jake refused to go with them.

General Price approached Corporal Moreno. "You still want to blow something up?"

"Yes, sir," she answered with a wide smile.

"I thought so, get some of your explosives and some help. I want to blow this place to bits"

Corporal Moreno saluted him. "With pleasure."

"Can you make sure it implodes so it doesn't raise too many questions?"

"Yes sir."

After Moreno and two others went off to set the explosives, the general walked over to Sam and Wendi, who sat on the floor, drinking bottled water and talking to Jake and Ellie. "You must be Sam Donaldson and Dr. Hamilton." he said.

Sam got up and shook the general's hand. "Yes sir, thank you for coming to get us."

Wendi also got to her feet and with tears in her eyes, hugged him. "Thank you."

General Price was caught off guard by her emotional response. Finally, he replied, "Um… of course, young lady, it's our job."

Wendi wiped the tears from her eyes. "No sir, it is not. This is more than your job. You came all this way to fight monsters and Nazis to rescue us."

General Price blushed. "You're welcome."

Sam nudged her and whispered to her, "I think you made him feel uncomfortable, he blushed."

Wendi smiled. It felt good to smile. She then looked at Jake with a somber face. "I heard that you saw Adolph in the control room?"

Jake nodded. "He gave his life to save mine. His last words were to tell you that he tried to help. Does that make sense to you?"

Wendi nodded. "That monster Herman lied to him about everything, but he figured it out and didn't want to be part of it. He may have had some of Hitler's DNA, but he wasn't the Hitler they wanted in the end. His heart wasn't in it."

"Tarnac pushed a button on a keyboard, but nothing happened." explained Jake.

Sam smiled. "Oops, my bad. I forgot to tell him that he needed a password."

They all returned the smile.

General Price turned to Jake and Ellie. "Your angel friends came through just in time."

Jake nodded. "They have a way of doing that. Sadly though, we lost some good people."

"Yes, we lost eleven good soldiers, but without the heavenly beings' help, it could have been a lot worse."

"God has a way of having perfect timing according to his will." commented Ellie.

Before the general could reply, Petty Officer Lawson walked up. "General, sorry for the interruption, but the storm has passed and we have radio contact with the coast guard."

"Excellent." replied the general.

"They've docked at the Nazis' dock. They'll rendezvous with the CATV full of injured. Funny thing is, they said there was quite a commotion in the sickbay when a giant man with wings holding Agent Williams appeared. She's being treated. They said it was touch and go for a few minutes, but they feel she'll survive."

"That's even better news, thanks." replied the general.

"Yes, thank you for the info." said Jake.

Eudora, Kong, and Soaring Eagle walked over to them. "We heard that Agent Williams will be ok."

"Yes, thanks to God, and his angel Malachy." said Jake.

Eudora nodded. "Yes, he seems to show up at the right time. Do you think there's hope for us?"

"What do you mean?"

"I mean, we're half demon, so can God care about us too?" asked Soaring Eagle.

"Absolutely," said Ellie. "You're also half human, and the demon part was not your choice. God loves all of us, you included."

Eudora smiled and nodded. "Thank you, I'll remember that."

Kong grunted, resulting in an elbow to the big ape's ribs from Eudora. He smiled.

———

GENERAL PRICE HAD several soldiers collect Wendi and Sam's paperwork and documents, along with any other documents they could find in the control room. Corporal Moreno returned and advised that her charges were set to cause an implosion.

"Alright people, let's load up and head out." yelled General Price.

The remaining group loaded into the CATV and drove out of the tunnel. When they were several miles away, General Price smiled at Corporal Moreno. "You may have the honor." he said.

Corporal Moreno smiled and pushed the detonator button. They heard a muffled series of explosions followed by a tremble across the frozen ground.

"Beautiful." said Moreno.

"Good riddance." said the general.

CHAPTER TWENTY-SIX

Admiral Berisso Integrated Naval Base Hospital
Ushuaia

FOUR DAYS LATER, Agent Williams opened her eyes and blinked at the bright sunlight coming in through the window. She then saw Agent Pyle's smiling face looking down at her.

"Oh no, I've died and gone to hell." she said.

Agent Pyle smiled. "Glad to have your rude self back." His face turned serious. "We were worried."

"You're not rid of me yet." She smiled a groggy smile, reached up, and patted his face, "Thanks for being here."

Agent Pyle squeezed her hand. "Hey, we're partners. Now I'll go tell the others." Agent Pyle left. She looked around and saw Tank asleep in a chair across the room, covered by a blanket.

Jake and Ellie came in, Ellie came over to her bed while Jake stood at the end.

"Stephanie, we were so worried about you." said Ellie.

"How long have I been out?" asked Agent Williams.

"It's been about four or five days." replied Jake.

"The last thing I remember is Malachy looking down at me."

Jake nodded. "Yep, he picked you up and brought you to the coast guard ship. It caused quite a lot of excitement when he appeared in their sick bay with you."

Agent Williams laughed, then winced. "I can imagine. So, what happened to your arm?"

Jake held up his right arm in a cast and shrugged. "Tarnac broke it."

"And cracked two ribs too." added Ellie.

"What did you do?" asked Agent Williams.

"I blew his head off." replied Jake dryly.

"Good." She looked over at Tank who was still sound asleep.

Ellie smiled. "He's been here the whole time. He refused to leave, except to use the bathroom. So has Terrell."

"You seem to have a fan club." added Jake.

"I should charge club dues." Agent Williams said with a laugh making her wince in pain again. "So, what happened after I was shot?"

Jake explained the battle, how the angels arrived to help stop the demons, and the subsequent destruction of the silo.

"Our angel friends come in handy." commented Agent Williams.

"Yes, they do." said Ellie.

"I hope that place stays buried forever. What about the Nazis still in Argentina?"

"Agent Contreras said that because of what happened, the Argentina authorities are helping locate any of their organization. I think they're embarrassed that they allowed them to do this under their noses." explained Jake.

"Now we'll leave and let you rest." said Ellie. "Terrell and Tank will watch over you."

"Don't tell them, but it's nice to have them around." said Agent Williams.

"It's our secret."

———

Palmero and Oro Apartments

Buenos Aires

AGENT CONTRERAS STOOD in the lobby of the apartment building. A few minutes later the elevator dinged, Eudora stepped out and approached him. She was wearing a bright-colored dress, yellow sandals, and a black wig with yellow tips. Agent Contreras' eyes widened and his mouth dropped open.

"Are you ok, Alex?" she asked.

Agent Contreras nodded, then realized his mouth was open and closed it.

"How do I look?" asked Eudora as she spun around in a circle. "Ellie and Pam helped me pick it out."

"You look beautiful, I mean, uh, I mean, you, you look fine." he stammered.

Eudora smiled. "Thanks."

"But why are you wearing the wig?"

"I thought maybe you wouldn't want to be seen with me without it, and it matches my shoes and my eye." she replied.

He looked at her one yellow eye. "You don't need to unless you just want to."

Eudora thought for a moment, reached up, and removed the wig. She tossed it into a trash can. "How about now?"

"Absolutely amazing." said Agent Contreras. "I'm sorry, I mean you look fabulous, er, I mean you look ok."

Eudora laughed and slipped her arm through his arm. "So, show me the sights of Buenos Aires."

"What about Kong?"

"Oh, I told Kong I'd protect you if something happened."

———

The White House
1600 Pennsylvania Avenue Northwest
Washington D.C.

FBI DIRECTOR CHISOM entered the oval office where President Campbell waited behind his desk. Upon his entry, the president got up and shook his hand. "Good to see you, Bill, have a seat."

Director Chisom sat in one of the chairs that faced the desk.

"I read your report on Antarctica." said the President. "I just wanted to meet with you in person and tell you how grateful I am for the success."

Director Chisom smiled. "Thank you, sir, but the credit goes to everyone that participated."

"Of course," said the President. "I read that Agent Williams is recovering nicely."

"Yes, she came back here yesterday accompanied by Agent Pyle and a Corporal Smith. I think he's one of General Price's men. Apparently, they wouldn't leave her side. She'll be out for a while."

"It's nice to have devoted friends, and I doubt she's out for long." said the President. "If I know her, she'll be back any day."

Director Chisom laughed. "Can you believe she's already called Oscar Ruiz wanting to come into the office?"

President Campbell laughed. "I do. I read about the bravery of our three extra-special agents. We couldn't have done it without them. I'd received some flack about hiring them as agents, but they've proven to be an essential element of your unit."

"Yes sir, Eudora, Kong, and Soaring Eagle are valuable members of my unit." replied Director Chisom.

"I saw that she and Kong are staying in Buenos Aires for a few extra days."

Director Chisom nodded. "Yes sir, Agent Contreras is showing her the beauty of the city. Kong is staying because he doesn't want to be far away from her."

The President smiled. "Good, they deserve a vacation. Kong seems to have become her self-appointed bodyguard."

"As if she needs one." answered the director with a chuckle.

"And Colonel Taft, Ellie, and Miss Martin have gone back home?"

The director nodded. "I guess you read where Jake received a broken arm and some broken ribs, so they're recouping at home."

"They too deserve a rest. He's once again pulled it off. If it wasn't for him and his connection to the heavenly beings, the operation might have been a disaster." commented the President.

"Their timing was impeccable as always."

"And I've been thankful for that." replied the president.

"Mrs. Taft said God has a way of having perfect timing according to his will."

The president smiled. "And Ellie's absolutely right. On a more serious note, I spoke to General Price. We talked about how the operation went and about the sad loss of eleven fine members of his team. I know we can't replace their lives, but they have our country's admiration for giving their lives to save the world, and their families will receive posthumous accolades."

Director Chisom nodded sadly.

"I know his orders were to rescue Mr. Donaldson and Dr. Hamilton and to secure the site, but he blew it up." explained the President. "I told him that I agree with that decision, but the official statement is that the demons and Nazis had a self-destruct system that caused it to implode. I don't want anyone trying to dig around there. As far as I can tell, there's nothing of value anyways."

"Yes, sir." said the director.

"I read that Lt. Colonel Wilkins lost part of his leg. I spoke to General Price who said he's recovering nicely and will get fitted for a prosthetic leg. Apparently, he's determined to return to active duty."

Director Chisom nodded.

"The cargo ship was towed back to Argentina for the ship's owners to deal with the mess in the cargo bay. Maybe they'll be more careful who they lease it out to next time."

"And the dock in Antarctica was dismantled." added the director.

President Campbell nodded. "I've got a handful of minor complaints from a few world leaders about us using military force there, but when it comes to us stopping demons and Nazis, they can't complain much."

"How are Mr. Donaldson and Dr. Hamilton?" asked the director.

The president smiled. "I spoke to both personally and assured them that there wasn't anything they could've done under the circumstances. They were united with their families a few days ago."

"Good, they went through a horrible ordeal."

"There will be an investigation, of course, into Mr. Donaldson's company, but I told him not to worry. It was his co-owner that caused it."

"And we were able to get to the last drilling rig they'd erected near Yellowstone." said the director. "It had been abandoned. We surmise that since the plan in Antarctica failed, they just left it."

The President nodded. "We got lucky, if that super volcano had erupted, we wouldn't have had a chance."

"Maybe we'll get luckier and it'll quiet down for a while." said the director.

"Until another demon comes up with another plan." said the president.

EPILOGUE

1911 Foxtrot Trail
Canyon City, Oregon

AN UBER STOPPED in front of a modest residence, and Wendi stepped out of the van. The driver, a student working his way through college, helped get her luggage out.

A dark-haired, five-year-old came running out of the house towards her. "Aunt Wendi, you're back."

Wendi bent down and hugged the little girl longer than she should have. "I'm so glad to see you, Krissy. I missed you."

"Why are you crying?"

Wendi wiped her tears away. "I'm just glad to see you, sweetie." replied Wendi.

"Mama said you went on a long trip."

"Yes, I had to go take care of some stuff, but I'm back now."

Wendi took her hand and walked towards the house. A woman who had been waiting on the porch smiled and hugged Wendi. "I'm glad you're back safely, sis."

"Me too, Nora."

Nora held her out by the shoulders as if she was examining her. "Are you ok?"

Wendi nodded her head. "Yes, I am now."

"Good, you can tell your big sister all about it inside." replied Nora.

"Me and Mama made you some cookies, but we have to save some for daddy when he gets home from work." added Krissy.

"I'm sure they're the best, and we'll save him one." said Wendi.

––––––––

14351 Glendale Park Drive
Odessa, Texas

JAKE, Ellie, Pam, and Roscoe returned home to a happy Roy and Ned. After resting for a few days, they drove up to Odessa at the invitation of the Donaldson family. They drove up in their newest Ford 350 crew cab pickup and parked in front of the Donaldson's home.

They rang the doorbell and Allison answered.

"Oh my gosh, I'm so glad you came." she said with a bright smile. "Please, come in."

They introduced Pam to her and then followed Allison through the house towards the backyard, but she suddenly stopped. She looked at Jake and Ellie and tears welled up in her eyes. "You promised me that you were going to do everything you could to bring my dad back, and you kept your promise. I can never thank you enough."

Jake removed his Stetson and held it in his hand. "Hey, us Texans have to look after each other."

Ellie laughed. "He would've done it for anyone, no matter where they live."

Allison stepped forward and gave them a group hug. "C'mon, everyone's out back."

Numerous friends, neighbors, employees, and others were congregating outside. Sam saw them, waved, and came up. He went to shake Jake's hand and remembered his broken arm. "Thanks for coming." he said. "So, how long do you have to wear that cast?"

"Doctor says only another three weeks." replied Jake.

Sam nodded as Mrs. Donaldson walked up.

"Thank you for coming. The last time you were here, it was not a pleasant occasion." she said.

"We're honored that you asked us, Mrs. Donaldson." replied Ellie. "This is Pamela Martin, my best friend, who was also part of the group that helped save Sam and Dr. Hamilton."

Mrs. Donaldson smiled and shook Pam's hand. "I remember reading your book last year, *The Demon Uprising*, about the President's daughter's kidnapping and your interview with him later. It was amazing."

"Thank you, Mrs. Donaldson." replied Pam.

"Please call me Sharon, and we're honored to have all of you. Y'all went through a huge ordeal to bring Sam home. I know a lot of good people were injured and died." She began to tear up.

Ellie reached out and took her hand. "Thanks, Sharon, but we had a lot of help."

"Yes, of course, and I invited all the FBI agents that were involved, but I was told Agents Eudora and Kong are still in Buenos Aires with Agent Contreras." She pointed towards Agent Pyle who waved and gave a thumbs-up sign. "He told me his partner, that wonderful Agent Williams, was seriously injured. She was so nice when she was here." said Sharon.

"Who?" asked Jake.

Ellie elbowed him in his sore ribs. "He's kidding. She's recovering and will be fine."

Sharon nodded. "I'm so glad." She pointed to Soaring Eagle who was down on one knee talking to a group of children and letting them touch his wings. "He is such a remarkable person. I called their deputy director and told him to tell the others who didn't make it how thankful we are."

"I'm sure he will." said Jake. "And Sam was brave for holding out hope and trying to stand up to demons and Nazis."

Sharon took Sam's hand and smiled. "He is. I heard that he tricked that monster at the end to try to delay the explosions."

Sam blushed. "Wendi and I delayed it as long as we could. I felt help would come, and it did. Did I tell you that I saw real angels?"

Sharon laughed. "Many times, dear."

"So, what are your plans?" asked Sam.

"We'll go back home, I'll work on our ranch while Ellie gets back to work at our church, and Pam has a newspaper and coffee shop."

"That is until the FBI calls again." added Ellie.

"How are the Peterson's doing?" asked Pam.

Sharon shrugged. "It's been hard on them. We invited them to come, but I'm not sure if Tammy and the kids will come."

"It'll take time, and love."

"Despite it all, Steve was still my friend." said Sam. "It was sad, but I was told that he gave y'all the information about Antarctica right before… the incident."

Jake nodded. "We may not have been able to get to you in time if he hadn't told us. He came through for us in the end."

"We'll miss him." said Mrs. Donaldson.

"Have you heard from Dr. Hamilton?" asked Ellie, trying to lighten the mood.

Sam smiled and nodded. "I talked to her yesterday. She's happy to be back home and was going to visit her sister and her niece. I think that will help her more than anything. I just hope it's all over."

Jake shook his head. "For you it is, but it'll never be completely over for us as long as demons are still around."

"Well, enough of that." said Sam. "Let's enjoy the party."

Jake and Ellie walked around and met the people attending. Later, they were drinking punch and eating cake when they heard a familiar voice.

"Greetings from the Most High God."

They turned to see Malachy and Kiara. Their golden-tinted skin, white clothing, and wings were surrounded by a bright aura.

"I'm so glad you made the party." Ellie said with a bright smile. Malachy noticed Ellie looking around because no one else seemed to notice the two heavenly beings.

"We're only appearing to you." said Malachy. "No one else can see us right now."

"We can't thank you enough for your help, without you, we wouldn't be having this party." said Jake.

"And we thank God for making you a part of our lives." added Ellie.

"We are pleased to serve the Lord." answered Kiara.

"And as you said moments ago, it will never be completely over for us as long as the fallen are free." said Malachy. "So in the future, you will be needed."

IF YOU LIKE THIS, YOU MAY ALSO ENJOY:
THE FINAL REMNANT
BY TERRY JAMES AND HEATHER RENAE

After the disappearance of nearly half the world's population, Caden Johnson is convinced God totally sucks. In fact, He can take His holiness and shove off. The world is crawling with mutant animals and invisible monsters—who all enjoy human being with a side of fries. And what is God doing? Watching it burn.

But when Caden hears his little sister might be alive—and stuck on the other side of the world—he decides things are *going* to change. Dragging his brother along, and armed with nothing but a baseball bat, he sets off to keep what's left of his family alive.

In a gang he hardly trusts, and enemies at every turn, Caden must face the Cosmic Bully he's learned to hate all his life… Or die trying.

A unique blend of genres, The Final Remnant is teen fantasy and apocalyptic Christian fiction at its best.

AVAILABLE NOVEMBER 2022

ABOUT THE AUTHOR

Kerry Adcock is a graduate of Angelo State University with a Bachelor of Arts degree. After serving in the U.S. Air Force, he then spent 37 years in law enforcement working in patrol, and as a detective in the Special Victims Section as well as in the Homicide unit.

He has lectured and taught classes on sexual assault and sex offenders to the police academy as well as local and national women's groups. He's received awards such as the Police Medal of Valor and Detective of the Year. He is currently retired and lives in Arlington, Texas.

Kerry is an accomplished artist as well, focusing primarily on painting acrylic on canvas.

www.ingramcontent.com/pod-product-compliance
Lightning Source LLC
Chambersburg PA
CBHW011427010726
47494CB00011B/2541